What People Are Saying
about the Left Behind Series

"This is the most successful Christian-fiction series ever."
—**Publishers Weekly**

"Tim LaHaye and Jerry B. Jenkins . . . are doing for Christian fiction what John Grisham did for courtroom thrillers."
—**TIME**

"The authors' style continues to be thoroughly captivating and keeps the reader glued to the book, wondering what will happen next. And it leaves the reader hungry for more."
—**Christian Retailing**

"Com! `nes Tom Clancy–like suspense with touches of romance, high-tech flash and Biblical references."
—**The New York Times**

"The most successful literary partnership of all time."
—**Newsweek**

"Wildly popular—and highly controversial."
—**USA Today**

"Christian thriller. Prophecy-based fiction. Juiced-up morality tale. Call it what you like, the Left Behind series . . . now has a label its creators could never have predicted: blockbuster success."
—**Entertainment Weekly**

"They can be fun and engaging, with fast-paced plotting, global drama, regular cliffhanger endings, and what has to be the quintessential villain: Satan himself."
—**abcnews.com**

"Not just any fiction. Jenkins . . . employed the techniques of suspense and thriller novels to turn the end of the world into an exciting, stay-up-late-into-the-night, page-turning story."
—**Chicago Tribune**

Tyndale House products by
Tim LaHaye and Jerry B. Jenkins

The Left Behind® book series
Left Behind®
Tribulation Force
Nicolae
Soul Harvest
Apollyon
Assassins
The Indwelling
The Mark
Desecration
The Remnant
Armageddon
Glorious Appearing
The Rising
The Regime
The Rapture (available 6/6/06)

Other Left Behind® products
Left Behind®: The Kids
Abridged audio products
Dramatic audio products
and more . . .

Other Tyndale House books by
Tim LaHaye and Jerry B. Jenkins
Perhaps Today
Are We Living in the End Times?
The Authorized Left Behind Handbook
Embracing Eternity

For the latest information on individual products, release dates,
and future projects, visit www.leftbehind.com

Tyndale House books by Tim LaHaye	Tyndale House books by Jerry B. Jenkins
How to Be Happy Though Married	*Soon*
Spirit-Controlled Temperament	*Silenced*
Transformed Temperaments	*Shadowed*
Why You Act the Way You Do	

THE REGIME

THE
EVIL ADVANCES
REGIME
BEFORE THEY WERE LEFT BEHIND

TIM LaHaye
JERRY B. JENKINS

Tyndale House Publishers, Inc.
CAROL STREAM, ILLINOIS

Visit Tyndale's exciting Web site at www.tyndale.com

Discover the latest about the Left Behind series at www.leftbehind.com

TYNDALE is a registered trademark of Tyndale House Publishers, Inc.

Tyndale's quill logo is a registered trademark of Tyndale House Publishers, Inc.

Left Behind is a registered trademark of Tyndale House Publishers, Inc.

The Regime

Designed by Jessie McGrath

Scripture quotations are taken from the New King James Version. Copyright © 1979, 1980, 1982 by Thomas Nelson, Inc. Used by permission. All rights reserved.

Scripture quotations are taken from the *Holy Bible*, New Living Translation, copyright 1996, 2004. Used by permission of Tyndale House Publishers, Inc., Carol Steam, Illinois 60188. All rights reserved.

Library of Congress Cataloging-in-Publication Data

LaHaye, Tim F.
   The regime : evil advances : before they were left behind / Tim LaHaye, Jerry B. Jenkins.
     p. cm. — (Left behind series)
   ISBN-13: 978-1-4143-0576-9 (hc)
   ISBN-10: 1-4143-0576-1 (hc)
   ISBN-13: 978-1-4143-0577-6 (sc)
   ISBN-10: 1-4143-0577-X (sc)
   1. Steele, Rayford (Fictitious character)—Fiction.   2 Rapture (Christian eschatology)—
Fiction. I. Jenkins, Jerry B. II. Title.
   PS3562.A315R44 2005
   813'.54—dc22
                                          2005018809

Printed in the United States of America

12 11 10 09 08 07 06

9 8 7 6 5 4 3 2 1

To the memory of
Dr. Arthur Peters,
faithful teacher of the prophetic Word,
who is now experiencing the
blessed hope
he taught so well

Thanks to
John Perrodin and Kari Dunaway
for research
and to
David Allen
for expert technical consultation

The Principals

Nicolae Carpathia, 24, multilingual, import/export business tycoon in Bucharest, Romania

Viviana Ivinisova (aka Viv Ivins), Russian-born spiritualist, Luciferian, adopted aunt of Carpathia

Reiche Planchette, regional director of Romanian Luciferian Society

Irene Steele, wife of Rayford Steele, new believer in Christ

Rayford Steele, 33, Pan-Continental Airlines pilot

Jonathan Stonagal, American, international banker and financier

PROLOGUE

From *The Rising*

By age twenty-one, Nicolae Carpathia was nearly finished with graduate school and ran an import/export empire with Reiche Planchette low on his payroll. Carpathia was on the cover of every business magazine in Europe, and while he had not yet made the cover of *Time* or *Global Weekly,* that couldn't be far off.

He lived in a mansion on the outskirts of Bucharest, not a half mile from where his biological fathers had been assassinated a few years before. Viv Ivins enjoyed quarters on the top floor and managed his personal affairs. She supervised his valets, his drivers, his household and garden staff. His every need was cared for.

Nicolae was in the middle of two projects: clandestinely hiring an off-the-books cadre of professional facilitators who would make sure his least cooperative competitors met the same fate his fathers and his mother had, and surrounding himself with the politically astute.

His next horizon was government. First he would get himself elected to the Romanian parliament. Then he would angle for the presidency. Next step, Europe. Ultimate goal: the world.

There was no such position yet, of course, leader of the world. But by the time he ascended, there would be. He just knew it. . . .

[Three years later] Nicolae Carpathia was awakened from a sound sleep. At least he thought he was awakened. Maybe he was still dreaming. There had been no noise, no light. His eyes had simply popped open.

As was his custom when a dream seemed too real, he reached under his silk pajamas and pinched himself. Hard. He was awake. Just like that, on full alert. He sat up in the dark bedroom and peered out the window.

What was that? A figure sitting on the roof? There was no way up there without a serious ladder. Another ten feet and the figure would have reached Aunt Viv's level. Nicolae was tempted to direct it that way. If the figure had an ill motive, better her than him, and he would have time to escape.

But the figure wasn't moving. Holding his breath, Nicolae slipped slowly out of bed, quietly drew open the drawer of his bedside stand, and pulled out a massive Glock handgun. As he crept toward the window, the figure turned to look at him, and Nicolae froze, though there was no light in the room, no way for the figure to see him.

He lifted the Glock to eye level, hands shaking. But

before he could pull back the firing mechanism, the figure lifted a finger and shook its head, as if to say he wouldn't need that. "I am not here to harm you," Nicolae heard, though not audibly. "Put down your weapon."

Nicolae set the Glock on the bureau and stared. His heart rate slowed, but he didn't know what to do. Unlock and raise the window? Invite the figure in? In the next instant he was transported outside, still in his pajamas, and now he and the figure, a male, stood in a desolate wasteland. Nicolae tensed at the growls and howls and whines of animals. He pinched himself again. This was real.

The figure was draped head to toe in a hooded black robe, his face and hands and feet hidden. "Wait here," the man said. "I shall return for you in forty days."

"I cannot survive here! What will I eat?"

"You shall not eat."

"Where will I stay? There is no shelter!"

"Forty days."

"Wait! My people—"

"Your people will be informed." And with that the figure was gone.

Nicolae wished the time would speed as it had when he had moved from the bedroom to this place. But it did not. He was aware of every crawling second, the heat of the day, the bone chill of the night. Nicolae had grown accustomed to creature comforts. He was not used to hunger, to fear, to darkness. He might have tried to walk home had he any idea which direction it was. All he saw was nothingness on every side.

After several days Nicolae thought he would go mad. He tried to mark the time by gouging the ground with a stick every sunrise. His hair and beard grew; his pajamas became tattered. He feared he was wasting away. Time and again he called out for the figure, finally screaming maniacally for hours, "I will die of hunger!"

Nicolae lost all track of time, not sure whether he had missed a day or two or added marks too often. At the end of a month he lay in a fetal position, his bones protruding, his teeth filmy. He rocked and wept, willing himself to die.

Hours and days passed long after he believed the forty days were up, until he despaired of ever being rescued. He slept for long periods, waking miserable, filthy, trembling, utterly surrendered to his fate. He had had a good run, he told himself. At twenty-four he was already one of the most promising, revered men in the world. He didn't deserve this.

Finally, at long last, the robed man reappeared. Nicolae tried to muster the strength to attack, to harangue, but the spirit again lifted a finger and shook his head. "Are you the chosen one?" the figure said.

Nicolae nodded, still believing he was.

"Look around you. Bread."

"Nothing but stones," Nicolae rasped, cursing the man.

"If you are who you say you are, tell these stones to become bread."

"You mock me," Nicolae said.

The spirit did not move or speak.

"All right!" Nicolae shouted. "Stones, become bread!"

Immediately the rocks all around him became golden brown and steaming. He fell to his knees and lifted one to his nose with both hands. He thrust it to his mouth and began to devour it. "I am a god!" he said, his mouth full.

"Are you god?" the spirit said.

Suddenly Nicolae stood at the top of the temple in Jerusalem, warm bread still in his hand. "I am," he said. "I am that I am."

"If you are, throw yourself down and you will be rescued."

Shuddering, wasted, standing barefoot in tattered silk, Nicolae felt full of bread and full of himself. He smiled. And threw himself off the tower of the temple. Hurtling toward the rocky Temple Mount, he never once lost faith in himself or the promise of the spirit. Twenty feet from impact he began to float, landing on his feet like a cat.

Suddenly Nicolae and the spirit were at the top of a mountain, barefoot in the snow. The air was frigid and thin, and Nicolae felt his chest heaving, fighting for enough oxygen to keep him alive.

"From here you can see all the kingdoms of the world."

"Yes," Nicolae said. "I can see them all."

"They are yours if you but kneel and worship me, your master."

Nicolae dropped to his knees before the spirit. "My lord and my god," he said.

When Nicolae opened his eyes, he was back in his bed. That the experience had been real was borne out by his own stench and filth and ratty garments. He staggered from his bed and noticed a sheet of paper under the door. It was in Viv Ivins's flowing script:

Shower, change, and come down, beloved. Barber, manicurist, masseuse, and cook are here and at your service.

ONE

THE WHITE BENTLEY glided beneath the canopy over the veranda of the most expansive estate in Romania. From the two-story foyer, Nicolae Carpathia watched through the draperies as the driver and a security guard stepped quickly from the vehicle.

The driver stood next to his door. The guard hurried to the opposite back door, awaiting Carpathia. Both, Nicolae knew, bore compact Uzis beneath their uniforms.

The approach of the car had triggered a coded signal inside the house and brought one of the maids hurrying to the door. She slowed, then stopped when she saw Nicolae at the window.

"I have it, Gabriella," he said without turning. He could see her bowing and retreating in the reflection.

He had to admit it was out of character for him to be impatiently waiting for his ride. Commonly his house staff would have to come find him in his office or the library or wherever. His was the only schedule that mattered.

But today Nicolae was eager. He'd enjoyed one full day and night since his ordeal—forty days fasting in a desolate wilderness that should have cost him at least twenty-five pounds. Indeed, when he had found himself back in his bed in his tattered silk pajamas, it seemed he could see every rib, feel every bony protrusion.

Nicolae had gathered his household and import/export business staff and had them quickly bring him up to speed. Meanwhile, he slowly introduced small meals throughout the day. To his amazement, his body seemed to fill out and strengthen, almost as if he had not endured the fast. By the end of the day he had felt himself again. It was as if the flesh had returned to his skeleton.

If he had never before felt like a man of destiny, Nicolae did this morning. Besides what had always seemed his superhuman mental acuity, after the encounter in the desert he now believed he had a mission. He had humbled himself, dedicated himself to a being greater than himself, submitted himself to the ultimate spirit guide, who promised Nicolae the world in exchange for his devotion. Such a great prize for such a small price.

His human counselors had proven inept, naïve, weak. Reiche Planchette was twice Nicolae's age and yet was easily bullied. His ersatz aunt, Viv Ivins, was immensely helpful and valuable, but too starry-eyed and fawning to take seriously as a counselor. Not that she didn't try. The staff knew she spoke for him and thus respected her; they didn't have to know he barely listened to her.

It was neither Planchette nor Ivins who suggested his course of action this day. Rather it was his own spirit guide. Nicolae was nearly drunk with the privilege of essentially going over the heads of other humans to communicate directly with the spirit world. He had not yet determined, this exercise being barely twenty-four hours old, whether the being he prayed to was the same one who had accompanied him to the wilderness. It didn't matter. He had access to what appeared unlimited power, a sea of resources. All Nicolae wanted was to know what was expected of him. He already knew what had become his entitlement: nothing less than all the kingdoms of the world.

Pan-Con Airlines heavy-craft captain Rayford Steele looked different, at least to himself. As he left the flight center at O'Hare well after midnight for the drive home to Mt. Prospect, he wondered if others could see in his face what he felt so deeply. The embarrassment of having to ride back to Chicago on another Pan-Con plane rather than pilot his own craft back was one thing. It was not uncommon for a pilot to be put on temporary leave as a near crash was investigated both by Pan-Con and the National Transportation Safety Board.

What had shaken Rayford, naturally, was his brush with death. He hated rehashing it, but missing a jet on the ground by inches refused to be set aside in his mind. All the what-ifs and why-nots swirled until they nearly drove him mad. Especially after having to rehearse it for hours at Los Angeles International Airport.

He had cried out a prayer when he believed he was going to die, and he couldn't just pass that off now. Rayford had meant it. He had made some promises. He had to at least talk to Irene about them.

His wife was a woman of insight; he had to give her that. Intensely loyal and loving, she seemed to know him better than he knew himself. And while they had had their fights and disagreements, he felt they were solid— despite his nearly having strayed once at an office Christmas party she couldn't attend.

That was far enough in the past that Rayford believed he had already made it up to Irene, though he had never confessed it and never would. But this—this whatever- had-happened-to-him—he couldn't keep to himself. And Irene was the only person he felt he could tell.

He'd never seriously considered God, even as a child when his parents took him to church every Sunday. It was just something they did. That was the way it was now too. Irene was more devout, it seemed. More inter- ested, anyway. Rayford didn't mind missing a Sunday due to work. Sometimes he found reasons to miss even when he was off. But Irene was determined to take the kids, and while she had apparently learned not to nag Rayford, she couldn't hide her feelings when he made her go alone.

Irene was waiting by the door when he arrived home.

The kids were in bed. "Peek in on them," she said, "but don't wake them."

"Okay," he said, "and then we have to talk."

"I can tell," Irene said. "Anything I need to worry about?"

"Nah. Just something I have to tell you."

———

"Good morning, sir," the bodyguard said, opening Nicolae's car door. "How's the most successful businessman in Europe this morning?"

"Bored," Nicolae said.

That was his typical response, but it jangled even in his own ears today. He was anything but bored now. He used to say it to indicate he was not at all satisfied with his prodigious accomplishments yet. There was so much more on the horizon, so many more battles to wage and win.

But to have the world at his feet and know it beyond doubt? Nicolae Carpathia was anything but bored. Drunk with intrigue was more like it.

The only reason he had not summoned the physician to his own home was that the clinic had all the equipment necessary for the complete physical assessment he coveted.

So far the spirit had not revealed any timetable for his ascendancy, but his entire life had aimed at this. Nicolae had assumed he would have to do it on his own, and perhaps he could have. But with these new resources, what chance did anyone else have?

———————

Rayford told Irene all about his new first officer, the engine oil light, the maintenance record that showed metal shavings, the seeming innocuousness of it all, and how he had been fully confident he could get the craft down safely in Los Angeles.

There had been no problem, even when he lost one engine. That wasn't common, but he had flown heavies that way before. The problem was the weather—not being able to see until they broke through a low cloud cover, committed to landing—combined with miscommunication with a US Air jet on the ground that thought it had been cleared for takeoff.

"I had to pull up and go around," Rayford said. "And I still can't believe I didn't hit that plane. It's likely we'd have lost everybody on board both craft."

Irene sat shaking her head. "I pray for your safety, you know."

"Well, it worked this time. I prayed too."

She took a breath as if to speak but hesitated.

"I did," he said. "I did everything I knew to do, but I was still sure we were going to collide, and I found myself calling out, out loud, in front of this new guy, 'God, help me!'"

"And He did, Rafe."

"He must have. The promises though, they were silent. Think they still count?"

She smiled. "The promises? What did you promise?"

"Church every Sunday and prayer every day."

Irene embraced him and laughed. "And you a straight

arrow who always follows through on his commitments." She released him and sat back. "I can tell you're shaken and exhausted, but I've got something to tell you too. Maybe I'll save it until tomorrow when you're up to it."

"I'm a little wired. I'll hear it now."

The female nurses and even some of the males seemed unable to take their eyes off Nicolae Carpathia as he made his way to the changing room at the clinic. He was used to that. Enough people had told him how attractive he was, how he had a matinee idol's look. He was less concerned with that just now than he was with how the forty-day fast in the wilderness had affected his health.

"Remind me," the doctor said as he prepared a stress test, "what made this exam so urgent."

"I got lost hiking and my people did not find me for forty days."

"I heard nothing of that. You'd think it would have made the news."

Nicolae smiled. "I could not have my competition so encouraged. My staff would not report my death until months after it occurred."

The doctor measured and weighed him. "Do you have a problem with fibbing, Mr. Carpathia?"

"Me? No. Why?"

"What did you eat while you were stranded?"

"Precious little."

"What?"

"Virtually nothing."

"Please. No small animals, plants, berries, other fruit?"

Nicolae held up both hands. "On my honor, I ate nothing. I do not recall even drinking water."

"A man cannot live without water. Food maybe, for a while, but not water. You had to have been getting hydration from somewhere."

"Perhaps. But as you can imagine, after a while I was delirious. In fact, I was amazed to find I had been out there for only forty days. It seemed months."

"Would it surprise you to know that you are down only three pounds since I saw you last year?"

"Yes, that is a surprise."

"It's also incongruous with your story, sir."

"I cannot fool science, can I?"

"No, sir. You cannot. And if you were literally twenty-four hours from having fasted for forty days in the elements, I would not be subjecting you to all these physical tests today. But your resting pulse is as low as a marathon runner's, and—"

"I have run marathons."

"But surely you did not exercise during your ordeal."

"Of course not."

"Your respiration seems normal. Your blood pressure. Sugar. Everything."

"Then crank up that treadmill."

Irene was nervous. Hopefully, because of what Rayford had just been through, he would be receptive to what had happened to her. But she didn't want to presume. She eased into it.

"I've told you about Jackie, the one at the park—"

"The religious nut who calls you Eye, sure."

"She's not a religious nut, Rafe."

He shrugged. "That's how you made her sound. Trying to get you to come to church, always talking about Jesus her personal Savior, that kind of stuff. Reminds me of an obnoxious friend I had when I was a kid."

Irene's shoulders slumped. "Forget it."

"No, I'm sorry, babe. Go ahead. I was just saying I know who you're talking about."

"Well, if you think she's a nut, you may not like what's happened."

"You didn't tell her we'd visit her church, did you? Please, not that."

"No. In fact, the truth is, Rafe, she almost pushed me too hard. It got to where I didn't want to hear it anymore. She said her church was full of born-again Christians trying to get other people into heaven."

Rayford stood. "See, that's just it. They ought to worry about getting themselves to heaven and let us take care of ourselves."

"But, no, they're born-again—"

"Whatever in tarnation that means . . ."

"—so they're already in. She says her pastor teaches straight out of the Bible."

"Sounds boring."

"And she wanted to know if our church taught salvation."

"Salvation? Well, 'course it does. Doesn't it, Irene?
I mean, isn't that what any church is about? You get
together, sing, worship, help people, learn how to be a
better person, and that makes you one of the good guys.
I know I've been lax about it, but now I've made these
promises, so I figure you don't have to worry about me
anymore, and neither do I."

Irene knew this wasn't going to go down easily.
"I didn't say we would come to their church."

"But?"

"Well, she started changing her tune a little. It must
have been obvious I was uncomfortable talking about it.
So she quit bringing it up."

"That's a relief."

"She talked about everything but that for days, Rafe.
Frankly, I started to miss it."

"You're kidding. All that pressure?"

"The fact is, hon, our pastor doesn't teach straight
from the Bible, and we don't talk about salvation. All
that is just sort of understood and assumed and not discussed."

"My kind of place."

"Anyway, she told me she cared about me and said the
last thing she wanted to do was offend me or push me
away, so would I just take a brochure and think about it."

"I've seen those. Weird."

"This one wasn't."

"Uh-oh."

TWO

NICOLAE WAS INVIGORATED by the stress test, which he could tell impressed the doctor. It appeared the man had something to say but was apparently saving it until all the results were in. For now he shuttled his patient off to the optical wing.

Besides all the typical tests, a young female aide supervised Nicolae's eye-chart exam. She lowered the cumbersome mechanism to his eyes and had him look through clear holes as she flashed the chart on the wall. It bore eight lines of increasingly smaller type from top to bottom.

"What is the smallest line you can read?" she said.

Nicolae moved the apparatus from his eyes and turned to face her.

"Through the holes," she said. "I'll try different lens strengths in a moment."

"No need," he said. And without looking back at the wall, Nicolae recited the entire chart from top to bottom, then added, "'Not to be copied without permission. All rights reserved.'"

"Where'd that come from?" the aide said.

"The very last line."

She moved to the wall and squinted. "That type can't be larger than four points. This is a trick. You're from the company that makes the charts."

"I assure you I am not."

"How'd you do that?"

"It is a gift, young lady."

She eyed him warily. "I'm finding this hard to believe. You've never seen this chart before?"

"I would have remembered."

"I have no doubt. You realize that besides being able to memorize fifty-six letters in perfect order in just seconds, being able to read all the lines puts your vision at, like, twenty-ten. And being able to read that copyright line would make you, like, twenty-five. That means you can read from twenty feet away what the normal person can read from five feet away."

"Is that so?" Carpathia flashed her his best smile, and he could see its effect.

Young and nubile, she had been eyeing him. His peripheral vision was good too. It was a strange thing about women, though. While he appreciated good looks and was attracted to lithe bodies, he had no desire for a real relationship. The truth was, beyond their ability to satisfy him physically, women bored him. There was no doubt of his sexual preference, but in every other respect he found men much more fascinating. Nicolae loved to psyche men out, read them, size them up, decide whether they were worthy of respect or disdain, deference or condescension. Women, on the other hand, were playthings.

While he assumed this young woman was ripe for the picking, he had little need to pursue this class of pleasure. He had long had his choice of women of any socioeconomic class or age. And he never wanted them more than once.

———

Now this was weird. Rayford sat on the couch across from Irene in the wee hours of the morning, his head in his hands. It had been one thing to acknowledge that maybe, yes, he had needed help from the Almighty in the face of death—and he still intended to make good on his end of the bargain. But her story? Oh, please.

"So you got saved?"

"I'm not entirely sure what to call it, Rayford. I got convinced; I'll tell you that. The little brochure and all the things Jackie had been talking about—even when she was coming on too strong—all kind of pushed me to look in our Bible. Do you remember that we have one?"

"Somebody gave us one for our wedding, didn't they?"

"You're kidding, right?" she said.

"No. What? I know we have one. Where'd we get it?"

"I can't believe you forgot."

"So sue me, Irene. And pray tell."

"You got it for me for our first anniversary."

"I did? I did, didn't I?"

She nodded. "I read a lot in the New Testament, Rafe. It can be confusing in a lot of places, but on this subject, it's really quite clear."

"This subject?"

"Salvation."

"Do we have to talk about this?" He could tell that had pierced her.

"It's only the most important thing that's ever happened to me, Rayford. I should think, especially in light of what you've just been through—"

"I prayed and God helped me, Irene. I'm not ready to become a Holy Roller and dance in the aisles of the church. Next you'll be expecting me to speak in tongues or get healed or something."

She stared at him. "How did we jump from this to that?"

"You're just sounding a little severe is all," he said. "I'm a Christian. I believe in God. I'm going to be better about going to church whenever I'm in town, and I will pray. Okay?"

She nodded. "It's a start," she said, holding the brochure out to him. "Would you just read this and think about it?"

He pointedly ignored it.

"There's more, Rafe. We need to acknowledge that we're sinners and that we can't get to God on our own. We have to—"

"Now, see? That's what I'm talking about. Nothing I ever say or do is quite enough, is it? Do we have to become extremists? Do you want to become known as a fundamentalist? Wars are fought over this stuff, Irene. Terrorist attacks are blamed on it."

"What?"

"What's the difference between a zealous Christian and a zealous terrorist who believes God or Allah or whoever has told him to bomb buildings or kill people?"

"Rafe!"

"What? Tell me. What's the difference?"

"Well, for one thing, have you ever heard of a terrorist attack by a born-again Christian, claiming God told him to do it?"

"Have you ever heard of the Crusades?"

"The Crusades? Rayford, come on! That's like comparing true Christians to Hitler or the Ku Klux Klan."

"That's what people are going to think of you, Irene."

"You're tired. You should get some sleep, and we can talk more about this later."

He stood. "You're right. I should get some sleep. But do we have to talk more about this?"

"It's important to me."

"I can see that. I'd like it to be just a little less important to you. Can't you get involved with something—anything—without it consuming you? Remember your Tupperware phase?"

"I made some money."

"Of course you did. You were a Tupperware dream. You going to become a nun now?"

"Rayford, we're not even Catholic."

"Okay, a saint then?"

"Go to bed."

———————

At the end of the day the doctor sat across from Nicolae, seeming to study him. The young man couldn't wait to be lauded for his physicality, and he wished the doctor would get on with it. He had places to go, people to see.

"We test everyone here," the doctor said. "Men and women of all ages, shapes, and sizes. This is where our Olympic athletes are screened. You should see the numbers produced by marathoners, sprinters, decathletes."

"Should I?"

"Yes, because yours outstrip them all. It took forever to get you up to the heart rate we needed for the stress test, and you maintained it nearly twice as long as anyone else ever has. Your recovery time was minuscule, meaning your cardiovascular system is off the charts.

"You have the strength of someone twice your size. And of course I was informed of your visual acuity. The young woman wants to know if you are single, by the way."

"Not interested."

"How about I say unavailable?"

"Even better."

"Mr. Carpathia, what will you do with this super-human body of yours?"

"What do you suggest I do with it, Doctor?"

"Become an Olympian or a professional athlete."

Nicolae waved dismissively. "No challenge. I ran a fifteen-hundred-meter race in physical education in college that would have won me a bronze at the Olympics, and I had never run one before, never competed on a track team."

"Impossible."

"You doubt me?"

"After today? No. I'm just saying . . ."

"I had all kinds of pressure to pursue track and field. A coach tried me out in various events. I could high-jump, pole-vault, throw the discus and the shot, run the hurdles."

"Then why not?"

"What is the challenge?"

"For the glory of Romania then?"

Nicolae sat back. Was the doctor serious? Actually doing something for the benefit of his country had never crossed his mind. It was a strange notion. He too would benefit from the visibility, but having to share the glory with a nation? It didn't compute.

"How about IQ tests?" the doctor said.

"I have taken them all," Nicolae said.

"And how did you do?"

"No problems."

"Meaning?"

"Except that the results were delayed while they pondered the implausibility of my scores, I was gratified to have apparently broken some records."

"I don't suppose you recall which tests you took?"

"Do I recall?" Nicolae said, smiling. He reached for a pad of paper on the doctor's desk and pulled a pen from his pocket. "Not only do I recall them, but four years later, I can reproduce them. All of them. Every question and every multiple-choice answer. I will not waste our time doing them all, but here is an example."

Nicolae scribbled furiously, perfectly reproducing three consecutive questions in the spatial-cognition portion, including five intricate drawings. At the end he wrote the name of the test, the company that produced it, and the full copyright line.

The doctor pressed his lips together and nodded as he read. "I know your reputation as a businessman, Mr. Carpathia. But you really have much more to offer. I realize this is outside my purview as your physician, so forgive me if I am crossing the line. But don't you have any lofty goals, any plan to benefit mankind, to better the world?"

"As a matter of fact, I do," Nicolae said. "I plan to take it over."

The doctor leaned back and roared. "And a sense of humor to boot! Well, I'll be looking for you on the cover of *Global Weekly* one of these days."

Nicolae wasn't laughing.

Rayford busied himself with Chloe and Raymie that Sunday to avoid any more uncomfortable talk with

Irene. She seemed positively serene, not to mention eager to get to church. To his horror, she had her Bible tucked under her arm.

"They flash the verse on the screen," he said in the car.

"I know, but Jackie says the best sound in her church is the rustling of the pages when the passage is announced."

"Thank God we're not going to her church."

"That's blasphemous, Rayford. Using God's name to—"

"I was being serious. I do thank Him we're going to our own church, but you're going to be the only one with a Bible."

"It should embarrass me to carry a Bible to church?"

"I just think it seems a little over the top, that's all."

Usually Irene worried what others thought. She might as well have been wearing a sandwich board announcing that the end of the world was near.

"We have only one, sometimes two verses on the screen for an entire sermon," she said. "This way I can at least study them in context."

"Isn't that the pastor's job?" Rayford said. "To put it in context?"

As he had promised in his airborne foxhole, Rayford tried to pray every day. When he forgot, he reminded himself as he was drifting off at the end of the day. He thanked God for protecting him and asked God to take care of Irene and the kids. And to make him a better man. He wasn't sure how possible that was, not that he wanted to brag. But he was doing all right for himself, and most people thought he was a pretty cool guy.

He was doing what he had always wanted to do. He had everything he had ever hoped to have. His wife was great and would be even better when this superreligious phase passed. And of course Rayford loved his kids.

To top it all off, he was fulfilling his promise to God, and here he sat in church. That was not new, except that only he and Irene knew he intended it to be the first of many Sundays when he would do the same.

THREE

As much as Nicolae was repulsed by Reiche Planchette, he could not deny that the man was loyal to the Luciferian cause and clearly had spirit-world connections.

Privately the younger man longed to usurp the older in influence in the netherworld, and Nicolae firmly believed that day would come. Perhaps it already had. Though he paid Reiche as little as he could get away with, Nicolae installed him as part of his cabinet. He would one day enjoy lording it over his elder that he had surpassed him in every endeavor—particularly the spiritual—but meanwhile, he needed to take advantage of what Planchette had to offer.

In a meeting with his top people, including Planchette and "Aunt" Viv, in the vast conference room in his home, Nicolae rehearsed his medical report and sat basking in their admiring smiles. "In all humility," he said,

"I feel as if I stand on a great precipice with unlimited vistas before me. I have maximized my physical and mental gifts and stand ready to use them to benefit mankind."

He was surprised to see Viv raise a hand. Could she not just listen? He ignored her. He had plans, strategies, ideas. On the screen behind him he would soon show the highlights of a project he had put together the night before, outlining the timeline for his next great conquests.

As his remarks moved closer to the media show, Viv again raised her hand.

"What is it?" Nicolae said, not hiding his pique.

"I just want to say that this is something your late mother and I talked and dreamed of. It was obvious from an early age that you—"

"Forgive me, Aunt Viv, but surely you of all people realize how little influence my mother had on my development."

"Oh, I am not implying that you are other than a self-made man. I just—"

"She had even less influence on my character and abilities than you did."

"Even less than I? What are you—?"

"If I may proceed." Using outlines, charts, and graphs projected onto the screen, Nicolae walked his brain trust—such as it was—through his ten-year plan. "Keep in mind, of course, that I may be underestimating my own appeal to the populace and, thus, this could very easily be accelerated."

He laid out a schedule that saw him gaining admittance to both the army and air force schools as a combination part-time student and adjunct business professor.

"Does such a role even exist?" Reiche Planchette said.

"Not that I am aware of," Nicolae said. "Do you consider that an obstacle?"

"No, sir," Planchette said. "A challenge, of course."

"Good. Then that shall be your assignment. Make it happen. If I have to donate a weapon of war or two, so be it."

"May I know your ultimate purpose, Nicolae?" Planchette said. "Just so we're all on the same page?"

Carpathia gazed at Planchette, closed his eyes, and sighed. "Surely you are assuming my plan has an overarching aim."

"Of course."

"Then listen and you will learn."

By the time the Steele family got home from church, Rayford was already wavering on the commitments he'd made to God during his crisis. If he could just drag himself out of bed on Sunday mornings and sit through church, fine. But to endure Irene and her higher-than-a-kite response to everything—that he wasn't so sure he could deal with.

"Reverend Bohrer is a wonderful person, no doubt," she said, sitting at the dinner table. "But did you really listen, Rafe?"

"I tried to, but the wind gusts alone from the turning of those big Bible pages drowned out half his words."

"Very funny. But that's just it. He was proof texting. Know what that means?"

"I went to college too, Irene."

"He used only two verses, but rather than tell us what they meant based on his own careful study, he worked at making them fit *his* point, which wasn't that profound."

"So we're going to have roast pastor for dinner?"

"I'm not saying a thing to you I wouldn't say to him," Irene said. "In fact, maybe we should invite him and his wife to Sunday dinner next week so I can get into this with him."

Rayford let his chin fall to his chest. "I'd rather be drawn and quartered."

"You don't want to talk about this stuff?"

"I don't even want to think about it. I thought his talk was fine today, hon. I felt uplifted, encouraged."

"Really?"

"Yes!"

"Refresh me. What was his point?"

"His point?"

"That should be easy, Rafe. It uplifted and encouraged you."

Rayford shrugged and shook his head. "Be nice to everyone and live in peace. Bottom line."

"Profound."

"Does he have to be profound every week? What do you expect?"

"You could have delivered that message, Rayford.

So could I. Is it wrong for me to expect some meat from a pastor, something from the Bible I wouldn't otherwise understand? Jackie says her pastor studied the original biblical languages in seminary, and while he doesn't overwhelm people with it, he tries to explain what things mean in the Hebrew or Greek."

"Sounds like a barrel of laughs."

"I don't want to just be made to feel good, Rayford. I want to be challenged, taught. I want to grow in my faith."

Rayford bit his tongue.

"What, Rafe? What's on your mind?"

He finished a bite and slid his chair back. "I just don't want to be this much into it, Irene. Can't you leave the rah-rah part to the professionals, the ministers, the full-timers? We go to church to worship and fellowship and get re-centered. I'm not going to be a missionary, a zealot, or an evangelist. And, I hope, neither are you."

———

"While I am studying warfare," Nicolae said, "I want to expand the business."

"Expand?" Planchette said, and Viv looked surprised too. "How much bigger can we . . . er . . . you get?"

"Oh, much!" Nicolae said. "We should never feel we have arrived. This business should grow by at least 20 percent a year or be considered a failure."

"But we're profitable, and will be even if we have flat growth for two or three years."

"Flat growth is an oxymoron, Reiche," Nicolae said. "And how can you say that with inflation the way it is? The markets in the West have reopened, and the only way to take advantage of that is to borrow a hundred million and start trading."

"A hundred million?" Viv said.

"You have to think big," Nicolae said. "If I did not believe I could parlay that into a gain of at least 20 percent, I would not dream of it."

"Mr. Stonagal has been most supportive," Planchette said. "But a hundred million?"

"I do not propose we go to Stonagal for any of this. I would put up a portion of the company as collateral and do it through a European bank."

Carpathia could not help but notice the skepticism on the faces of his entire team. But he wasn't worried. That was merely fuel. He enjoyed surprising and impressing them as much as he did convincing them. They would be bowing and scraping a year from now.

"My political advisers tell me that the fastest route to the Chamber of Deputies would be through the Social Democratic Party. The Greater Party or the Liberal Party is less attractive, and the Hungarian Democrats are out of the question. I, however, would insist on running as an independent."

"Independents don't win, as a rule," Viv said. "Are you sure that's the best route to the Adunarea Deputatilor?"

"I will run as a pacifist."

That had the desired effect. The staff looked at each other, scowling, then back at him.

"A pacifist," Planchette said. "Then why the military training?"

"To be a dichotomy, a conundrum; to have to explain myself. The more people wonder about you, the more press time you get. I will be a military expert who has decided war is futile and hopeless. The wave of the future is peace. What could be more popular than that?"

"You realize that your major benefactor is huge into armaments."

"Do you assume I work for or cater to Mr. Stonagal? What do I have to do to disabuse you of that notion?"

"I believe you just did," Planchette said.

———————

"Jackie has been inviting me to weekly meetings, Bible studies," Irene said. "Maybe that would give me what I need."

"That's a rather transparent way to get you thinking about switching churches," Rayford said.

"Oh, I don't think Jackie has ulterior motives," she said.

Rayford stood and began clearing the table. "Well, I do," he said. "If going to little meetings like that will keep you from complaining about our church, feel free. But let me go on record right now: I'm not switching. I like where we are, and I said I would keep going, so I will. But nowhere else, and no extra meetings."

FOUR

Carpathian International Trading's purse strings were tended by a swarthy little man who went by merely Ion. On their way to the Intercontinental Bank in Bucharest, it appeared to Nicolae that Ion had never been in a Bentley before.

With his briefcase in his lap and files that wouldn't fit inside stacked precariously on top, Ion looked everywhere but at his boss. His ill-fitting suit was buttoned all the way up.

"You are certain that I need to be along, Ion?"

"Oh yes, sir," he said. "It would be easy for them to turn me down. But having to face you in person, well, I believe they will be impressed."

"You can prove my business is more than good collateral?"

"Of course. In fact, you will likely need to put up only a portion of it."

"Do you speak English, Ion?"

"Not so much, no, sir."

"You know, in English your name is not pronounced *E-on*. It is pronounced *Eye-on*. An atomic term. And when the American wants something watched over, he 'keeps an eye on' it, which sounds the same. That is the role you will serve today. Once we secure the financing, of course."

It was clear the play on words was lost on Ion. "I was named after the Romanian playwright Ionesco." He busied himself peeking at file summaries he said he had finalized late the night before.

When they reached the bank and Ion opened his door, he knocked it into the bodyguard who was trying to open it for him. Then he didn't seem to know whether to wait for Nicolae or simply to hurry into the bank and ask for the officer with whom he had made the appointment.

Nicolae caught up to him, and it became clear that their meeting was with several of the brass.

After pleasantries, the senior lending officer said, "Mr. Carpathia, we have your prospectus, of course, but perhaps you would care to personally walk us through your plans, should we see our way clear to front your company one hundred million."

Jackie and Irene sat at the park, watching their kids while chatting. To Irene it seemed Jackie could barely contain herself. "If you've received Christ, Irene," she said, "you must get into a Bible-believing, Bible-teaching church that will help you grow."

"I know. And yours sounds wonderful. But Rayford is dead set against it. I'm tempted to go anyway."

"I don't recommend that," Jackie said. "No sense alienating him. How about one of our weekly Bible studies?"

"He says that's okay if it keeps me from switching churches, but I know it will annoy him."

"I've got it!" Jackie said. "One day a week you bring Raymie to my house at nap time, and I'll put Brianna down at the same time. Then I could mentor you through a simple formula our church uses one-on-one and in small groups all the time."

Irene smiled. "Would there be homework?"

"You bet there would." Jackie outlined a plan that called for Irene to read at least one chapter from the New Testament each day and keep a daily journal of what she learned. She was also to read one of the very short New Testament books each day—like 1 John or Philippians. "You also make a list of ten people you're concerned about and pray for them. Then we'll get together every week and debrief."

Irene could only imagine how that would all sound to Rayford. Maybe she wouldn't tell him until the time was right. To her, it sounded perfect.

Nicolae was glad to have the floor at the bank. "I want to take advantage of globalism," he said. "I want to buy and sell and trade at the touch of a button. I am particularly intrigued by the new electronic technology originating in the United States and want to contract to bring oral-cellular communications to Europe. Have you heard of it?"

"Where they implant sensors in your teeth?" an officer said.

"Exactly. You hear the vibrations and tones directly in your mouth and inner ear, and no one else can hear them. It is sweeping the States, and I aim to corner the market on it here. Ion can show you in a matter of minutes that my company is worth well more than what I am seeking."

It turned out to be almost too easy. Ion was nervous but thorough. The bank agreed that time was of the essence. They prepared documents outlining the schedule of payouts and paybacks on the money, and Nicolae left with assurances that the first fifth of the amount would be in his business account by the close of the next day.

Twenty-one-year-old Cameron Williams lounged in ancient Nassau Hall on the campus of Princeton University in New Jersey, idly leafing through *Global Weekly* magazine while waiting for his date. She lived in student housing a few blocks south but insisted on meeting him here. His own dorm was to the north.

Cameron read *Global Weekly* every chance he got.

His dream was to win an internship there before leaving Princeton, his ultimate goal working for the magazine. *Time* or *Newsweek* would be all right too, but he considered *GW* the ultimate.

A short piece in the People section caught his eye. A Pan-Con Airlines pilot was being lauded for averting a crash in Los Angeles, certainly saving the lives of hundreds aboard both his and a US Air craft on the ground. Captain Rayford Steele had gone from being suspected of procedural improprieties to hero status when the airlines and the National Transportation Safety Board concluded their investigations. Apparently the craft had been deemed sound before takeoff, a minor issue having been taken care of, and the captain had followed protocol. But after losing an engine and facing limited visibility, he'd had to manhandle the plane to safety.

Cameron glanced at his watch and tossed the magazine on a table. He stood and checked his longish blond hair in a mirror. He missed Tucson, but the Ivy League was the place to be if he wanted a career in frontline journalism. Sure, Princeton was known for its emphasis on architecture, engineering, and science, but its preceptorial approach, fostering self-study and individualism, fit Cameron perfectly. The journalism track in liberal arts should prove to be a stepping-stone to the career he wanted.

Cameron Williams didn't want to just read about heroes. He didn't even care to be one. He just wanted to write about them.

———————

Something was happening with Rayford, and he couldn't make sense of it. After three consecutive weeks when he was coincidentally off work on Sundays and able to attend church with Irene and the kids, he found himself restless, uncomfortable.

He was too young for a midlife crisis, and yet this had all the earmarks. It was as if he had settled into the life he had dreamed of and was now wondering if this was all there was. He had an attractive, even vivacious wife, a perky blonde daughter who reminded him of himself, and a young son, on whom he pinned many dreams. They had a nice home and two cars they shouldn't have stretched to afford.

Rayford had even enjoyed a brief season of celebrity. His heroics at LAX—though they had hardly seemed so at the time; desperate measures were more like it—had earned him a squib in all three major newsweeklies, appearances on two Chicago TV news shows, a spot on one of the network morning shows, and a summons to Washington for him and his boss, Earl Halliday. They gained an audience with none other than the president of Pan-Con himself, Leonard Gustafson.

In truth, Rayford had thought Earl's secretary was kidding when she called to tell him of the invite. "Yeah, Francine, and I'm the Easter bunny."

But it had been true, and he enjoyed the ride with Earl, as first-class passengers, and the privilege of meeting the legendary Gustafson. He proved shorter than Rayford—most men were—and even thinner than the wispy Earl, but being ex-military, Gustafson had that bearing that commanded respect.

Rayford had always been a bit of a Boy Scout—formal, courteous, moderate in his appetites. So it hit him strange that both Gustafson and Halliday thought nothing of having a stiff shot of scotch in Gustafson's office in the middle of the afternoon. On the other hand, he didn't want to seem rude by rejecting the offered drink.

"You can imagine," the president said at last, "that I can't have a sit-down with every pilot who does what he's been trained to do."

"Yes, frankly, I was wondering what all the fuss was about," said Rayford.

"Well, that's just it," Gustafson said. "Had you reveled in the attention, I would have let that be the extent of it. That would have been your reward; know what I mean? But Pan-Con looks for examples, men and women we are proud to have wearing our wings. Your feat was extraordinary. Not unique, but special nonetheless. But how you've handled it has been exemplary. You didn't make it into something it wasn't. And what you said on the *Today* show about it being the thing that any trained pilot would have to try, that was spot-on. So congratulations, thanks, and be aware that I have put your name on the short list as a substitute on *Air Force One* and *Air Force Two*."

"Sir?"

"As you know, occasionally we get asked for referrals if there is ever a need for backup for the president or the vice president. Such opportunities are rare, because the full-time job always goes to a military pilot, and there are several pilots ahead of you on the sub list. But a lot goes into a recommendation. Even a man's looks. How he wears the uniform, carries himself, deals with the press. There might be a hundred men more qualified than you on our team across the country, but your little brush with notoriety made you visible. So, good for you."

Rayford was flattered, of course. He didn't expect anything to materialize from the *Air Force One* thing, given that substituting was mostly honorary and there were several ahead of him. But it did get him thinking about whether a big honor like that should be a career goal. He'd not had a dream higher than where he sat every few days—in the cockpit of a 747. And yet he couldn't shake the feeling that something had been nagging him. Had he peaked too soon, achieved his goals, realized his dreams?

On the flight back, since he had already had a couple of belts in Gustafson's office, Rayford surprised himself and wondered if he noticed a double take on Halliday's part when he accepted a couple more hard drinks.

"Glad you're just a passenger," Earl said.

Rayford laughed a little too loudly. "Don't worry," he said. "You know me."

"Thought I did."

"C'mon, Earl. We're celebrating, aren't we?"

In truth, Rayford had never been a problem drinker. He rarely got drunk, even on the golf course, sipping beers for four or five hours at a time on Saturdays and as soon as he could get away from home after church on Sundays.

Maybe that was his problem. He felt guilty leaving Irene with the kids for the better part of the weekends he was home. And yet he told himself—and her when she mentioned it—that he deserved his own time. He worked hard. His job was high stress.

So many shots of the good stuff in one afternoon was unusual enough for Rayford that they knocked him out and he slept soundly, even through dinner—normally pretty good in first class.

"That's quite all right," Halliday said later. "I needed your butter and your dessert anyway."

"Not like me," Rayford said. "I usually sleep light enough that smells wake me, especially hot food right under my nose."

Still logy, Rayford was long enough from his last drink to trust himself to drive home. But this was the day Irene had her meeting with Jackie. Well, the women saw each other almost every day, but this was the official one, the study one, their own little mentoring-and-accountability group. Deep down Rayford wished he had a friend like Irene did. But still he dreaded her rambling accounts of all that had gone on.

These days there was a light in Irene's eyes, a glow he both resented and envied. Rayford decided to just settle in and listen, because he was going to get both barrels anyway. He was not, however, prepared for today's account.

"Jackie had some stuff to do today," she said at dinner. "So she gave me a practical assignment." Irene paused, as if waiting for Rayford to ask what that meant.

He would not bite. It was enough that he was giving her eye contact and not showing his boredom.

"I was to pick someone on my prayer list and do something specific for them today."

She's going to say she picked me. And I wonder what she did for me.

"I chose your parents."

"My mom and dad?"

"Those would be your parents, yes, Rafe."

She had his attention. "Yeah, I know, but what? What did you do?"

"I visited them."

"In Belvidere?"

"Where else, hon? It's not like they get out much."

"You drove all the way to Belvidere?"

"No, I took our helicopter. Thanks so much for providing that."

"Stop being so snippy, Irene. I mean, seriously? You drove to Belvidere on a weekday, without me, to see *my* parents?"

"I thought you'd be pleased."

"Pleased? I'm . . . I'm speechless. I'm dumbfounded. Frankly, I didn't know you cared. That much, I mean."

"You know what, Rayford? I never did care that much before. I mean, they were your parents and I liked them all right. But your father has not really been with us mentally for years, and your mother is hard on his heels. But ever since I started praying for them, I—"

"What do you pray for them? It's not like they're going to be healed of Alzheimer's."

Tim LaHaye & Jerry B. Jenkins

"No, I know. I pray for their souls. I pray they'll have moments of lucidity and that when they do, someone will be there to interact with them. I pray they'll have more good days than bad, that God will comfort them, that they will have peace and safety, and that the staff at the home will be kind to them."

Rayford didn't know what to say. He was moved. Touched deeply, actually. "Thank you, Irene," he said, surprised by a catch in his throat. "That was a very nice thing you did for me. For my parents, I mean."

She hadn't said it was for him. It was for his parents. They were the objects of her prayers. But it also *had* been a gift to him. That his wife would see him off to the airport, get Chloe to school, bundle up Raymie, and make that drive . . . well, talk about above and beyond the call.

FIVE

THIS WAS THE DAY. And Nicolae was ready. He had risen early and followed a hard, sweaty five-mile run with a vigorous half hour on the rower and a weight-lifting set. In the shower he rehearsed his pitch and could barely wait to get to the phone. He had to wait until midafternoon to allow his target in the United States to begin his workday, so Nicolae filled his morning checking in on staff and staying atop everything.

When the appointed time came, he rubbed his hands together, sat back with his feet on his desk, reminded himself of everything he knew about his prey and the product, strapped on his ear set, and called the CEO of Corona Technologies in New Orleans, Louisiana.

Nicolae spoke fluent French and even tossed in a Cajun flavor, clearly impressing the man. "Jimmy!" he began. "How are things in the Bayou today?"

"Couldn't be better, Mr. Carpathia," James Corona Jr. said. "Just closed my biggest sale ever."

"Well, you will be able to break that record in a few moments if we can come to an agreement. This will be your lucky day."

"It already is, my friend. But you'll be hard-pressed to top a one-hundred-and-one-million-dollar deal."

Nicolae froze. A hundred and one? What were the odds? He buried his pique and calmed himself.

"What can I do for you?" Corona said.

Deflated but determined not to show it, Nicolae outlined his plan to purchase enough hardware and licensing to tie off the Romanian markets first, and then to become the exclusive distributor of Corona's oral-cellular technology in all of Europe.

Corona responded with a throbbing silence.

"This makes your other sale appear insignificant now, no?" Nicolae said, suddenly suspicious.

"No."

"Really? You must be on a roll, Jimmy."

"A roller coaster is more like it, Nicolae."

"How so?"

"I cannot sell to you."

Nicolae swung his feet from the desk and stood. "You are joking."

"I'm not. I wish I were."

"Why?"

"Your territory has been taken."

"By whom?"

"You know I'm not at liberty to reveal—"

"Tell me who, Jimmy, or never get another dime's worth of business from me."

"You're a friend, Nicolae, and a treasured customer, but I cannot violate trade laws like that."

"You know I will find out soon enough."

"I have no doubt, and more power to you."

"What else do you have, Jimmy?" Nicolae said, having switched to English now.

"I don't follow."

"What is on the horizon? Give me something cutting-edge, something I can use to break the back of my competitor."

"But you said you would never do business with me again."

"Do you want the money or not? I have a hundred million to burn. And I will add two to it just for good measure."

"That's the trouble, Nicolae. It would be too much of a risk. This would be something I have not even dreamed of offering anyone yet. It's too embryonic."

"Try me."

"We're just in the development stage."

"Then you could use a hundred million. A hundred and two."

"Could we ever. But I wouldn't do that to you, Nicolae."

"I insist. At least tell me what it is." Carpathia was pacing now, gazing out his glass walls at the mountains that bore his name.

"Cellular-solar technology."

"Tell me more."

"This is classified."

"You can trust me. I have just been kicked in the teeth by an unnamed competitor, Jimmy. I am what you would call a motivated buyer."

"*Investor* is more accurate. If you buy product, it's on you to succeed with it. If you invest in this, we become partners and we could both lose everything."

"Fine. Stipulated. What is cellular-solar technology?"

"Just what it sounds like. We launch proprietary satellites far enough from the earth that the sun reaches them twenty-four hours a day, allows them to relay energy and signals and information to each other, and they power your electronic gadgets for free."

"I am in."

"Nicolae, you're responding emotionally. I haven't even bid this out yet, haven't talked to our top people, haven't—"

"Money is going elsewhere if you let this slip through your fingers, Jimmy. Tell me I am in."

"Okay, all right, you're in. I'll get back to you as soon as possible with the details. You know, of course, there are zero guarantees on this one. We have no idea where it will go, whether it will work, whether there'll be a market for it—anything."

"If it does what you say it will do, there will be a market," Nicolae said. "And if there is not, I will create one."

———————

Irene had always been a creative, fastidious homemaker, but after what she had told Rayford about her new inter-

est in and care for his parents, he began to notice more
and more around the house that impressed him. Like
any other mother of young children, Irene had often been
frazzled, short-tempered, not averse to raising her voice
at the kids and him. He rarely saw that anymore.

It wasn't that she was perfect. She was not. But she
was quick to apologize, to make up for outbursts, to
soothe hurt feelings, to break and ease tension. He
couldn't deny it. She really was becoming a different
person.

That had a strange effect on Rayford. On one hand,
he was drawn to her the way he had been when they
met. On the other, getting too close to her scared him.
It was as if she were a mirror to his own soul, and he
didn't like what he saw there.

Rayford had always considered it a gift to know how
to look out for number one. He hadn't seen it as self-
centered. Real men called this ambition and drive.
Nobody handed anyone anything in this life. You had
to reach out and take what you wanted, become master
of your own destiny, captain of your own soul. He had
earned everything he had achieved, including time for
himself. It was time to do something for Rayford.

So when his buddies wanted to play golf Sunday
mornings instead of Sunday afternoons, he told Irene
he was going to ask the church brass to consider adding
to the schedule what was known among his Catholic
friends as "Fisherman's Mass."

"A Saturday night service," he said. "Lots of churches
have them. They originated for men who went fishing

before dawn on Sundays. Well, it ought to hold that they would accommodate us golfers too."

"I can't see it," Irene said. "You know how long it took to get the new foyer carpeting through all the committees. It would take months to move on something like this, and it would require a congregational vote."

"In the meantime, I may have to miss a few Sundays."

"Really."

"Don't look at me like that, Irene. I didn't promise *you* I'd go to church every Sunday."

"No, but you promised Someone, and if I were you, I'd be more worried what He thought about this."

"I think God understands. And He helps those who help themselves."

"Does He really? I don't suppose you can support that with chapter and verse."

"It's in there somewhere."

"No, it isn't. Because I tried that line on Jackie, and she caught me on it. It sounds good. Even seems to make sense. But it's not there. You know what though, Rafe? I would support your Saturday night church attendance and even be happy to see you off to the golf course at dawn the next day."

He stopped and squinted at her. "What's the catch?"

"Small as New Hope is, they have a Saturday night service."

"Forget it."

"I thought you wanted my blessing."

"I don't need your blessing, Irene."

"My permission then?"

"I'd better not need that either." That made her cloud over, but right then Rayford didn't care. "I shouldn't have to ask my wife if I can go out and play."

———————

Their mild tiff niggled at Irene for hours. Rayford could be so frustrating. And yet was trying to match him jibe for jibe the way to reach him? She feared not.

SIX

NICOLAE CARPATHIA became consumed with ferreting out his competition at Corona Technologies. He had an idea, of course. And when Reiche Planchette came to report on his task of getting Nicolae into the Romanian military academies in a hybrid role, Carpathia changed the subject.

"You wanted a civilian student and adjunct instructor position," Planchette began. "It might interest you to know—"

"Someone is leaking information from somewhere, Reiche, and I want to know who."

"Leaking, sir?"

"From within Carpathian Trading or from Intercontinental."

"Oh, I doubt the bank would risk that, Nicolae. And I'd hate to think you face treachery from within."

"That kind of naïveté will result in more of the same, Reiche. Get Ion in here. Let us find out if he has an opinion regarding anyone from the bank meeting the other day."

"Ion?"

"Yes! Ion!"

"Well, I was under the impression he had left us."

Carpathia cocked his head. "Left us? Without my knowledge? Impossible."

"Actually, I am quite certain. He has taken a similar position with a firm in Moldova."

"This cannot be! No notice? No one informing me?"

"I just assumed that if I knew, you knew. Would not Personnel have kept you in the loop?"

"Apparently not, Reiche. When did Ion leave?"

"Just days ago."

"No severance, I hope. I mean, not giving any notice. Amazing. Tell me he did not join a competitor."

"Oh, he did indeed, Nicolae. I am so sorry you were not informed. I would have told you myself, had I only known—"

"You should have!"

"—that you would have been left out of the normal protocol. From now on I will be sure you are kept informed of every eventuality."

"Not Tismaneanu. Tell me Ion did not go to work for Emil."

"Good call, sir. That is precisely where he has gone."

Nicolae stood and slammed a fist on his desk.

"Tismaneanu Tech is owned by a crook, and everyone

knows it. Emil lives here so he can serve in the Adunarea Deputatilor, and yet everyone knows he really lives in an apartment in Galati, just this side of the border from his headquarters in Moldova!"

Planchette sat nodding solemnly, which only infuriated Carpathia more. If Reiche knew all this, why didn't he do something about it? Why didn't Nicolae himself?

"Well, I am *glad* he lives here, Reiche. Do you know why?"

"Tell me, Nicolae."

"Because I live here too."

Reiche looked blank. What a dolt for a man so revered in spiritual circles.

"He is looking for a third term as a deputy in the lower parliament," Nicolae said. "How would he like to be soundly defeated by a newcomer?"

"You're not saying—"

"Of course I am saying! Hold on a minute." Nicolae sat at his desk and called Corona Technologies in the States. "Jimmy," he said at last, "Nicolae Carpathia here. All right, I found out it was Tismaneanu who got the contract with you for Europe."

"You didn't hear that from me, Nicolae."

Carpathia glanced at Planchette and raised a fist. "No, you are in the clear. But I need to know they have only the oral-cellular deal and are not privy to cellular-solar."

"That is correct. I have told no one but you about the latter. And frankly, my people are excited about your confidence in us."

Irene was more than curious. She was desperate to know. "Jackie, can people with dementia or even full-blown Alzheimer's become believers?"

"In a lucid moment, who knows? It would obviously have to be a work of God in more than one way. They would have to be clear of mind long enough to understand what someone was saying, and that someone would have to be there at the right time. And then the patient would have to be receptive."

"You can imagine what I'm praying for, Jackie."

"Of course. How bad is Mrs. Steele at this point?"

"She has the most promise. There's little doubt it's Alzheimer's, but for now she has just short-term memory loss, a lot of confusion. And she's starting to get agitated."

"And Mr. Steele?"

"We're losing him. He's not with us much of the time, but rather than being spaced out like a lot of his fellow patients, he's upset. It's as if he knows he should be able to remember things, express things, all that. But he just can't."

"Not at peace then."

"Not at all."

Carpathia walked Planchette onto a balcony over his veranda. The wind whipped through a cloudless sky, and the sun highlighted the mountain peaks on the horizon.

"I never asked how you took care of my fathers, Reiche."

"It was prudent that you did not. It was one of the most distasteful assignments I ever had, and I don't wish to revisit it."

"I need you again, Reiche."

"Please, no. Emil Tismaneanu has extensive security, not unlike yourself."

"I will defeat Emil politically. But an example needs to be made of Ion."

"Ion? Surely you can't be serious."

"Think, man. I can live with disloyalty to a certain degree. A man wants to move on, finds a better deal, does not want to face me, all right. That proves he is independent, has his own mind. Maybe someday I hire him back. But if you think that is the extent of what Ion did to me, you are a *prostovan* with such *naivitate* that I must question your intelligence. Ion is a traitor, Reiche. If I were to let him get away with costing me a hundred-million-dollar deal, my reputation would be worthless. I would be seen as a weakling, easily trampled upon."

"And yet if something happens to Ion, you will become the immediate suspect."

"I was not suspected in the deaths of my fathers."

"You were just past childhood, and that was a very expensive, very professional job. And, as I say, one I do not wish to revisit."

"We *are* revisiting it, Reiche. Ion will be dealt with in such a way that it will be clearly an accident. No one will even suspect me. You will make it happen."

Reiche moved away, staring into the distance. "If it is done so well, how will that protect your reputation? A man who has seemingly done you wrong is befallen by an unfortunate accident. It will be seen as a coincidence, karma at best."

"Those who need to know will know. Or at least they will wonder. This might even discourage Emil from running against me."

———————

Irene could not have been more stunned if her mother-in-law had told her she had been a contortionist in a former life. After a couple of typical episodes of forgetting where she was or which way to turn to get back to her room, she asked what time lunch was.

"We just came from there, Mom," Irene said. "You enjoyed the coleslaw, remember?"

"Oh yes! That was today?"

It had been ten minutes before.

"Mom, do you ever pray?"

"Why, yes, of course I do. I pray every day. I am a Christian, you know."

I know you think you are, Irene wanted to say. But the woman was fragile.

"I worry so about my husband. I don't think he really knows the Lord."

"You don't?" Irene said.

"Not like I do, no. My son either."

"How so?"

"You have to have Jesus in your heart," she said, sounding so much like a little girl that Irene was taken aback.

"And how do you get Jesus in your heart?"

"Not physically, you know," the old woman said. "It's just an expression."

"I understand."

"I found it in the Bible. Our church never talked about it. That we're all sinners and separated from God. That Jesus died for our sins. I mean, we heard that a lot, but it seemed to refer to the whole world. He did die for the whole world, but you have to receive Him for yourself. I have a favorite verse."

"You do?"

"Oh, what's the reference again?"

"I don't know, Mom. What is it?"

"I like when you call me Mom. I'm not your mother, am I?"

"You're my mother-in-law."

"You're Rayford's wife. I was at your wedding."

"You sure were."

"When are you going to give us grandchildren?"

Irene pulled out pictures and reminded her of Chloe and Raymie.

"Of course, I remember."

"And your favorite verse? What is it?"

"I can't remember the address."

Irene had never heard that term for a Bible reference. "Just tell me the words then."

"'As many as received Him, to them He gave the right

to become children of God, to those who believe in His name.' I believe in His name, Chloe."

"I'm Irene."

"I believe in His name, Irene."

Irene could barely speak. What a gift this was!

"Everybody stops after Romans 3:23," Mrs. Steele said, astonishing Irene anew.

"So that address you remember."

The old woman nodded. "They need to read the next verse too."

"Do you remember it?"

"Of course. Both of them. 'For all have sinned and fall short of the glory of God.' But here's the best part: 'being justified freely by His grace through the redemption that is in Christ Jesus.'"

"That is beautiful, Mom."

"Yes, it is. John 1:12."

"Beg pardon?"

"That's the address of the first one, Chloe."

"Irene."

"Irene."

SEVEN

Ion was killed in rural Moldova when his brakes failed and he plowed into first a gas truck and then a horse-drawn wagon.

Nicolae attended the funeral, sent a lavish spray of flowers, and attempted to console the grieving widow, who clearly wanted nothing to do with him. He thawed her by whispering that he was establishing a fund for their only child, a sixteen-year-old son, so his college expenses would be covered. She reached to embrace him, and over her shoulder, Nicolae caught Emil Tismaneanu's eye.

Tismaneanu was more than twice Carpathia's age and dressed and comported himself like the successful businessman and politician he was. Nicolae excused himself from the widow and made his way to Tismaneanu for an awkward handshake.

"Thanks so much for informing me before raiding my ranks," Nicolae whispered.

"Raiding?" Tismaneanu said softly with a smile. "It's not like I stole one of your cabinet. I wouldn't do that to you without your knowledge. As quickly as Ion was available, I assumed you knew he was not happy there."

"Little gets past me," Nicolae said. "But let me assure you, should I ever come after one of your employees, you will hear it from me first."

"Don't bother. No one who works for me would want to work for you."

"They might when I am a deputy from Bucharest."

Emil stepped back and raised an eyebrow. "Is that an announcement?"

"Apparently to you it is."

"Your mother is a born-again Christian, Rayford," Irene said.

He closed his eyes and rubbed his face. "You don't say. Like you?"

"I do say, and yes, like me."

"So I'm surrounded."

"Yep. Might as well give up and give in." Irene smiled, trying to keep things light.

"Not a chance."

"Rafe, I'm only teasing you. Don't make it a competition where you feel like you would be losing if you decided to do the right thing."

"Meaning pray to Jesus and tell Him I want to be like you."

"I really don't like when you're sarcastic about this. You know how much it means to me."

"I sure do. And you should know by now how much that annoys me."

"It shouldn't. Your mother was quite—"

"So you weren't kidding about my mother."

"No, she was very clear and—"

"My mother is demented, Irene. Alzheimer's is on the horizon. Half the time she doesn't know who or where she is. How can you put stock in anything she says?"

"Because she quoted verses and knew their addresses."

"Their addresses?"

Irene explained.

"She's pulling memories from her childhood at random," Rayford said. "She doesn't know what she's saying, what she believes, even what she remembers. Her brain is like a jukebox, and the selector arm reaches into her memory banks for a slice of this and a slice of that, putting them together in jumbles that sometimes seem to make sense. I'm surprised you give her any credence."

"You should hear her."

"That's not fair. You know how busy I've been."

"I'm not commenting on your visitation habits, Rafe. I'm just saying you should hear what she says and decide for yourself. You know there are visiting hours every day of the week, even on your off days. Even Saturdays and Sundays."

"When I'm playing golf, you mean."

"She'd love to see you."

"Thanks for that guilt trip."

"If the shoe fits . . ."

Rayford stormed from the room.

Irene chastised herself. There had to be a better way to communicate with him.

———————

Nicolae was intrigued but also confused.

"The naval academy has a man in a position similar to what you are seeking," Reiche Planchette said.

"The naval academy? I said army and air force."

"I just assumed you meant all three."

"Really, Reiche. How important is a navy to a largely landlocked country?"

"Important enough to have a naval academy. Anyway, you don't have to attend there if you don't wish to. But that is where I discovered the scenario you outlined."

"I might like to have all three academies on my résumé when I run for deputy. So they have a combination civilian student and instructor?"

"In a manner of speaking." Planchette pulled out his notes. "An Italian in his middle forties, with a background in religion, teaches cadets international diplomacy, protocol, and religious distinctives among various people groups. Name's Leonardo Fortunato."

"Fortunato," Nicolae said. "Does that make him *norocos*—a lucky man—or an opportunist?"

Reiche shrugged. "I've not met the man."

"Meet him. Feel him out and see if you think I would benefit from meeting him. But also use his precedent to get me a similar position at one or two or all three of the academies."

Irene found Mr. Steele most difficult to talk to. He seemed to look through her and then, every few minutes, would discover her anew. "My son is a pilot," he said for the fourth time, breathing heavily through his nose and looking all about the room.

"I know. And you're proud of Rayford. Do you remember that I am his wife?"

"I could use a glass of water, young lady. Now, please."

"I just got you one. There it is."

He sighed and shook his head, clearly embarrassed. "Thank you." He sat scowling at her.

"Do you remember your grandchildren?"

He shrugged, then nodded, clearly not comprehending. "My wife died."

"No, she didn't. She's here too. She will come see you later this afternoon."

"Does she have grandchildren?"

"Of course, the same as you." Irene showed him the pictures.

He pointed to Raymie. "Rayford," he said.

"Rayford Jr.," she said.

"He's going to be a pilot."

"He might. That would be fun, wouldn't it?"

"My son is a pilot."

EIGHT

NICOLAE DIDN'T NEED to know all that went on behind the scenes to get him an invite to teach as an adjunct at each of the three Romanian military academies. All he knew was that it would look great on his résumé, and that when he flipped to a pacifist position, he would have more credibility than ever.

That Reiche Planchette reported that Nicolae would have to endow a chair at each of the academies hit him as strange. He hadn't been aware of private endowments to government-run institutions, but on the other hand Planchette had made it clear that these arrangements were to remain off the books. It cost Nicolae only a few million total; a small price, he decided, to secure his future.

"You are free to attend any classes anytime you want at any of the three institutions, and you are invited to speak on business and international relations on a schedule that fits your calendar."

"Excellent work, Reiche," Nicolae said, feeling suddenly magnanimous. Surprise registered on Planchette's face. Admittedly, Nicolae's praise of the man was rare. "Really, Reiche. I appreciate it."

Planchette bowed slightly. "An honor to serve you, sir."

Carpathia studied him. What a passive, cutting victory. To elicit emotion from an older man, a former mentor, with a compliment. That had to hit Planchette like a razor, slicing more deeply, humiliating more effectively than a tongue-lashing, than reminding the man overtly how they had so thoroughly switched roles.

"Now, then, Reiche. This Italian you mentioned."

Planchette pulled a dossier from his briefcase. "Did some background work on him, Nicolae. Quite a pedigree."

"Do tell."

Reiche riffled through his stack of papers. "An impressive fellow. Varied, eclectic background. Began his education as a religion major. Catholic. Has left the church for some reason. Appears to be a devotee of Theosophy. Served in the military with many decorations, always for service to his superiors. Seems to know how to make the man above him look good.

"You know the Italian government is a model for ours. Two houses of a bicameral parliament: the *Senato della Republica,* Senate, and the *Camera dei Deputati,* Chamber of Deputies. Interesting thing here. Fortunato was elected first to the Senate and served five years. Then, despite his popularity, he *chose* to run for the lower house, the Chamber of Deputies, and served two five-year terms there."

"What do you make of that, Reiche?"

"Hard to know. Maybe that servant attitude again? Enjoys elevating others for some reason."

"Strange."

"Since then the man has begun his own business; traveled the world consulting with and advising heads of states; trained politicos; coached political parties; taught diplomacy, protocol, and—where allowed—something he calls 'religious sensibilities.'"

"I would love to meet him. Get a handle on my teaching role. Set it up, would you, Reiche?"

———————

Rayford began to dread coming home. Oh, the kids were fine, if a little bothersome. Chloe, twelve, was so much like Rayford he found it scary. She didn't miss a thing, and he often overheard her using the same arguments with her mother that Rayford used. She was smart and articulate, loved science, and was a show-me person. If you couldn't prove it, you'd better not get into it with her.

Rayford could tell that Irene was, of course, worried about Chloe's soul. She needn't be, he decided. Chloe was no worse than anyone else and better than most. Oh, she could be kinder to her four-year-old brother, who naturally *loved* everything having to do with Sunday school and church.

That was another thing. Now that Raymie *had* to go not just to church but also to Sunday school, they all had to go.

Rayford and Chloe fought it tooth and nail, and often the family arrived at church red-faced and not speaking, yet pasting on their Sunday smiles. Rayford had failed to talk the higher-ups into any semblance of Fisherman's Mass, so every other Sunday or so resulted in yet another go-round with Irene about whether he went to church (*and* Sunday school) or played golf.

He was tired of losing that battle, and the day would come soon when he would confront her about it. Rayford was tired of the teasing from the rest of his foursome. He didn't find it funny to be accused of being henpecked, or worse, whipped. The fact was, his commitment to church had been made to God, not to Irene, and he was going to stop being parented over it. He could worship God just as well in nature as he could in some cold, hard pew. Probably better. Most of all, this was his life, and he was going to do as he pleased. He didn't tell Irene what to do, and he'd be hanged if he was going to let her tell him what to do.

There was no one else in his life, and he had never considered divorce. But when he imagined the confrontation with Irene, he had to play it out to its potential conclusion. If they came to loggerheads, what were his options? Would he leave her? Could he? He didn't want to. But he didn't want to live this way either.

And while he had not been on the prowl, there *were* other fish in the sea. Rayford wasn't blind to the way women looked at him, looked up to him, talked to him, smiled at him. He had colleagues who had taken advantage of almost every member of their flight crews. He didn't doubt he could do the same if he was of a mind to.

But that wasn't the point. He just needed a little shift in the balance of power at home. Not only did he want to do what he wanted to do, but as the sole breadwinner he also felt entitled to his own time, and he was finished being made to feel small over it.

How could so many things be going right in her life while her marriage seemed to be stagnating? Irene prayed for Rayford every day, mostly for his salvation. But lately she had been pleading with God for patience and under-standing. She and Rayford had become strangers, awk-ward, alien beings who seemed to spin in separate orbits. They weren't even united about the kids.

Irene kept a tight rein on Chloe and Raymie, though Raymie didn't need much. Chloe tested her mother, mostly verbally, seemingly all the time. Everything had to be explained or defended, or Irene could be made to feel like the most ignorant woman on the planet.

Rayford, on the other hand, was largely disengaged from the kids. When he was home he wanted them quiet. He spent a little time with them and was good with them when he did, but usually he begged off after half an hour or so.

Irene began mustering her courage and making a list for a confrontation. It wasn't working this way.

———

Leonardo Fortunato accepted Nicolae's invitation—through Reiche Planchette, of course—for a late dinner on a Thursday night with Nicolae's Aunt Viv and Reiche at the estate. This time Nicolae selected the black Bentley to pick up the guest, who was to be delivered to the front door at 10 PM.

It was arranged that Reiche and Viv would wait in the parlor and summon Nicolae when Fortunato arrived. By the time Nicolae came down from his study, wearing his most sedate and understated classy dinner jacket, Reiche had introduced Mr. Fortunato and Ms. Ivins.

Fortunato—"Please, call me Leon"—was very dark and stocky, wearing a tailored but not expensive suit and tie. He reminded Nicolae of a bodyguard in a bad movie. He looked older than his years, though his hair remained thick and black. Perhaps it was because of his jowls. His black eyes carried a world-weariness, but Nicolae thought he detected shyness as well, despite the man's varied background.

Fortunato presented Nicolae with an expensive bottle of Italian wine, insisting that he enjoy it himself at another time. "No doubt you have already selected one for tonight."

"More than one, actually," Nicolae said, thanking him.

The four sat to a formal meal at a small square table,

Fortunato immediately apologizing for not speaking Romanian. "That has made it difficult to teach here, but I do my best."

"Well," Nicolae said, "it happens that Italian is not one of my mastered languages, so let us choose, say, English, and see if we can make that work, shall we?"

As the staff served, Fortunato stage-whispered to Planchette, "How many languages has he mastered?"

"Nine."

"Nine! My heavens!"

"And enough of them," Nicolae said, "are close enough to Italian that I could do the best I can."

"English is fine," Leon said. "And what have we here?"

"Oh, just a little *delicateţe*—some *fruct*."

"A delicacy of fruit?"

"See, you speak Italian, English, and Romanian!"

They spent a long while enjoying a multicourse meal; then Nicolae excused Viv and Reiche and ushered Mr. Fortunato into a screened-in anteroom that looked out over the mountains. A fireplace roared.

Nicolae had Cuban cigars delivered. "Do me the honor of selecting that one," he said, pointing to one of the thickest in the humidor.

"Gladly," Fortunato said.

Nicolae chose a duplicate. He snipped the ends and lit both cigars.

After a long, slow pull, Fortunato seemed to savor it before slowly exhaling. "I can die now," he said, chuckling. "Thank you for a wonderful evening. You have a beautiful place, everything perfect."

"Oh, the night is young; do you not agree?"

Fortunato shrugged and smiled, as if up for anything.

"I thought we might talk at length," Nicolae said. "But I would not want to be a rude host."

"I have all the time you need, sir," Leon said.

———

Rayford didn't know what to think when Irene informed him of her plan for the next time he returned from a long trip. She had arranged for Jackie to take the kids, and she had booked a room at a local hotel. That was not new, but when she had done it before, it had been either Valentine's Day, their anniversary, or Rayford's birthday. This time there was no special occasion.

During his flying and idle time, Rayford tried to come to some conclusion about what this was all about. While their love life of late left something to be desired, it had not been all that bad. She was tired, stressed, over-worked. He was distant, not entirely happy, clearly with something unresolved on his mind.

Maybe it was a test. Maybe she was going to ask him if he had remained faithful. For that he was grateful. He didn't need real guilt atop what she already tried to induce in him with her looks, body language, and comments about his parenting, his responsibilities to his parents, and his fast-deteriorating Sunday commitments.

Rayford decided to take his list with him. Maybe it wasn't fair to ambush her, to spring a confrontation on her when this was a party she had planned. There was obviously something on her mind. He would enjoy putting her at ease, but at some point, if the timing and atmosphere were right, he was going to haul out that list.

That she had planned this at a hotel, plainly with romance as part of the milieu, meant she was not totally on the warpath. He wouldn't be either. But it was time to be honest. He would be clear with her that he had not strayed but also that he had good reasons for the emotional distance he had allowed between them. The fact was, this was as much or more her fault than his, and she was going to have to face that and deal with it.

"I'll have a bag packed for you, hon," she had said. "You don't even need to get out of the car unless you want to. I'll be ready to go, and we can head straight for the hotel as soon as you pull into the drive. How's that sound?"

"Suspicious," he said.

"I'm sure glad you said that with a smile," she said. "There can't be anything wrong with a woman wanting to seduce her husband, can there?"

"I'll rack my brain," he said.

NINE

Nicolae Carpathia couldn't help but be intrigued by the dichotomy that was Leonardo Fortunato. During the meal he had listened to the man but had not really taken him in visually. Nicolae was always more concerned with how he looked than how others did.

But now, trying to get to know the man, he surveyed him more carefully.

Fortunato was probably five inches shorter than Nicolae, and yet was so thick and compact that he appeared a solid mass. The little things were not lost on Carpathia. The suit, dark and conservative, was plainly inexpensive and yet tailored. French cuffs with diamond links protruded from the sleeves. Fortunato wore two rings on one hand, one on the other.

His tie was an iridescent red and seemed to pulsate, even in the dim light of the screened-in anteroom.

When he crossed his legs—no small feat—socks that matched the suit showed a red stripe that almost matched the tie. Nicolae decided this was a man who had to fight flamboyancy.

A soft breeze kicked up and Carpathia edged closer to the fire. Fortunato did the opposite. Not only did he lean away, but he asked if his host minded if he shed his suit coat.

"Not at all," Nicolae said, snapping his fingers and calling out, "Peter!"

A valet appeared.

"Oh, I'll just drape it over the back of the chair," Fortunato said, "if you don't mind."

"I do mind," Nicolae said. "Peter, please hang Mr. Fortunato's suit jacket and bring him a smoking jacket just in case."

Peter soon returned with a burgundy felt-and-satin number and draped it over the arm of a divan near Fortunato.

Leon leaned toward Carpathia, spreading his feet and resting his elbows on his knees. In the low light Nicolae noticed sweat rings under the man's arms. Nervous or truly overheated? He never touched the smoking jacket.

The men talked for hours, and by about three in the morning, Carpathia began to feel a strange bond. Fortunato seemed to know a lot about a lot. In fact, he seemed to know everything about everything. Had Nicolae enjoyed such a wealth of experience and exposure, he believed he would have long since been one of the most revered men in the world.

"I need to ask you a few questions, Mr. Fortunato, and I beg you to not take offense."

"Please."

"How is it that you have remained so anonymous? Why have I never heard of you before?"

Fortunato smiled as if Carpathia could have paid him no higher compliment. "That, my young friend, is by design. I like to think of myself as a kingmaker."

Nicolae sat back. *A kingmaker?* "You get great satisfaction in giving others the tools they need to excel."

"Exactly!" Fortunato said. "I don't know why myself. I don't even understand it. Many have asked me why I am not a leader, why I don't seek the limelight for myself. I don't know, but I'll tell you this: my life is a calling. I can't tell you that the heavens opened and a light appeared or that I heard voices. All I know is that I come alive when my behind-the-scenes work results in the elevation of someone I have discovered, someone I admire and trust. At times like that, when my candidate wins or my client gets the promotion, I couldn't feel more fulfilled if I were king of the world."

"Fascinating."

"Thank you, Mr. Carpathia. Frankly, it fascinates me."

Nicolae asked Peter to bring the humidor, and he chose a smaller, milder cigar. "Mr. Fortunato?"

Leonardo declined.

Carpathia lit up. "You will tell me if I keep you too long."

"No, please. I am a night owl, and who doesn't like to talk about himself?"

Nicolae chuckled. "I am curious about your spiritual background. Mr. Planchette tells me you were raised Catholic and studied for the priesthood."

"Well, I was a religion major in a Catholic university not far from the Vatican, but I don't believe I was ever truly priest material. I loved the church and all the trappings, but I was not humble enough."

"Not humble enough?"

"I am a transparent man, Mr. Carpathia. I will tell you the truth. What appealed most to me about my inherited religion was the formality and the pageantry. I never felt close to Christ, the object of the church's worship. Many of my classmates and colleagues did, and I respected that and envied them. And yet I knew why I fell short in that regard as well."

"You wanted to be pope."

Fortunato lifted his head and roared. "Close! Close! I wanted to be Jesus!"

Carpathia laughed along. "We would make quite a pair, Mr. Fortunato. I want to be god!"

The men enjoyed a good laugh.

"Are you up for a walk, Mr. Carpathia? I feel like a rude guest suggesting it, but I'd like to get up and move."

"Certainly, but we must both agree to drop the formalities. I can tell we are going to become friends, and so let us get on a first-name basis. Fair enough?"

Fortunato reached for and shook Carpathia's hand, standing and pulling the younger man from his seat.

"Would you like Peter to bring your suit coat, or do you prefer the smoking jacket?"

"Frankly, Nicolae, I am fine. I love a bracing breeze in shirtsleeves."

"Suit yourself."

Rayford Steele was not a man to look a gift horse in the mouth. Irene had booked the honeymoon suite at the finest local hotel, and they enjoyed a late dinner served on their balcony. A couple of hours later they lounged in bed in the dark, talking.

He couldn't shake the feeling that he had been set up, that she had used everything she knew to soften him for something. For what, he did not know. But he had an idea. By midnight he wished she'd just get on with it. Yet she was still going on with memories, reminiscences of how they met, fell in love, courted, got engaged, married, moved, had kids.

It *was* fun to rehearse and grow nostalgic over years that seemed so recent and had flown so quickly. Rayford could tell Irene was easing into her real subject, the true reason for this getaway, when she waxed melancholy about Chloe.

"I'm worried about her, Rafe. She's too much like you. . . . I didn't mean that to sound the way it did, but she's only twelve years old. I had always hoped our kids would remain tender longer than most. Tender doesn't describe her anymore, does it?"

"No, but it describes Raymie," Rayford said, "and that troubles *me*."

"Rafe, he's only four."

"A very soft four."

"He ought to be soft at four. And don't worry; no son of yours is going to grow up soft."

Rayford liked the sound of that.

"We'll get to Raymie," she said. "We need to talk about Chloe. She's a skeptic already, challenging everything, believing nothing."

"Not believing like you, you mean."

"Well, there is that. A kid her age ought to have no trouble believing in and loving Jesus."

"Unless she doesn't," Rayford said.

"What does that mean?"

"Well, as long as we're getting into this—I mean, you want to, right?"

"More than anything."

"That's what I was afraid of."

"Rafe, don't do this."

"Okay, let's just talk. But since you've gone to all this trouble, let's be frank."

"Can we be kind at the same time?"

"Sure. I'll try. But this is as much a hot button for me as it is for you, Irene. We've been dancing around this for months, and it's time to get it all on the table."

Irene clasped her hands behind her head and sighed. "Fire away."

"You don't want to hear it. I can tell."

"No, I do. I just think I've heard it all before."

"Fine. Then I won't repeat myself."

"No, Rayford, please. I shouldn't have said that.

I hope you can surprise me with some new insight. Really, I do."

He turned to face her and leaned up on an elbow. "Chloe's okay with God and church and all that. Just like I am. We're simply not as into it as you are. You're the most religious person I know."

"It's not—"

"Irene, listen to me." His voice had an edge of annoyance he didn't care to blunt. "If you get into that business of its not being about religion but being about Jesus, I'm going to explode. I know, okay? I know. You say it all the time. Religion is our attempt to reach God. Jesus is God's attempt to reach man. I've heard it so many times that it's just words by now. It's something—forgive me—that a religious person would say! Don't you see? You come off like a nun or a saint or a Bible student or something. We all have to be as religious as you or we don't qualify."

For once he had silenced her, and he wasn't so sure that was a bad thing. Now he could turn and, he hoped, sound more reasonable.

"Think of what you could have for a husband. An abuser. A womanizer. A drunk. Someone who *never* goes to church. I go to church, Irene. Maybe not as much as you think I should, but I go. I believe. I believe in God and I even like hearing about Jesus. That stuff's all okay with me. I just don't want to be a weirdo. I don't want it to overwhelm my life, make me awkward around my friends. They have their beliefs and I have mine. It's a free country."

Rayford wanted to fill the glaring silence with his views on when he was and wasn't going to church and how he planned to go less and play golf more, but that could wait. He didn't want to press his luck. He knew he was saying other than what Irene hoped to hear. In fact, he was likely fulfilling her worst nightmare. Well, this had been her idea. She wanted to know where he stood, and this was where.

"We were talking about Chloe," she said quietly.

"We were? Okay. What about her?"

"She worships you. You're her hero. She wants to be just like you."

"Is that so bad? She could do worse. Wouldn't you love for her to be a successful pilot someday?"

"That isn't the point. She's a brilliant student. She can write her own ticket. She'll be fine that way. You're a grown man. You have the right to make these decisions on your own, even if I disagree. Even if I hate the consequences. But she's twelve, Rafe. Challenging the existence of God, saying I can't know the Bible is true, fighting going to church and Sunday school every week. She criticizes her Sunday school teacher, slouches and folds her arms and closes her eyes during sermons."

"She hears them."

"Oh, I know well she hears them, because she picks them apart."

"So do you, Irene."

"I give up." She turned away from him.

"No, don't do that. At least we're talking. Do you really want me to feel like you've given up on me?"

She turned back. "No, I don't. But I want you to encourage Chloe to give me a chance. Give the Bible the benefit of the doubt. Make an attitude adjustment about Sundays."

Rayford sat up and swung his feet off the side of the bed. "Can't do it," he said.

"Oh, Rafe!"

"I can't, Irene. I have to be true to myself and do what I believe is best. You're not going to browbeat your own child into a life decision this important. You can't force her to share your beliefs. She has to come to them on her own. I want her faith to be based on her own study and conclusions."

"Like yours."

"Yes, like mine! What's wrong with mine?"

"You don't have any, Rayford. You attend church the way you go to the club. If you were serious about your relationship with God, you would study the Bible, go to a church that teaches and preaches it. And you'd be sure you raised your children the same way. No, I don't want to give Chloe an inherited faith. I just want to see her more open, more teachable, more malleable. She's too young to be so rebellious, so antieverything."

"She's not a rebel, Irene. She's a good kid, a great student, never in trouble. I asked you to imagine the kind of husband you could have. Imagine the kind of daughter you could have."

"So I'm supposed to be thrilled with my husband and my daughter—despite their nonexistent relationships with God—because of what they're not? Well, Rayford, let me tell you, I'm just so thrilled that I thank God every day you're not like Hitler. And isn't it wonderful that you're not a mass murderer? That could really put a crimp in a marriage."

"Now it's my turn to give up," he said.

With that, Irene was out of bed and pulling on her robe. She turned on the lights and sat before the television.

"You know," he said, "that thing you said about my going to church the way I go to the club?"

"Um-hm," she said, not looking at him.

"That's one of the reasons I don't want to switch churches."

She turned to look at him, bewilderment on her face.

"You realize our church is where we met our doctor, our dentist, our insurance guy, and even the man who put my name in for membership at the club?"

Irene turned back to the TV.

TEN

NICOLAE CARPATHIA and Leon Fortunato walked and talked until dawn, stopping to take in the beauty of the Romanian sunrise over the Carpathian Mountains. Peter and a bodyguard discreetly stayed about a hundred feet behind them.

The men traded life stories, hopes, dreams, plans. While Nicolae had not yet said it in so many words, it had to be clear to Fortunato that he was being vetted for a role in Carpathia's future.

The more they talked, the more specific Nicolae became and the more questions he asked. Fortunato soon sounded like a man selling himself, but he was subtle. It was, Nicolae decided, as if it was clear to both men what each wanted, but neither would put it on the table.

Finally they retired back to the anteroom, where Leon slipped on the smoking jacket and Peter had plates of fruit and toast delivered.

"I do not like to play cat and mouse," Nicolae said at last.

"I figured as much."

"You are the ultimate kingmaker, Leon. And I want to be king."

"I know."

"You know?"

"Surely you are not surprised to know that I did my homework before accepting your invitation. Your rise in business has been meteoric. Your intelligence has already been celebrated. Your physical prowess is legendary. While you have not announced it publicly, it is getting around that you are restless, eager to expand your horizons, grow your business, widen your influence. Politics cannot be far off."

"Let me ask you something, Leon. How far would you go to help a man achieve his dreams?"

Leon pushed his plate away a couple of inches and leaned back, crossing his arms. "Ah," he said. "The true test."

"I am just curious."

"Oh, it is more than that and you know it. It is the crux of the matter. I told you I did my homework."

"Meaning?"

"Meaning I have an idea how far *you* will go to achieve your goals."

"Really? How far?"

"Let me stall by telling you what got me booted from the Catholic university."

Carpathia loved such stories.

"I told you I loved the pageantry. I never forgot the funeral of one pope and the election of another and all that went with it. What is more beautiful than the red, red, red of the cardinals' vestments? Even as a student, I always had businesses on the side and, thus, more money than my classmates. Once I had it in my head that I wanted a cardinal's vestments, nothing could dissuade me. I rushed to the shop at the Vatican, only to have to lie to be able to purchase what I wanted. I was informed that I had to have special permission to buy such garments, so I immediately spun a yarn about it being a gift for my bishop. I said we were the same size, and I was overjoyed when the questions stopped and the measuring began.

"When the vestments were ready and I tried them on before the three-way mirror, I could have gone straight to heaven. I had to harness my emotions to continue the ruse and insist that my bishop would be as thrilled as I was. I wanted to wear them back to my dormitory, but that would have given me away. I couldn't wait to get back and don them again.

"I wore them everywhere, like a costume. Classmates *ooh*ed and *aah*ed. Upperclassmen scowled and derided. I outwitted a professor by telling him I was wearing a rented costume for a masquerade party. He didn't find it amusing but neither did he imagine it broke any rules. Which was not true of my wearing the getup to classes the next day. *Class*, singular, would be more like it. By the time I entered my second class, the authorities were waiting for me. I was brought before an administration council, where I was scolded, reprimanded, and instructed to return the 'costume' posthaste.

"I tried to tell the council that my true motivation for wearing the elaborate habit was genuine admiration and respect for them. They weren't buying. They said my devotion belonged to Christ. And you know, Nicolae, it hit me in that moment. While this had all really just been a lark—a compulsion to have and to wear the beautiful garments—I had no real devotion to Christ. I knew He was the object of the worship of the church, was purported to be the Savior of the world, the Son of God. But I simply didn't believe it."

"And so?"

"When I was seen, hours later, still traipsing about campus in my vestments, I was summarily expelled."

"And excommunicated?"

"No. That was threatened. I accomplished that on my own."

"On your own?"

"I simply stopped being Catholic. No Mass. No prayer. No rosary. No nothing. I had read widely in Theosophy, and while I determined to remain a-religious for the rest of my life, its tenets most resonate with me."

"And those are, in a nutshell?"

Fortunato turned and stretched his legs, crossing them at the ankles. "The beauty of Theosophy, which is not yet two hundred years old, is that basically everything is okay with them. You can bring your own religion into the mix, as long as you agree that everything you believe from here on out comes from your own intellectual study and not from dogma or tradition or single authorities. We believe all religions are part of man's effort to relate to one another. And everyone can cooperate."

"But surely there must be some commonly held beliefs. Otherwise Theosophy becomes everything and nothing."

Fortunato nodded. "These are not fixed beliefs but rather a way of looking at life. We believe in reincarnation, karma, worlds beyond the physical, consciousness in all matter, physical and spiritual and mental evolution, free will, self-responsibility, altruism, and the ultimate perfecting of human nature, society, and life."

It sounded like blather to Carpathia, but he wasn't ready to say so. "Oneness," he said.

Fortunato nodded. "Oneness is very much a part of it. Our second president, the late Annie Besant, wrote the Universal Invocation. Would you care to hear it?"

"Of course."

> "O Hidden Life, vibrant in every atom;
> O Hidden Light, shining in every creature;
> O Hidden Love, embracing all in Oneness;
> May all who feel themselves as one with Thee
> Know they are therefore one with every other."

Carpathia couldn't help himself. He howled with laughter.

Fortunato smiled with only his mouth. "What am I missing? This is funny?"

"Hilarious! Has this mishmash of silliness had an iota of impact on the world?"

"It has an impact on its adherents."

"Really. What impact has it had on you, Leon?"

Finally he truly smiled. "It gives me something to teach. To talk about. It's harmless."

"And toothless."

"Unless—and this is the beauty of it—you bring a bit of your own belief system into it. For instance, among the founders and early leaders are women who were religious, then atheistic, then into Theosophy."

"As for you, you bring a bit of Catholicism?"

"No. I told you, I never bought into the central theme of that. I believe in the spirit world."

Nicolae stiffened. He was eager to get back to the subject of the extent to which Fortunato might go to achieve his client's goals, but now they were getting somewhere.

Irene finally reached the part Rayford had feared and dreaded. She switched off the TV and stood to face him. "The fact is, dear," she said, "this is not working. We're not together in the most important areas of life, and something has to change."

Really. Was she honestly prepared to present an ultimatum, to throw down the gauntlet? "What do you propose changes, Irene? Let me guess. I go whole hog with Jesus, start going to the fundamentalist church, never let golf get in the way of church, and use my influence on Chloe to get her on board too."

"That would be a start. No, that would be heaven."

"You're joking."

"No," she said. "Were you? I think you have assessed the situation perfectly."

"I think you have a blind spot the size of Texas. This isn't going to happen, Irene, and I'll tell you why. Chloe is going to make up her own mind with influence from us both. I am not switching churches. And I am not giving up golf or having you tell me what I can or can't do or when I can or can't do it. If I miss church for six months, that doesn't mean I don't believe in God or I'm not as spiritual as you. And if you think this gives you license to go to the other church behind my back, I forbid it."

"There's a twenty-first century man for you. You *forbid* it?"

"You heard me. It's embarrassing enough to have you God-talking all the time, even when we have guests. Now enough is enough. I can't tell you what to believe or how seriously to take it. But you know where I stand, and this is how it's going to be."

ELEVEN

NICOLAE HAD THOUGHT he finally detected fatigue in the eyes of Leon Fortunato until they got on the subject of the spirit world. He wasn't ready to dump his whole story on the Italian, but he told him enough that Leon would know they were both on the same page.

Still, he wanted to get back to the other subject. Maybe this was the route. "You have a spirit guide?" Nicolae said. "A contact?"

"I believe I do," Leon said. "He has never steered me wrong yet. Every impression I get seems solid. Even his leading me to you."

"You discussed our meeting with a being in the nether-world?"

"I consult the spirits for everything."

"And?"

"Let's just say I came with great anticipation."

"Now let me ask you this, my friend," Nicolae said. "Is there any length to which your spirit guide might tell you to go that would make you uncomfortable, make you hesitate, make you resist?"

"No!"

The answer was so immediate and forceful that Nicolae flinched. "Indeed?"

Fortunato made a fleshy fist. "Some things are solid, and you just know. Like you knew what to do about your competition."

Now this was getting eerie. "My competition?"

"You think you didn't get Mr. Tismaneanu's attention?"

"Sorry?"

"I thought you eschewed cat and mouse," Fortunato said. "You're trying to tell me that your former employee's unfortunate demise was coincidental?"

Carpathia's mind was reeling. He had to hold out the possibility that this had all come from Planchette. Rule out all conventional explanations before giving credence to a man's intuition. He was tempted to excuse himself for a bathroom break and get Planchette on the phone.

"No one told me this," Fortunato said, "if that's what you're wondering."

"Told you what?"

"Oh, very good. Deny as long as you can. If we have a future together, Nicolae—and I'd like to think we might—don't sit there and look me in the eye and with a straight face tell me that your accountant jumped to the enemy ship and then was *accidentally* killed within days. Do you think Emil Tismaneanu believes that?"

Nicolae couldn't hide his smile. "I hope not."

That made Fortunato laugh. "I hope not too. It should be rattling in his brain all during the campaign for the lower house, wouldn't you say?"

"You know about that too."

"That you have not hidden. And I can help you win. My first bit of advice is on the house. Trumpet your military exposure, which begins soon. Then run as a dove."

This was uncanny. How could they think so similarly? Was it possible they shared the same spirit guide?

Nicolae stood, finally feeling he needed a bed. "Normally I would play it safe with a new acquaintance," he said. "But I must ask you flat-out. How far would you go to ensure my victory over Emil Tismaneanu?"

"How far would you want me to go?"

"As far as necessary."

"As far as, shall we say, Ion?"

Carpathia stared at him. "What if that was my request?"

Fortunato stood and stretched. "I need to beg your leave," he said. "But let me say this. My response to your requests—*any* requests—will be determined by how deeply I believe in my client and his cause."

———

Rayford sounded asleep, and he had never been good at faking it.

Irene slipped out of the hotel-room bed and sat by the window, staring at the streetlights. So this was how it was going to be. Well, at least there was some closure, some sense of satisfaction in even knowing that. She could quit banging her head against a brick wall and hoping for better. On the other hand, she hated herself for failing at this yet again.

Irene couldn't wait to talk with Jackie. What was she supposed to do with all this? That part in the Bible about the husband being the spiritual authority and the head of the home was misunderstood even when both spouses were believers, she knew. But what about when the man was not a true believer? Was she supposed to obey him?

Irene knew she could never do something she believed was against the will of God, even if Rayford commanded it. But he wasn't that type. He didn't browbeat her, didn't bully her. He simply told her how it was going to be, and she could do what she wanted in light of that, except he really didn't want her to go to New Hope.

Well, if he was going to have everything his way on Sundays, Irene was going to insist that Chloe be in Sunday school and church with her every week until she left for college. And if they paid for college, they should be able to expect her to live by their rules there too. That was unlikely, she knew. She could worry about that later.

So Irene was going to be a golf widow. And what kind of marriage could she expect from here on out? Her husband pegged her a religious nut. How attractive could that be? He was out and about all the time with beautiful young flight attendants on every flight. She wasn't about to lose him to them, no matter what.

Maybe it was time for self-examination. Was there a

way she could be faithful to Christ without so alienating her husband? What if she accepted his decision and more than resigned herself to it? What if she helped get his equipment ready, had his clothes laid out, reminded him of things she'd read about the weather or upcoming tournaments? What if she skipped a Sunday morning once in a while to watch him play in a special event? That would knock his socks off.

She heard him stir, then turn. He reached for her and found her gone. "Irene?" he said.

"I'm here," she said. "I love you, Rayford."

"You do?"

"You're a stubborn old creep, but I love you."

"Well, thanks. You're a Bible-thumpin' door-to-door evangelist, and I love you too."

"Do you really, Rafe?"

"I do. I like being married to you and want to stay married to you. I've remained faithful to you and plan to keep it that way."

"That means a lot to me."

"I mean it, Irene. Now come back to bed."

She joined him and they lay there in the darkness, Irene staring at the ceiling. "What if I learned to play golf?" she said.

"What?"

"How long would it take me to get good?"

"I've been playing all my life, and I'm still no good."

"You know what I mean. How long, if I took lessons, until I would quit embarrassing myself and you would let me play in mixed matches?"

"Mixed matches? I didn't even know you knew what those were. Thing is, it could take forever, and I don't think your heart is in it. I appreciate the effort, but you wouldn't be doing it for you. You'd be doing it for me, and that would never work."

Irene sighed. *Can't blame a girl for trying.*

TWELVE

Nicolae Carpathia became such a hit at the naval academy as both a student and an adjunct instructor that he was at first a concern for the brass, then soon ingratiated himself as one of their favorites as well.

He had been called on the carpet by an admiral who cautioned him against becoming too much a friend of the cadets. "You're also a student, yes, but you're just enough older than these young men and women that they could tend to idolize you. So maintain a bearing of authority and maturity."

"I understand, Admiral," Nicolae said. "I want to be an example to these people. I want them to see the possibilities for them, within the service of their country and again when they are civilians."

"You understand, of course, Mr. Carpathia, that our

wish is that graduates of this institution make the Romanian navy their lifelong occupation. Try not to make the private sector *too* inviting."

Nicolae smiled. "I will do my best," he said. "But it is not like I am unknown to them. They read the news."

"And they see you get dropped off every day in one of your many Bentleys. How many colors do you have to choose from?"

"Oh, not that many."

"I have seen at least three. How many?"

Nicolae shrugged. "I see them as simply vehicles, sir. Equipment. Conveniences."

"My life should be as convenient."

"Perhaps I should be talking to *you* about considering the private sector."

"Don't tempt me."

Nicolae put Leon Fortunato on a monstrous monthly retainer and provided him an office. It was soon clear that both Reiche Planchette and Viv Ivins viewed Fortunato with skepticism and wariness, but Nicolae chalked that up to jealousy. He was careful not to put Leon in charge of any staff. Leon was wholly a behind-the-scenes adviser, but it was hard to hide that Nicolae did nothing without his counsel.

Irene Steele had to face it. Her pain and resentment toward Rayford and his new resolve to do as he pleased affected her view of his parents. It was cold and small and petty, and knowing that about herself made her feel like scum. She confessed it to Jackie.

To her credit, Irene's friend did not immediately react, though Irene could easily read her look. "I've terribly disappointed you, haven't I?" Irene said.

Jackie smiled but looked away. "You're human, Eye," she said. "You remind me of me. I have to admit, for a long time I've wondered if you were too good to be true. You try so hard. You're so devout. You're growing and thriving in a difficult situation with a difficult husband. Yes, the right thing to do in this circumstance is to love these people with the love of Christ, regardless of who they are or how they are related to you."

"I'm just awful, aren't I?"

"You need to do the right thing; that's all."

"But I have to feel it."

"God feels it. He loves the Steeles."

"And so I should too."

"You do. I know you do. You've proven it over and over."

"But maybe I've done all that hoping to impress Rayford. It *has* impressed him too. Sometimes he's actually moved that I have taken the time and effort and energy to visit his parents."

"That's all right, but you well know that can't be your motive. This is either a selfless act of love and compassion, or it's something else."

"How I feel right now makes me wonder if I've ever had the right motive," Irene said.

"You're not planning to abandon them now, are you? Just to get back at Rayford? to show him?"

Irene had considered that very thing. "I need to pray about this," she said.

"No, you don't."

"Sorry?"

"This is not something you need to pray about. You already know the answer. God wants you to do the right thing, regardless of your personal feelings and pain, and you know it. If you want to pray about something, ask forgiveness for temporarily getting your focus off the Steeles and onto yourself."

"Leave it to you to cut to the heart of the matter."

Jackie smiled. "Just here to serve."

"Willing to watch Raymie the rest of the day, or were you just saying you're here to serve?"

"Happy to."

Nicolae should have known the news would be hard when the arrangements for a phone call from James Corona in Louisiana were made well in advance to be sure Nicolae would be available. Carpathia was celebrat-ing—though his largesse had made these inevitable—not just his appointment to similar teaching assignments in both the army and air force academies but also the pub-licity for the same in local papers and magazines.

He had been riding high, learning from Leon, putting the pieces in place for announcing his candidacy for the lower house of Parliament against none other than his major business rival, Emil Tismaneanu. He took the call in his own office.

"This is the most difficult call I've ever had to make, Nicolae," Corona began.

"Talk to me, Jimmy."

"We chose to match your investment funds dollar for dollar."

"I know."

"What we make, you make, and what we lose, you lose."

"I was fully aware."

"Today we have each lost half our investment."

"You are not saying . . . ?"

"Fifty million each, Nicolae. I'm terribly sorry."

"You are sorry? What happened?"

"We partnered with a private propulsion firm and launched two satellites simultaneously. They are not sure what went wrong, but something malfunctioned and both were shot off course, never gained orbit, and plunged into the sea."

"But insurance . . ."

"Covered only a percentage. The loss was actually much greater than the fifty each."

"Jimmy, surely you had no illusion that this was my own money, that I could just consider it easy come, easy go."

"I figured as much. I'm sorry."

"I am into a lender for the whole amount. Now I want the other fifty back right away, and—"

"Nicolae! You must know I can't do that. The documents are clear and binding. Our only hope to salvage this loss is to make the project work. We're starting from scratch, and it will take your remaining fifty and our fifty to have a chance."

"I cannot and will not default on a hundred-million-dollar loan, Jimmy. Get serious."

"I hope you don't have to sue us, Nicolae. I tried to warn you of the risks. I even tried to talk you out of this. But your enthusiasm was shared here, and I'm still confident—"

"Sue you? Jimmy, I will destroy you! Whom do you think you are talking to?"

"I hoped a friend."

"Friendship is left at the door when a hundred million is on the table. Did you expect me to just sit and take this? Do not dare touch the other half of my investment if you do not want an injunction slapped on you this very day. You will be hearing from my lawyers regardless, but I warn you not to proceed with the rest of my money."

"Nicolae, be reasonable. My counsel tells me the investment from you is secured and that we are free to proceed, which we plan to do."

Nicolae slammed down the phone and summoned Leon.

The older man arrived and sat passively taking notes, letting Nicolae rave.

Nicolae paced about his office, staring out at the mountains.

Finally Fortunato got his attention and raised a hand. "Sit, sit," he said. "You have options. Legal ones, no. Mr. Corona is right. You can tie them up, but they could countersue and win damages if you unduly delay them from trying to salvage this."

"So what options?"

"One big one."

"Just tell me, Leon."

"Stonagal."

"Oh no. I could never. First, I would have to explain why I went elsewhere for the original funds."

"And why did you? Just to exercise some independence?"

"Of course."

"Noble but foolhardy. Don't look at me that way, Nicolae. I mean no offense. Hindsight and all that. You must agree it would be much easier to be into Jonathan Stonagal for this money than the Intercontinental. He has the muscle to get it back. The bank has only the law, and the law is on the side of Corona."

Carpathia dropped into a chair. "I cannot fathom bringing Stonagal into this. I want the bank to use its muscle. And I want to ruin Corona *and* Tismaneanu."

"No, you don't."

Carpathia looked up, surprised. "I do not?"

"Tismaneanu, yes. He used your own man to hurt you. Corona, it seems to me, acted in good faith. Losing an investor's fifty million is egregious, of course, but ruining them only hurts you more. Help them. Get them what they need. More money, if possible, maybe from

Stonagal. And if you believe in their technology, they could make you rich beyond your dreams."

"But I do not want to be so beholden to Stonagal! To anyone!"

"You would not be beholden to him. He would merely see it that way. He likes to keep people under his thumb. You do not respond well to that, nor should you. Play his game in order to get what you need, and when the time comes, pay him off and turn your back on him."

"Right now that does not seem possible. Dig myself out of a one-hundred-million-dollar hole?"

"Fifty."

"Oh, that makes it more manageable."

Fortunato smiled. "That's my future king. But tell me, Nicolae. Are you truly unaware that Stonagal owns the lion's share of Intercontinental Bank?"

"Oh, he does not! His affairs are quite public."

"Apparently not all of them, if one of the leading businessmen in Europe is unaware."

"The Intercontinental? I have been using his money all along? Are you serious?"

Leon nodded.

"Do you think he knows about my loan?"

Fortunato shot him a double take. "Do I think Jonathan Stonagal knows who has secured a hundred-million-dollar loan from one of his banks? Yes."

"Do you think he has an inkling that I did not know of his involvement?"

"Now *that* is a great question. It would behoove you to convince him you were fully aware all along."

Since her salvation, Irene had to admit that she had not
experienced a plain, otherwise-unexplainable answer to
prayer. Until she walked into the care facility that housed
her in-laws today. The first step over the threshold saw
her awash in unconditional love and compassion for Mr.
and Mrs. Steele that made her temporarily forget how
their son was treating her.

She felt even worse for considering using them as
pawns in her game of getting back at Rayford. Where
had her altruistic plan gone, the one that called for her
surprising him by *encouraging* his golfing?

Irene found Mrs. Steele napping and so visited her
father-in-law. She was surprised to find him other than
agitated. Usually he was bound to the bed or locked in
his room or being followed by aides as he wandered.
Now he lay in his bed, gazing out the window.

"Hi, Dad," Irene said softly, so as not to startle him.

Rather, he startled her. He turned with a smile and
said, "Irene. How kind of you to visit."

"You remember me?"

"Of course. How're Ray and the babies?"

"Everyone's fine. But they're not babies anymore."

"I know. Chloe has to be twelve by now."

"Very good."

"How bad am I when I can't remember?"

There was a question for the ages. How honest should
she be? He deserved the truth. "Pretty bad, Dad. I miss
you when you're not really with us."

"And that's fairly often?"

She nodded. "And you're often agitated."

"That part I'm aware of," he said. "So frustrating. So embarrassing. Irene, it's terrifying. I am sort of conscious of what's going on, but I can't make things come together in my mind."

"How often are you lucid, Dad?"

He cocked his head. "Not often, I'm afraid, and not for long. I worry each time will be the last. Sometimes I awaken in the night and I feel clear as a bell. I start reminding myself of everyone's names and their ages, and I fight to keep it all straight. Then I fall asleep and wake up in a fog again."

"No wonder you're agitated."

"That's not the only reason."

"It's not?"

He shook his head. "Sometimes I wonder if my life was wasted."

"Wasted? You were a good husband and father and businessman. You provided jobs and goods and services. You raised a successful son."

He looked away. "Yeah. But . . . something. I don't know. Something was missing."

"I know that feeling," Irene said. "For a long time I felt something was missing from *my* life. Wondered if that was all there was."

He turned back to her and nodded. "Sometimes."

Irene felt the urge to hurry, believing she had just a brief window of opportunity. She didn't want to overwhelm him, but when might she get another chance like this?

"Dad, I came back to God. That's where my peace and contentment and satisfaction come from. Do you feel like you're all right with God?"

"I don't know," he said, looking down. "And now, see, you've got me confused."

"No! I don't mean to do that. We're just talking here. You said something seemed to be missing from your life. I'm telling you I felt the same and what made a difference for me. That's all. We can talk about it another time."

"I want to talk about it now, but—"

"But?"

He shook his head and his breathing came faster. "I'm . . . I'm . . . I can't, ah—"

"It's all right, Dad. We can take a break."

He pressed his lips together and looked at her pleadingly. "You see?" he said. "You see what happens? Words are hard. I—I have a son, right? And, and my wife. Is my wife all right? See? I can't even remember her name. Is she here?"

"She's napping, Dad. She'll be in to see you later."

"And you are?"

Irene was crestfallen and apparently couldn't hide it. "I'm your daughter-in-law, Irene. Married to your son, Rayford. We have two kids. Chloe is twelve. Raymie is four. You want to see pictures?"

The old man's face contorted and his lips trembled. "No," he rasped. "No thank you." And he swore. "This is what happens."

Irene stood and gently touched his arm, but Mr. Steele

wrenched away and rolled onto his side, his back to her, still shaking his head.

"I'm sorry, Dad," she said. "I didn't mean to trouble you. I just want you to know that God loves you and wants to be everything you need. He cares about you and doesn't want you to feel empty."

Mr. Steele fell still and his arm slipped from his side, his hand flopping onto the bed in front of him. Irene tiptoed around to see if she could detect any light, any life, any response in his eyes.

But he was asleep.

THIRTEEN

CAMERON WILLIAMS was a bit of a loner. He had his
friends on the Princeton campus, primarily international
finance student Dirk Burton of Wales, whom he had
interviewed for a school-paper feature. But Cameron had
finagled his own private room as soon as he could manage it, and by the time he was an upperclassman with his
sights on an internship—and eventual position—at
Global Weekly, he had become one single-minded young
man. Literally.

He still enjoyed dating, but he ran from any girlfriend
or even acquaintance who hinted at caring for him in a
real way. Girl pals accused him of fear of commitment.
Maybe they were right, but he didn't think so. He had a
one-track mind; that was all. There weren't many Princeton students with as modest a background as his, and
had it not been for his stellar college test scores, his high

school journalism awards, and his extensive extracurricular involvement, he likely never would have gained admittance to an Ivy League school. He had been involved in every club and activity he could find—except the choir, because he couldn't carry a tune in a barge.

Once at Princeton, Cameron had become determined not to just stay, but to make and leave his mark. He had to work, of course, but to kill two pigeons with one pebble, he took a job as a stringer for a local paper. He shone there so early that they kept offering him a full-time job. Cameron didn't want to offend his boss, so he brushed aside the offer with the excuse that he had to finish college first.

The truth was, his sights were set much higher than a local paper. He told Dirk Burton, "If I graduate from Princeton and have no other offers, I will feel like a colossal failure."

"No worries," Dirk said. "Somehow I think you'll succeed all right."

That said, Cameron Williams threw himself into every assignment for the little rag. He started covering high school sports and school-board meetings, of all things. The full-timers resented the attention he got from editors when his little stories seemed to gleam with import. He eschewed the standard who, what, when, where, why, and how inverted-pyramid formula and got to the point in the first paragraph.

Old-timers on the staff would start a high school basketball story with something like: "The Arlington Cougars extended their win streak last night with a 64–60 victory over the visiting Wheeling Falcons behind a 20-point effort from senior guard . . ."

Cameron's bosses would circulate his story of a similar game for everyone to see, especially with a lead like: "Jim Spencer's four-point play with less than a minute to go in the third quarter proved the turning point in last night's basketball game between . . ."

"You see?" the grizzled sports editor would tell the rest of the staff. "Get to the heart of the matter right away. These other stories are fill-in-the-blanks, and I've seen 'em a thousand times."

Cameron peppered his pieces with quotes not only from the coaches and players but also from fans and even referees. And his coverage of what might otherwise have been dead-boring school-board meetings crackled with drama, even if he had to embellish it.

> The fly vigorously rubbing his forelegs together on my knee during last night's meeting of the District 211 school board was the highlight until council member Fred Kinsella referred to the chairwoman with a gender-based epithet. That woke the rest of the board, the fly, and me. The inciting issue was . . .

But the story that launched Cameron Williams's career was one of those serendipitous events that falls into the lap of the person who finds himself in the right place at the right time. He found no joy in the circumstance, however, because the event was tragic almost beyond words.

He had been lounging in the editorial office, gassing with a couple of photographers, when one was summoned to the scene of a horrible accident. "Wanna come, Cam?" the photog said, strapping on his cameras and grabbing his coat.

Cameron checked his watch. His ball game didn't start for another hour, and the scene of the accident was on the way. He followed the photographer to a tiny suburban subdivision that had seen better days. They picked their way around and through emergency vehicles to where an ambulance waited, its lights off. A man leaving for his evening shift at a local factory had backed over and killed his own toddler son in the driveway.

Cameron immediately began interviewing the first cops on the scene. He was informed that the victim and the father were in the kitchen, and everyone was just giving him a moment before they transported the body to the morgue.

He signaled the photographer, and they slipped in the kitchen door. The curtains were closed and the room was dark, save for a light directly over the kitchen table, where the tiny body lay, wrapped head to toe in a dirty white sheet. The father sat before his child with his back to Cameron and the photographer, his forehead on the table, shoulders heaving. It was clear he had not heard them enter.

Cameron glanced at the photographer, who lifted his camera and aimed at the poignant scene. Just then the father slowly lifted his hands and put one atop the covered head of his son and the other over his ankles.

Cameron could only imagine the perfection of the composition in the frame of the camera.

The picture would tell the whole story. The room was dingy; the overhead fixture isolated the dead boy and his grieving father, abject with guilt, gently touching—blessing—the child he had killed. Cameron waited and waited for the click of the shutter and hoped it would not interrupt the man's reverie.

The photographer stood there for what seemed hours while Cameron remained transfixed, thinking only how sensitive he would have to be to ask the man a question or two once the boy was carried away. It was awful work, a terrible obligation, and yet it was his job.

Finally Cameron turned and noticed the photographer frozen in the moment. The man lowered his camera, lips pressed tight, and slipped behind Cameron and out the door. He had never pressed the shutter.

Cameron followed him out. They could fire him, but there was nothing to ask the father. Rather, Cameron followed the photographer all the way back to the office and interviewed him. His short feature entitled "The Greatest Photo I Never Took" was picked up by wire services and papers all over the country, won nine journalism awards, and was a Pulitzer finalist.

A month later Cameron stood at the window of his dorm room taking in a spectacular lightning-and-thunder storm that threatened to flood the quad. There was little he enjoyed more than such displays of natural phenomena. He would soon have to make his way across campus to the student newspaper office, and if the rain didn't let up, that would be fine with him. To actually be out in it with only an umbrella and a jacket, that was best of all.

As he was gathering up his stuff to leave, he took a call from his brother, Jeff, in Tucson. Jeff was the homebody, the commoner, the sensible one, not off chasing dreams out of his league on the East Coast. He was already married and had two young kids.

"Hey, Jeff," Cameron said, ever trying to ignore the tension and maintain family ties. "How're Sharon and my niece and nephew?"

"Oh, you know. Good, but Sharon's still trying to get me saved."

Cameron laughed. He'd wondered, as had many others, when Jeff married a thoroughgoing church woman. Jeff and Cameron had been church and Sunday school kids all their young lives but quit going as soon as they had a choice. On that they were agreed. It just didn't seem to make sense. They saw no connection between what was being taught and how the family conducted itself at home. Their parents were honest and pleasant enough, but whatever they got out of church seemed for Sundays only. It wasn't even discussed during the week.

Cameron's parents were still faithful attendees, but they resented that their church was apparently not good enough for their daughter-in-law. Sharon continued to go to the church of her youth, and she took the kids. Jeff went on special occasions, and it was plain to all that Sharon, wonderful as she was, considered him lost.

"I've got to get going, Jeff. What's up?"

"It's Ma."

"What about her?"

"Looks like cancer, Cam."

"Cancer? I didn't even know she was sick."

"She wasn't. It was sudden, but it's also bad. I'm pretty much running the business now so Dad can be with her most of the time, but they're giving her only a few months."

"A few months!"

"You'd better plan on being here over the holidays, Cam. Probably be the last time you'll see her."

"Oh, man."

"What?"

"I'm dead broke, Jeff. Maybe you or Dad could lend—"

"Things are no better here, Cameron. I'm driving one of the trucks myself, the Oklahoma run, every week. Gas prices are eatin' us alive, ironically."

It was ironic because they were gas-and-oil haulers, running crude from Texas and Oklahoma into Arizona for refining. Many Arizonans resented importing the crude from other states.

"I'll do what I can, Jeff, but I don't know how I'm going to pull this off."

"Your own mother, Cam."

"I said I'll try."

"You'd better call her."

"Jeff, I'm not a complete idiot."

FOURTEEN

IT WAS ANOTHER MONTH and four visits to the Steeles before Irene was gifted with another lucid moment with her father-in-law. She had begun to despair of his even recognizing her again. He had been blank or very upset every other time, including the one Sunday evening when she had finally shamed Rayford into coming along.

To Irene's surprise, Rayford hadn't resisted. It was clear he was still impressed that she took the time to do this, and it had been a long time since he had been there. "Dad doesn't know whether I'm there or not," he would say. "And all Mom wants to talk about is getting him saved."

"Well, you know that's on my heart too," Irene said.

Rayford said, "Yes, I *know that's on your heart too*," he said, mimicking her voice.

It was all Irene could do to keep from lashing out at him.

At the home Rayford's mother went on the offensive. "Well," she said, "glad you could find time in your busy schedule to visit the woman who raised you."

"Your memory seems good today, Mom," he said.

"It's hard to forget a son who forgets his mother."

"I haven't forgotten you, Mom. I could never do that. Now let's not fight. I'm here, aren't I?"

"Sure, but for how long? And for how long will this salve your conscience? It'll probably be another month or more before I see you again."

"I am flying a lot—and a lot farther—these days. I thought that would make you proud."

"Proud of a son who is gone too much to see his mother? What about your own family? You see them much either?"

"Of course."

"I'll bet you don't. I'll bet you're off doing your own thing when you are home."

Rayford shot Irene a glance, and she felt accused of talking out of school. She shook her head.

"Why don't you go see Dad?" Rayford said. "I'd better stay here awhile."

"Yes, you had better," his mother said. "You owe me."

"I know. I owe you a lot, Mom."

"Now you're patronizing me."

"I can't win."

Today an aide approached Irene in the hall. "You coming to see Mr. Steele?"

"Yes. Is he all right?"

"He's been asking for you."

"For me, personally?"

"By name, ma'am."

Irene hurried. She found Mr. Steele watching for her, a serious sense of purpose in his eyes. "Hi, Dad," she said, pulling a chair next to his bed. But he reached for her and took her hand in both of his, pulling her close.

She stood and leaned awkwardly over him as he talked softly, earnestly, his face close to hers. Irene fought to ignore his bad breath. He jumped into the middle of a conversation as if they had never left it.

"Irene," he said, "I think I know why I've felt so empty."

"You do?"

"I thought for a long time that it was because my son wouldn't take over my business."

"He wanted his own career, Dad."

"I know. He's a pilot now. And that's good. Not a lot of people can do that. But the way he turned me down. So mean. I don't know what I did to make him hate me so."

"He doesn't hate you, Dad! He really doesn't. He loves you."

"Well, maybe. But it's all right. I think I got over that. I'm proud of him, so I must be over it; don't you think?"

"Sounds like it."

"So I had to figure what else made me feel so empty, and I think you were right. I don't think I ever got the God thing right."

"The God thing?"

"It was never personal for me. It was just something

I did. Something I was raised in, felt comfortable with. But it never really meant anything to me. There had to be more. I mean, if there's really a God, there has to be more."

"He loves you."

"I know. You told me that. And it keeps coming back to me. Every so often when I can concentrate, that echoes in my mind and I don't know what to make of it. Jesus died for the sins of the world, but does that make me a sinner? I've never been perfect, Lord knows. But I never felt like a sinner before either. Maybe I do now."

"Do you?"

"Well, sure. I must be. Everybody must be. Otherwise, what's Jesus dying for? That's what's got me so off-kilter. I can't get my mind around it. I always saw God as a concept, a belief system, something you do on Sundays, and all that. But if He loves me, I ought to love Him. I don't love God, Irene."

"Why not, Dad?"

"I don't know. I guess I should. Sure. If His Son died for my sins. That proves He loves me."

"I couldn't say it better myself. You should pray, Dad."

"I have."

"And what did you say?"

"Just that I'm sorry and that I don't get it and could He explain it to me somehow."

"Explain what?"

"What it all means. What He's all about. What more there is if He really loves me."

"And what does He say?"

"He sent me you."

"Then listen to me. Are you listening, Dad?"

"I'm listening."

"Tell God you know you're a sinner and that you need His forgiveness and that you needed Jesus to die for your sins. Receive Him into your life and you'll be assured of heaven."

"I want to go to heaven."

"Of course you do."

Rayford entered.

"Son," Mr. Steele said.

"Hi, Dad," Rayford said, and he and Irene traded places.

"Irene here's been telling me about God and Jesus."

"I'll bet she has. You just try to rest. Don't get so worked up."

"I'm not worked up."

"I can tell you are. Now relax. You need a nap?"

"I'll have plenty of time to sleep when I'm dead. I'll sleep in heaven. Sleep will be heaven."

"I'm sure it will. Listen, Dad, work's going well. I'm flying longer routes, seeing more places. Wish you could go with me sometime."

"Don't make me laugh. You didn't invite me when I was healthy. And now you know I can't go, so it's easy to invite me."

"You see right through me; don't you, old man?"

"Always have. Always will. So you're a pilot. My son is a pilot."

"I'm your son, Dad," Rayford said, glancing at Irene.

"I know. 'Course I know. Who doesn't know that?"

Within a minute, Mr. Steele had drifted off again.

On the way home, Rayford was stony. "You're using them to get to me," he said at last.

"I wouldn't do that, Rafe."

"You think I'm dumb enough to believe my mother came up with that guilt trip without a little input from you?"

"I didn't say a word, Rayford. I swear."

"And you have to badger my dad with religion when he's fast fading? The man was with us there for a few minutes. We could have really communicated with him, logged some memories in his brain, shown him pictures of the kids, brought him up to date. But no, you've got Scripture verses you're trying to slam him with."

"I didn't quote any Scripture. And besides, he brought that discussion up on his own."

"Oh, I am so sure."

All Irene could do was pray she had gotten through to the old man before he lost touch with reality again.

"Mom, I'm trying everything I know how to find a way out there for Christmas," Cameron Williams said.

"Oh, Cam, don't go to any trouble. I know you're busy and money is tight. Maybe you can see me on spring break."

He hesitated. Didn't she know she was not expected to last that long?

She must have read his worry in the silence. "I'm going to beat this thing, Cam. I'm fine. I'm not even feeling any pain yet. They say that comes with the treatment, which is worse than the disease."

"I want to be there with you and for you, Mom. I'm working on it."

"Really, hon, you just concentrate on what you're doing. We can talk by phone. Daddy's taking good care of me, and Jeff's got the business under control. And you know Sharon. She's praying for me."

"I know that's true."

"I'll take whatever I can get at this point. The grand-kids want to know if I'm going to go bald. They're fasci-nated by that."

"I'll bet."

"And of course, I am. Already choosing wigs."

"Go blonde, Mom."

"I was thinking the same thing."

Cameron was in the student newspaper office that eve-ning when a call came for him from the *Boston Globe*. After pleasantries and congratulations on all his awards, the woman said, "Are you going to be around over the holidays?"

He told her of his hope to get to see his mother.

"I'm sorry to hear that for two reasons," she said. "First, for your mother. We'll keep a good thought for her."

"Thanks."

"And second, the *Globe* is honoring promising young journalists, and we'd like you to be our guest at a banquet. You'll get to meet our top people, take home a plaque, that kind of thing. We'd fly you here and put you up overnight, make it a nice deal. There are a dozen being invited, so it's a special opportunity."

"I'd love to," Cameron said. "Of course I would. Could I get back to you?"

"Sure. But don't delay. We'll want to fill your slot if you can't make it."

"Let me ask you this," he said, "at the risk of impertinence. If I chose to drive, would you still reimburse me for a plane ticket?"

"You're in New Jersey. That would be less than two hundred fifty miles. Sure. We could do that."

"Maybe that could go toward my little collection to see if I can get to Tucson to see my mother after that. Listen, count me in."

"You're sure? You don't need to get back to me?"

"No, I'm honored. I wouldn't miss this for the world."

FIFTEEN

NICOLAE CARPATHIA, to no one's surprise, proved a quick study in politics. Having never run for any office, he soon became the favorite to unseat the incumbent Emil Tismaneanu in the lower parliament. Carpathia, through Fortunato and Planchette, of course, hired the best public relations firm in Bucharest and assembled a crack team of youthful idealists, who were soon persuaded that Nicolae was the answer to all of Romania's ills.

Carpathia soundly defeated Tismaneanu in a pair of debates hosted by the University of Romania, after which Leon Fortunato insisted it was time to "start turning the screws."

Nicolae sat with him and Planchette and Viv Ivins in the mansion late one night. "How do you mean?" Nicolae said.

"He will be loath to debate you again, so resounding

was the response for you and against him. So now you go widely public with your insistence on another debate. He cannot accede to it without committing political suicide. You will box him into a corner. He has to refuse, but he will be desperate to save face. That will produce some kind of a foolish response, and you will capitalize on all the momentum."

The three men nodded, but Viv appeared stony.

"What is it?" Carpathia said. "You do not like the idea?"

"I agree it's good strategy," she said. "I just worry about Tismaneanu's desperate measures. He may spread a falsehood, or worse, a damaging truth."

"I have no skeletons, Viv," Nicolae said. "What could he possibly say to embarrass me?"

"I can think of three things."

"Do not keep us in suspense."

"Women, Ion, and Corona."

The men glanced at each other.

Fortunato nodded. "I wouldn't put it past him."

"Come on!" Nicolae said. "On the first matter, I am discreet. On the second, raising the Ion issue will make him look more than desperate. Tismaneanu has zero evidence, and I would immediately respond with a threat to sue for defamation. He will look terrible, especially when the educational trust fund for Ion's son is revealed."

"That is all in place and ready to go?" Leon said.

Nicolae looked to Planchette, who blanched. "It will be," he said.

"What has been the holdup?" Nicolae said.

Reiche shrugged. "Ion's wife did not seem impressed, and you told no one else."

Nicolae stood. "Reiche! What if she went to the press, telling them I promised something and never delivered?"

"She wouldn't. She's a simple widow—"

"She is a grieving, angry mother, man! And I believe she suspects me. Get on that first thing in the morning and leak it to the press. Very subtly. If we can get something out about that that appears not to have come from us, it will preclude Emil trying to use Ion's death against me. Now, Viv, what could he say about Corona? The satellite failures are on them, not me."

"You invested in a failed effort. And you have said yourself that you have about a 50 percent chance of defaulting on a huge loan."

Nicolae sat back. "And of course Tismaneanu knows all this."

"Of course."

"We need to preclude his using that against us too. But how?"

"Take advantage of our relationship with Mr. Stonagal," Reiche said. "Get him to cover the loan, make the debt appear to go away through some sort of personal agreement between you two. Then if Tismaneanu claims you are deep in debt, risking a default or bankruptcy despite your lavish lifestyle—sorry, but a case could be made for that—you can somehow prove you are thoroughly solvent and Stonagal can vouch for it."

Nicolae let his head fall back, his face pointed to the ceiling and his eyes shut, as if sleeping. "Tell me

something, Reiche," he said, his voice strained due to
the position of his neck. "Did you know Stonagal owns
the majority of Intercontinental?"

"Of course. Mr. Stonagal and I go back a long—"

"A long way, yes, I know. He is the angel behind your
organization; is he not?"

"One of many, yes."

"The primary one, no?"

"Yes."

"In fact, with him you need none of all the others
combined; am I right?"

"Yes."

Nicolae lowered his head and stared at Planchette.
"Stonagal also owns the laboratory from whence came
the sperm from my mercenary fathers, implanted in my
mother and resulting in me."

"Who told you that?"

"Tell me I am wrong."

"You are right, but it would behoove you not to reveal
to Mr. Stonagal that you know that. If he even suspected
you might have gotten that information from me—"

"You need not worry about Mr. Stonagal, Reiche. You
need worry about me."

"That's not fair, Nicolae. Who has been more loyal to
you than I?"

"Keeping from me the truth of my origin? That is your
idea of loyalty? Not telling me that Stonagal carried the
paper on my hundred-million-dollar loan all along? Why
would you have kept that from me, Reiche?"

"I thought you knew!"

"You thought no such thing. Are you also aware that Stonagal is behind a huge move to reduce the world's currency to just three denominations?"

"Well, no . . . well, I—"

"You probably know every detail."

"Well, that has been in the news, Nicolae. No one believes it will actually—"

"Oh, it will happen. And we are on our way to a single global currency. It may take time, but if Stonagal has his way, all of Europe will join Russia in doing away with the euro and moving to the mark. Asia, Africa, and the Middle East will trade exclusively in yen. North and South America and Australia will deal in dollars."

Reiche looked stricken. "That is the plan, I believe, yes. But nothing has been decided, and—"

"It is only a matter of time, Reiche. The question is, with the kind of access you have to Stonagal, why would you not be my source for such information? Why do I have to hear this elsewhere?"

"I'm sorry. I didn't know you wanted or needed to—"

"To be kept updated on international financial matters? Are you mad? Have you no concept of what I am trying to accomplish here?"

"Well, as I say, I apologize, and in the future I will—"

"Do you seriously believe you have a future with me, Reiche?"

"I certainly hope so. I—"

"I would have to be insane."

"Now, Nicolae, you must know that Mr. Stonagal and I are close, and—"

"And you believe that because I am into him for a hundred million and you knew him before I was born, that gives you some sort of protection—"

"No, I am not saying that! I want to emphasize that I believe in you. I am loyal to you. I may have fumbled the ball a time or two here, but it has not been with an ill motive. I just need to know what you need from me, and I will do all I can to—"

"You would like to prove your devotion to me?"

"Absolutely. I'll do anything—"

"Well, we shall see about that."

"Try me, Nicolae. You will see."

"You would be willing to meet privately with Emil Tismaneanu?"

"I would be honored."

"And you would speak for me?"

"A double honor."

"You might wish to withhold judgment on that until you know what I want communicated."

"I am puzzled, however, sir. How did you know these things without my telling you? Does Mr. Stonagal—?"

"Confide in me? Hardly. But the day may come when he wishes he had."

———————

Rayford didn't know what to think the first time Irene seemed to encourage his early Sunday morning golf game. He had been aware of her getting up in the night and quietly working in the closet and downstairs, but that was not unusual. She often had trouble sleeping. He was surprised at dawn, however, to discover that she had laid out his golfing clothes, put his golf bag next to his car, and even packed him a little goody bag with a frozen bottle of water, a couple of energy bars, and a love note.

In the note she also wished him a good game and said she and the kids would like to join him for lunch in the clubhouse after church. Rayford felt guilty that that didn't sound like such a good idea. Hanging with his golfing buddies for a sandwich and a brew was all part of the milieu, but he could hardly turn her down after all this.

Should he beg off from the guys and tell them he had lunch plans elsewhere? He didn't really want the kids in the clubhouse, especially at lunchtime. Rayford considered leaving Irene a note suggesting that he meet her and the kids at a fast-food place for lunch.

Ah, there was no point in upsetting her. He could live with her plan this once. Maybe he'd even have the rest of the foursome join them. Surely Irene would see that it was awkward and not suggest it again.

SIXTEEN

IRENE WAS SITTING IN CHURCH when her cell phone vibrated. She peeked at the caller ID and recognized the number of the health-care facility in Belvidere. Slipping into the foyer, she returned the call to find that Mr. Steele was in critical condition.

"What in the world?" she said. "We just saw him."

"Actually, this is not unusual, ma'am. Alzheimer's patients often have internal problems that don't come to light except for random testing. They don't understand or recognize pain, and often they complain of things that don't exist while missing serious problems that do. Mr. Steele is undergoing renal failure and has already been moved to the hospital wing. He may soon be reclassified as grave. We have not succeeded in reaching your husband."

"I'll let him know, and we'll be there as soon as we can."

Irene called Jackie, who said she would come right over from New Hope and take Chloe and Raymie to her home after church. Irene informed the kids' teachers and rushed to her car, dialing Rayford's number. She immediately got his voice mailbox, which reminded her that cell phones were verboten on the course at his club. She left a message, then called the clubhouse. They agreed to track him down.

By the time Irene pulled into the parking lot of the health-care facility, a hearse was parked at the curb. She prayed it wasn't for her father-in-law and told herself there were a lot of old and potentially terminal patients here. On the other hand, she had never before seen a hearse here.

Rushing into the hospital wing, she was intercepted by her in-laws' caseworker.

"I'm sorry, Irene," the woman said. "He's gone."

Gone? "This makes no sense," she said, reaching for the wall to steady herself. "So sudden."

"I've made arrangements for you to talk with the physician, and there's an aide who wants to talk to you."

"Where's my mother-in-law?"

"In her room. Sedated. You can imagine her tailspin."

"I should see her."

"She's sleeping, last I heard."

The doctor told Irene basically what she had been told when she was first called. "With Mr. Steele not being bedridden, we knew of no reason to monitor his urine output. He didn't complain until this morning, but apparently he had been unable to eliminate for some time. His color was bad, and he was suffering by the time we diagnosed the problem. We moved him over here, but he had already suffered a kidney shutdown, and it was a race against time, which we obviously lost."

Irene wanted to be waiting at the entrance when Rayford arrived, and she had to be reminded that an aide wanted to talk with her too. He was a young, fleshy Asian man wearing institutional blues. She asked him to join her in chairs near the door.

He introduced himself as Erap from the Philippines, and Irene noticed a faint blue tattoo of a tiny fish between the knuckles of his index and middle fingers. "I am a Christian," he said.

"I am too," Irene said.

"I know."

"How?" she said. "Do I know you? I don't recall meeting you."

"My cousin works in the supervised care unit," he said. "She told me she thought you were. But I know from Mr. Steele."

"What? Mr. Steele told you?"

"Not in so many words."

"I'm listening, Erap."

"I could see that your father-in-law was dying. In fact, I called in the code blue. In the few seconds before they rolled in the crash cart, I asked Mr. Steele if he was conscious and could understand me. He was barely speaking, but he nodded. I told him he needed to get right with God and receive Christ.

"I asked if he knew he was a sinner and separated from God. He nodded. I asked if he believed Jesus died on the cross for his sins. He nodded. I asked if he was willing to pray and accept Jesus into his heart. He said, 'I already did.' I said, 'You did?' He said, 'Yes, when my daughter-in-law told me how.'

"Mrs. Steele, I was there until they finished trying to save him. And those were his last words. I thought you would want to know."

Cameron Williams told his mother he was going to try to get home during the holidays. "With the money for the plane ticket from the *Globe* and a little loan from my Welsh friend, Dirk, I should be able to make it."

"Don't go to any trouble, Cam. There's no rush."

How he wished he could believe that. Of course, his brother, Jeff, didn't like the idea. "She's not going to tell you how bad off she is, Cameron. And Dad can't talk with her sitting right there. She looks terrible, hardly eats, can't get around well. She doesn't want to go to the hospital, but that's where she ought to be."

"That's her call, isn't it, Jeff?"

"'Course it is, but I'm telling you, she's fading fast."

"She sounded pretty good on the phone."

"So you're calling me a liar?"

"Come on, Jeff. We're not in junior high anymore.

I'm just saying she sounded fairly perky. And she was so proud of this honor I'm getting. She wants me to bring her pictures and news clippings."

"So you're coming when?"

"If I can find a few more bucks, I'll book a flight for the day I return to Princeton from Boston."

"How much more do you need?"

"A couple hundred. I can get one of those supercheap nonrefundables if I book it this week."

"I'll put a check in the mail today."

"Jeff, I can't ask you to do that. I—"

"You didn't ask. Come on, Cam. This isn't for you or about you. It's about Mom. You should be here tomorrow to be safe. What're we looking at now, ten days?"

"Twelve."

"Gimme a break."

"I'll see you then, Jeff. And thanks."

"Whatever."

Irene was not sure how the loss of his father truly affected Rayford. He was shocked, of course, at the suddenness of it, but he quickly seemed to go into business mode, making sure his mother was taken care of and that the funeral did justice to his father's memory.

Unfortunately, the funeral was held at the family's longtime church, Central Church. "I swear," Irene told Rayford as they prepared to leave for the church, "if there is no mention of your father's faith during the eulogies I'm going to say something."

"No."

"No? What are you saying?"

"Don't embarrass me or the pastor."

"It would embarrass you to have people know that your father was a true believer?"

"A deathbed convert is more like it, Irene. After your browbeating and that Filipino kid's badgering, what choice did a confused, dying man have? Anyway, he's already known in this church as a true believer for a lifetime."

"This won't be doing justice to your father." This was the last thing she wanted to fight over, but it was as if she couldn't help herself.

"Just promise me you won't do anything weird, Irene."

"You'd consider it weird if I merely told the truth?"

"I'd be humiliated."

She pressed her lips together and shook her head, despising that she felt so weak. "I won't humiliate you, Rayford."

"Thank you."

"I do wish your mother could be here. You couldn't stop her from telling the truth."

"Depends on your idea of truth," he said. "People would pass it off as the ravings of an Alzheimer's patient."

"But I would know better. And so would you."

"You know what I think, Irene. The truth is my dad has always been a Christian. He didn't just get religion before he died."

On the way into the service, Rayford was accosted by his childhood Sunday school teacher. She tearfully wrapped her arms around him. "I'm so sorry, dear. Your father was a great man."

"Yes, he was, Mrs. Knuth. Thank you."

Irene couldn't keep from weeping throughout the service. It was worse than she expected. While all the familiar Scriptures about death and rebirth were employed, nothing that was said explained them or brought the point home. Mr. Steele was revered, but there was no mention of his coming to a saving belief in Christ, no mention of his ever repenting of sin and putting his faith in God.

Irene was still crying on the way home, quietly grateful that the weather had finally turned and she would not be a golf widow again until spring. Rayford surprised her by putting a hand on her knee as he drove. "I do appreciate all the time you took with my parents," he said. "I really do."

His voice sounded quavery, and it was as close to tears as she had seen him in years.

"That's not over," she said. "I'll keep seeing your mom, of course."

"But they're saying she's already almost as bad off as Dad was mentally. Incoherent, and refusing to come today unless Dad came with her."

"All the more reason."

SEVENTEEN

"IS HE YOUR PARTNER?"

"I beg your pardon?" Cameron said.

"How would you like us to list Mr. Burton?"

"He's a classmate."

"You're not lovers then?"

"Um, no. Are we supposed to bring only significant others?"

"No, I was just wondering. We'll put him down as 'friend'; how's that?"

"Accurate."

Cameron was thrilled to be allowed to bring a guest to the *Boston Globe* event. Apparently others were bringing family members or lovers.

"There's another reason I ask," the woman said. "The executive editor of the *Globe* and a few of his associates would like a moment with you in his office after the banquet. Are you able to accommodate that request?"

"Well, sure. That'd be great."

"Your friend would not be included in that, unless he *was* your significant other."

"Really? Why?"

"I couldn't say."

"I mean, you don't think they're talking about something I would want to inform my loved ones about."

"I have no idea."

"Well, okay."

"He would be joining you then?"

"No. No. He'll wait. That will be no problem."

"The *Globe* is just up the street from the banquet site, and I don't expect your meeting will be long."

Irene could tell Rayford felt trapped. With the weather no longer conducive to golf, he no longer had an alternative to church on Sunday mornings. He still had some Sunday flights, but there were only so many. And when he was in town, there was really nothing else to do.

"You know what, Rafe?" Irene said. "I'll bet you'd enjoy attending New Hope, and it wouldn't be such an ordeal to talk yourself into going."

"No you don't. You haven't even been there. How do you know?"

"I can tell from what Jackie says. It's like I already know the pastor, Reverend Billings, even though I've never met him. And there's an assistant pastor, Bruce Barnes, whom everybody loves. All kinds of good things happening there."

"Don't start, Irene."

She hadn't meant to press; she really hadn't. Irene knew her motives were pure. If only she could find the right approach to the man she loved and worried about.

"I'm just saying," she said, "it might be worth a try. I sure would like to go and take the kids, especially when you're not in town."

He shook his head. "I'd never get you back."

"What do you mean?"

"It sounds like a cult to me. You know the leaders' names without even having been there? Let's just stay where we are, and I'll go when I can."

"Let him go, Nicolae," Leon Fortunato said, sitting across from Carpathia in the younger man's home office. "I'd encourage it."

"You would?"

"I would. You have nothing to fear from Jonathan Stonagal. Sure, he has the drop on you right now because you owe him a lot of money. But that will change. You have more potential in your little finger than he has in his whole body, and besides, he's not a young man."

"My strategy is not to fight him though, Leon. My plan is to endear myself to him."

"Then let Reiche accept his invitation to represent your interest. What are you worried about? Planchette being on Stonagal's turf?"

"Of course. You have seen the magazine spreads of Jonathan's Manhattan office; have you not?"

"I've been in those offices. They do make one's jaw drop. Planchette will be in way over his head. But I don't think they will be in league against you. Stonagal believes he, in essence, created you at the behest of the spirit world."

"Maybe he did."

"Maybe. But he will serve you one day, as we all will."

"I like the sound of that."

Leon stood and moved to the window. "I'm glad, because it's time for a tune-up of your image."

"What is wrong with it?"

"In many ways, nothing. You are in the thick of this race now and favored. But I have seen candidates lose in the final days on the turn of one phrase, sometimes one word. With you, it's all about tone."

"I am listening, Leon."

Fortunato returned to his chair. "Consider this question: who was the most influential person who ever lived?"

"Jesus."

"Excellent. As you know, the world has been impacted more by Him and His teachings than by any other. Our very calendar is based on His birth. What was His one most dominating character trait?"

Nicolae liked this kind of a challenge. "He could

perform miracles. At least that was claimed. I do not believe that."

Fortunato cocked his head. "That was something He was known for, yes. But I am talking about a quality He was seen to possess."

"Divinity."

Fortunato drew out a long "Hmm . . ."

"No?"

"Others have claimed the same."

"I doubt them all, of course, Leon."

"Of course, and while Jesus' adherents believe He was the only divine human, again that is not a character trait."

"All right, great one, I am ready for your all-knowing wisdom. What is the singular trait of Jesus you wish me to emulate?"

"In spite of everything He said and did and remains known for, two millennia after His death, Jesus' defining quality was humility."

Carpathia could not suppress a smile. "I will tell you the truth, Leon. I believe I am more than fairly self-aware. I know how I come across to people; I know myself. Frankly, I have nothing to be humble about and detect not a shred of humility in my personality."

Fortunato seemed to study him. "You *are* self-analytical."

"Humility is for weaklings. I know who I am and what I am capable of, and I am determined to do it."

"That's all well and good, but would you call Jesus a weakling? I submit that the ethereal paintings of Him as effeminate and cherubic are all wrong. This was a man of the earth, a man of the hardscrabble first-century Middle East. He was a carpenter, a man's man. A revolutionary. A preacher of paradoxes. An enemy of the establishment.

"You don't believe His entire résumé, fine. Neither do I. But His story is compelling. If He truly came from the throne room of heaven to be a mere mortal, it was the greatest act of humility ever. He had no reason to be humble either. His followers believe Him divine and perfect, self-sacrificial to the point of death. That is what makes His humility so attractive, so magnetic. You would do well to conjure a bit of it to round off your image."

Carpathia laughed, and the more he laughed the funnier the whole idea sounded to him, so he laughed all the more. "Think of it, Leon! What could be more egregious than *false* humility? I believe I may be unique among mankind. I have a combination of gifts and talents and knowledge and confidence that sets me far above perhaps anyone who has ever lived—including Jesus. And I should compound that with humility? What should I be humble about?"

Cameron Williams nursed his ancient Volvo north along the East Coast toward Boston through a light rain that turned to sleet and then a beautiful snowfall.

"Care to drive at all, Dirk?" he asked the Welshman.

"Not on your life. I would be on the wrong side of the

road within a minute. You just keep steering and I'll keep pedaling. Sure you have enough tread on these tires?"

"It's not the tires I worry about, Dirk. It's the heat gauge and the oil gauge. One is high, the other low."

"Seems a simple solution then, Cameron."

They stopped for oil. And antifreeze. And windshield-washer fluid. And a brush/scraper. A hundred miles later they stopped for more of the same, including the scraper, which had broken after two uses. Cameron was tense from peeling his eyes through the growing flakes and trying to sense whether his speed was right for the increasingly slippery roads.

He tried again to talk Dirk into driving, at least for a stretch. But Dirk was busy forming a snowball and hurling it, cricket style, with a long, looping left-hand delivery. Cameron barely evaded the missile, then dived into the car, laughing.

This was just another of the kinds of storms he loved. And while he had no interest in getting stuck or being late, this was an adventure, one he would long remember.

Cameron was relieved when they finally pulled into the covered parking garage of the hotel and banquet center. Once settled into their room with a couple of hours before they needed to be dressed for the bash, Cameron called his mother.

She wanted every detail, but she sounded terrible.

"You doing all right, Ma?"

"A little tired today. I'll be okay. Looking forward to seeing you in a few days."

"Two to be exact. Me too. Dirk just got back from

sneaking a peek at the banquet hall, and it appears they have pulled out all the stops. Lots of color and lights and sound. I couldn't afford to rent a tux, so I've borrowed Dirk's. It's a little snug and a little long, but I doubt anyone will notice or care."

"What about him?" Mrs. Williams said. "Doesn't he need his tux?"

"Nah. He's all tweedy like a Welshman should be, and anyway, he's just my date."

"Oh, Cameron!"

"That's what they think."

"Who's 'they'?"

"The powers that be at the *Globe*. They actually asked if we were lovers."

"Oh, they did not! Don't think you can pull one over on your naïve mom just because you're an Ivy Leaguer now. I know better than that."

"You're right, Ma. I was just teasing."

The banquet turned out to be even more than Cameron had hoped for. Copies of the honorees' articles were reproduced and circulated in a colorful brochure, and professional actors read some of each aloud. He may have been dreaming or just hoping, but it seemed to Cameron that his drew the loudest applause. Dirk agreed. The recipients were lauded individually and presented plaques commemorating the occasion.

The guest speaker was a horror novelist who had gotten his start in newspapers and never lost his affection for journalism. He regaled the crowd with stories everyone could identify with, and by the end of the evening Cameron was wondering if a newsweekly should really be his career target. Newspapering was still the stepchild of the publishing biz, but if you could land on the staff of a big metro daily, well, that would be exciting too.

The aide to the executive editor of the *Globe* made a beeline to Cameron at the end of the evening. "I know it's late and that you want to get going," she said, "but Mr. Rowland would still like a word with you. And you might want to consider staying the night and outlasting this storm."

A walk up the street confirmed her wisdom. Several inches covered everything. But Cameron didn't have the luxury of time if he wanted to get back to New Jersey in time for his flight the next morning.

He gave his keys to Dirk and asked if he could manage getting the car onto the street and parked in front of the *Globe* building. "Have it warm, defrosted, and ready to go, and I'll make it worth your while."

"You will, eh?" Dirk said, accepting a single dollar from Cameron. "Never saw a tip like this on the London Exchange."

EIGHTEEN

RAYFORD DID NOT see himself as a womanizer. Except for his Christmas party indiscretion a few years before, he had never been unfaithful to Irene, though he had to admit that if she had had a necking session like the one he'd had, only technicalities would keep him from calling it adultery.

His conscience had bothered him so much since that time that he had sincerely gotten his act together. Rayford wasn't blind. He could tell when women found him attractive. But the bad taste had lingered for so long after that holiday dalliance that he had been able to play dumb and deflect flirtatious advances.

Now he wasn't so sure. Hattie Durham had been a teenager when she became a Pan-Con flight attendant, and any heterosexual man with eyes agreed she was the total package. Head to toe, side to side, hair, face, and personality, she quickly became every passenger's favorite attendant and every crew member's dream.

She could be ditzy, but Rayford was convinced that was an act designed to manipulate. Interestingly, unless she was being reprimanded—which was rare, as she seemed to love her job enough to be conscientious—she never played that game with him. She plainly looked up to Rayford, and maybe he was being naïve, but it seemed genuine, not as if she was just flattering him because he was the captain.

Rayford was able to talk himself out of any less-than-honorable intentions by reminding himself how young she was. She had senior flight attendant written all over her, though it would be a few years before she reached that status. Other attendants, particularly women, acted less than impressed with her at first—jealousy, Rayford decided—but she soon won over even them. Her superiors seemed to look for minor offenses, but she was so good that they had trouble finding fault.

Rayford simply liked thinking about her, and he was always pleased when he saw her name on the crew list.

He was heading for the parking garage at O'Hare one evening when he heard heels approaching quickly from behind. "You live in Mt. Prospect, don't you, Captain?"

He turned, still moving. "I do, Hattie. Why?"

"You know I'm not far away. In Des Plaines. Just got a call that my roommate can't pick me up, and I hate to take public transportation at night. Would you mind—?"

"Of course not."

Hattie seemed to chatter nervously as they headed toward Des Plaines. It was all Rayford could do to keep his eyes on the road. He was certain he had never had as beautiful a woman in such close proximity.

He called Irene. "I'm going to be a few minutes, hon. Running a stranded teammate to her place in Des Plaines."

When he pulled up in front of Hattie's condo, Rayford started to get out.

"No need," Hattie said. "If you'll just wait to be sure I get inside before the boogeyman gets me, that will be fine." She took his hand in both of hers. "I really appreciate this, Captain. You're a doll."

At home a few minutes later Irene said, "So who was the stranded flight attendant?"

"That teenager with the funny name. I've told you about her."

"Hattie, the ditz?" Irene said.

"That's the one."

"Lock her keys in the car?"

"Wouldn't put it past her."

Rayford foresaw nothing untoward with Hattie Durham in the future. But he sure liked remembering her perched in the passenger seat, right beside him.

———

Dizzy Rowland, executive editor of the *Boston Globe*, welcomed Cameron into his spacious office and introduced him to three of his top people, two men and a woman. Their names flew past Cameron and he would have failed a quiz, but they all certainly looked the part. In banquet finery and at ease in the presence of the big boss, they exuded confidence and friendliness. All had nice things to say about Cameron's work.

Rowland pointed to a chair at a conference table away from his desk, and the five of them sat, four staring at Cameron. He finally felt conspicuous in his ill-fitting tux, and he was tempted to explain it.

"I just wanted a few minutes," Mr. Rowland said. "First, congratulations on your Pulitzer nomination and this award, not to mention your classwork. My spies at Princeton tell me you're a dean's-list student."

"Far from straight A's," Cameron said. "But I do feel obligated to give it all I've got."

"Admirable. Laudable. May I ask your career goal?"

"*Global Weekly*," Cameron said.

"Wow," Rowland said. "You didn't even have to think about that."

Cameron cocked his head. "It's been my dream for years."

Rowland sat back and seemed to study him, smiling.

Cameron's gaze darted at the others, who appeared bemused. Was admitting that lofty goal exposing himself as a rube, a dreamer? Well, the man had asked.

"You're sitting in the company of four career newspaper people," Rowland said. "Journalists, curious people. It wouldn't surprise me if one of them had a question."

They all seemed to speak at once, but the woman

prevailed. "Just wondering," she said. "Did you feel a check at all in your mind, blurting your magazine dream to a newspaper executive?"

Cameron thrust out his lower lip. "I guess I didn't. Should I have? Was that politically incorrect? impertinent? rude?"

The rest laughed. "It was commendable," Rowland said. "A lot of people would have worried more about diplomacy."

"Sorry," Cameron said. "I wasn't thinking. I certainly didn't mean to offend."

"Offend?" the woman said. "I found it refreshing. A little naïve, perhaps, but refreshing."

"Naïve?"

"Let me put it to you this way," she said. "A lot of our colleagues, even at our level, apply to the newsmagazines at least once a year, trying to get out of the daily grind—"

"—and into the weekly grind," one of the men said, and they all laughed again.

"The competition for jobs at *GW, Time, Newsweek,* and *U.S. News* is fierce. Your career goal is neither a surprise nor unique. Just lofty."

Cameron didn't know what to say. The Ivy League— Princeton in particular—was way past where he should have looked for college too. He wasn't about to give up a dream because it looked unlikely. He wanted to live an unlikely life.

"Did you wonder what I wanted to see you about, Mr. Williams?" Rowland said.

"Well, sure."

"Or did you just think it was to meet you and congratulate you?"

"I didn't have any idea."

"That's refreshing too," Rowland said. "I confess an ulterior motive. We want to hire you."

Cameron wondered where his mind had been. Why was this such a surprise? He simply hadn't considered it.

"Lest you think we say this to all the award winners," the woman said, "we don't. Of this year's crop, you are the only one."

"Well," Cameron said, suddenly feeling like an inarticulate bumbler. "Wow. Thanks. I had been hoping for a good internship."

"We're not talking about an internship, Mr. Williams," Rowland said. "For the rest of your senior year you would remain on the staff of the student paper and continue stringing for the local paper, but you would make yourself available for the occasional assignment from us, should a regional story hit in your area."

"Sure, I could do that."

"But upon graduation, maybe after a week or two to get your affairs in order, we would expect you to relocate here for a full-time reporting position."

"Full-time?"

"You are a gifted young man, Mr. Williams. We believe you have the stuff of a good newspaperman. Here you'll get a chance to find out if we're right. You'll get grunt work and have a deadline every day. This kind of work separates the pros from the dilettantes."

"And," the woman said, "the *Global Weekly* wannabes from the real deals."

Taking a solitary predawn stroll with his bodyguards at a discreet distance, Nicolae allowed Leon Fortunato's strange counsel to dance in his mind. Long a sports fan, Nicolae had always been entertained by the braggadocios, especially those who backed up their boasts. He agreed with the adage, "It's not bragging if you can do it."

The strutting confidence of young physical geniuses inspired Nicolae, and he wanted that same image as a politician and leader. But if Leon was right, the populace would soon tire of a self-promoter, a cocky show-off. Where did one go for examples of humility or to practice the art? One thing was certain: if Nicolae was going to appear humble, it would be more than art. It would be an act.

Cameron made his way onto the snowy street in front of the *Globe* building, not knowing how to feel. He was chagrined at his starry-eyed dream of landing even an internship with *Global Weekly* and high on the rush of being offered a job with the *Globe*. He couldn't wait to tell Dirk, let alone his family, particularly his mother.

The Volvo was idling, and while huge, soft flakes lit

on the car, they melted quickly. He opened the door to greet Dirk, but he wasn't there. He couldn't be far. He wouldn't leave an unlocked car on a busy street.

Cameron stood and turned to look, just in time to take a huge snowball in the chest that exploded all over his face and in his hair. Dirk came staggering across the street cackling so loud that Cameron feared he would pass out.

Cameron knelt and scooped snow he quickly formed into a ball, and before Dirk could dodge him, he fired away.

Dirk ducked and it splatted atop his head.

"Truce!" Cameron called out. "We've got to get going, and I have news!"

They brushed off and climbed into the car. Cameron had never understood this about himself, but besides loving storms, he didn't mind driving in them. They could be scary, but he figured he'd drive for as long as he could and get as far as he could and try to outlast the blizzard.

Being in a warm car with a full tank and a good friend, well, what could be better than that? Getting through the city and onto I-90 took just a few minutes, and while traffic was slow, the plows seemed to be keeping up with the snowfall.

At the first tollbooth the attendant said, "How far you going?"

"Jersey."

"Good luck. You got chains?"

"Do I need 'em?"

"You might the farther you go south. Don't be a hero."

A couple of hours later it was well past midnight and Cameron was merging onto I-84. At first it looked clearer and the traffic was lighter, so he hoped to make up some time. Dirk had been holding forth on conspiracy theories the whole way, and when Cameron could concentrate, he found his friend amusing.

"I didn't know the British Isles produced conspiracy theorists too," he said. "I thought those Illuminati and Bilderberger and Trilateral Commission freaks were all stateside."

"You don't believe in any of that?" Dirk said. "If you'd worked under Joshua Todd-Cothran at the Exchange you might change your tune."

"Or exchange it."

"Hilarious."

"Seriously, Dirk, you believe all that?"

"I don't know what to think, but it makes a lot of sense to me. Jonathan Stonagal is a secret member of a lot of organizations, and when he and Todd-Cothran and a bunch of other muckety-mucks are rumored to be meeting, major financial decisions follow that affect the whole world."

"Glad I'm not in economics."

"Don't kid yourself, Cam. We're all in economics. It's all about economics. You'd think a journalist would know that. Want to find the source of change, the source of trouble, the source of anything? Follow the money."

NINETEEN

NICOLAE LOOKED over his shoulder and found his bodyguards chatting among themselves. That was just as well. He felt safe in his own compound. And he didn't need them watching his every move, noticing all he was doing.

He wanted to pray, but that was private. He didn't need to kneel or bow, though he felt some obligation toward his spirit guide, whoever that was. Once he had deigned to admit his dependence on the wisdom of his guide and had the temerity to ask to whom he was communicating. He was met with obnoxious silence and took that to mean it either wasn't his to ask or wasn't the right time.

Just now he didn't care about the identity of his netherworld communicant. All Nicolae wanted was some confirmation that his counsel from Leon Fortunato was worthy of consideration.

He peeked back again and believed he was far enough away to avoid detection. He walked slowly toward the rising sun, whispering. "My lord and my master, tell me how to comport myself so the masses will be drawn to me and give me what I want."

He stopped and listened, knowing he would hear nothing audibly. He was opening his spirit to impressions, messages from beyond the mortal coil. Nicolae's face flushed when he believed a message was delivered to his soul. "Let others praise you," it said. "Make your gifts available, but exhibit no effort to strive."

It was the wee hours of the morning by the time Cameron finally merged onto I-91 South. Normally it would take him less than half an hour to reach I-95 South and the one hundred ten or so miles that would get him into New Jersey. But the going was slow and treacherous. Cars had slid off the road, some overturned. The occasional snowplow provided something to follow slowly at a safe distance. Cameron did not understand how Dirk could sleep at a time like this. He had to tell himself to loosen his grip, to relax his shoulders, to blink, to breathe.

Anytime Cameron felt a slide or even a hint of fishtailing he let up on the accelerator. He spent another two hours on I-91, and when I-95 finally came into view, he believed he was halfway home. It was hard to imagine he'd be in the car many hours longer.

———————

Jonathan Stonagal sat up in bed, suddenly awake a few hours before dawn in his Manhattan penthouse. Something was niggling in his brain. Carpathia, his hope for the future. According to Reiche Planchette, the young man was all and more than they could have hoped, except that he was clearly beginning to feel his oats.

Stonagal pushed a button on his bedside table, and within seconds his night-shift valet knocked softly and cracked the door open a couple of inches. "Do something for you, sir?"

"What time is it in Bucharest?" he said.

The valet entered and used the light from the hallway to illuminate his watch. "Late morning, sir."

"Get Fredericka on the phone."

"It's just past four here, Mr. Stonagal."

"I know what time it is here, Benny."

A couple of minutes later Benny informed the billionaire that his secretary was on the line.

"You awake, Fredericka?" Stonagal said.

"Well, I am now," she said. "Is there an emergency?"

"I want to know when Planchette is coming."

"And you need to know now."

"Soon."

"I'll call you."

Stonagal hung up without saying good-bye or thanks or sorry for waking her. He had never apologized to a subordinate, and he wouldn't start now. He paid Fredericka more than enough that she could be on call twenty-four hours a day without letting that pique invade her tone. He didn't call her off-hours that much. She ought to learn to roll with it.

When she called back a few minutes later, Fredericka reported, "Mr. Planchette can be here by this afternoon. He has cleared it with Mr. Carpathia, but he would like to talk to you now if he can."

"He cleared it with Carpathia? Whatever for?"

"I didn't ask, sir. Can he call you now?"

"Heavens no! Ask him if he knows what time it is here. Tell him I'll talk to him when he arrives, and keep me posted on the details."

Cameron became aware that his blinking had become more and more deliberate, his eyes staying closed longer than they should each time. He opened his window a sliver and slapped himself in the face. This was no kind of weather to be driving through with other than complete attention.

"What the—?" Dirk said. "It's freezing."

"I'll close it and keep you toasty if you want to try driving," Cameron said.

"Sorry I said anything. Carry on. How are the gauges looking?"

Cameron hadn't even thought to check. He had enough fuel to make it to Princeton, but he was alarmed to find the temperature gauge pointing straight up and the oil gauge the opposite. "Uh-oh," he said.

"How far to the next oasis?" Dirk said.

"Half an hour maybe."

"Not good." Dirk wrenched around in his seat and stared out the back window. "You're already burning oil," he said. "You're going to lock up the engine."

"I should pull over?"

Dirk shook his head. "I don't know. We're in the middle of nowhere and we'd be low priority for emergency workers. Better try to limp to the next rest area."

The daily papers in Romania were full of the story of the largesse of Nicolae Carpathia having established a trust fund for the education of the teenage son of his recently deceased accountant. The stories made an issue of the fact that the victim had recently left Carpathia's employ to join the firm of his biggest competitor and political rival, Emil Tismaneanu.

By the time the story made the television news, Tismaneanu was being grilled about why this should be Carpathia's responsibility. "In all fairness," Tismaneanu said, "the man had barely begun with me. I believe Mr. Carpathia owed him more than I did."

Nicolae was tempted to rail against his opponent and challenge him to match the educational fund, but when he ran his response through the grid of Fortunato's counsel and what he believed his spirit guide had impressed upon him, he changed his mind.

"Mr. Tismaneanu has enough problems right now," Nicolae said. "He appears to be trailing in the race, and there are many issues over which we vigorously disagree. I do not choose to add this spat to the mix. I am happy to fully fund the educational trust myself and would not want to burden my opponent with the responsibility."

Fortunato called. "Brilliant, Nicolae," he said. "Just wait until tomorrow's polls. You will surge even more because of this; you watch. And with your permission, I will plant challenges everywhere for another debate with Tismaneanu. Accepting could be his death knell. Declining would be the same."

Everything associated with the Volvo went at once. Cameron had been proud that he'd kept the thing on the road, and suddenly all the gauges lit up, the dashboard lights went out, the headlights dimmed, and the car shut down. With the power steering gone it was all he could do to wrestle the car into a snowbank.

"We have no source of heat," Dirk said, "and I'm not interested in cuddling."

Cameron dug through his luggage for a dirty T-shirt and tied it to the top of the car. He and Dirk stayed inside until they saw headlights. Then they jumped out and waved for help. The first several cars either didn't see them or ignored them.

Forty minutes into their ordeal, the cold beginning to reach Cameron's core, he came dangerously close to a snowplow that buried the car and him and Dirk in freezing slush. The driver must have seen them at the last minute, however, because he quickly slowed and pulled over, carefully backing up to them.

"Sorry about that!" he called out. "What's the trouble?"

"Out of oil and overheated!" Cameron called back.

"Hop in!"

Cameron and Dirk grabbed their stuff, wondering what the plow driver could do to help. "Do you have radio contact with a towing company or anything?"

"I do, but they're all tied up. I can take you to the next lodging exit, about an hour south, and you can take your chances at one of the inns. You're not going to get help for that car for a couple of days at best."

TWENTY

JONATHAN STONAGAL was not the type of man who
deferred to anyone, even old acquaintances, partners,
and friends. When Reiche Planchette was ushered into
his office late in the afternoon, looking sweaty and
disheveled from the long flight and the cab ride through
a snowy New York City, Stonagal didn't even rise.

Planchette rushed the desk and leaned over, extending
a hand. Stonagal grabbed it lightly with one hand,
straightening what Reiche had displaced with the other.

"Thanks for inviting me. Long flight. Bad traffic."

Stonagal pointed to a side chair, and Planchette
dropped into it, his coat and briefcase in his lap. "Is
there a place for this?" he said apologetically, holding
his coat aloft.

Stonagal scowled and pushed the intercom button.

"Fredericka, come and take the man's coat, would you? What's the matter with you?"

"I'm sorry, Mr. Planchette," she said, hurrying in.

As soon as she was gone, Stonagal got to the point. "Tell me how things are at Casa Carpathia. How is Ms. Ivinisova doing?"

"Well, she goes exclusively by Viv Ivins these days, and—"

"Whatever for?"

"Hiding her Russian ethnicity, I guess."

"Again, why?"

"No idea. Nicolae has drawn Leonardo Fortunato close as an adviser. Gave him an office in the compound."

"Good, good. I know Leon. Has the potential to be a sycophant, but he'll be an asset."

"Business was great until the dustup with Intercontinental."

"More than a dustup, I'd say," Stonagal said. "Will I ever see my hundred million again?"

"That's way beyond my area of expertise," Planchette said. "Corona is confident, but the failure hit them hard too. If Carpathia had to default, it couldn't happen at a worse time. His political opponent could use it to crush him. If he doesn't, Nicolae seems a shoo-in."

"He needs to remain a shoo-in. Assure him I will cover the loan. I want it back, make no mistake, but I will temporarily personally guarantee it. That way he can categorically deny any charge brought by Tismaneanu. I can't wait for the election. When is it?"

"First week of March."

"It'll be so good to have that old fool out of there."

"And our man in."

That made Stonagal smile. "And our man in. It's just the first baby step of many great strides, Reiche. Does it seem like a quarter century since we launched into this?"

"Time has flown, Mr. Stonagal. It's been a privilege."

"Tell me about our boy. What kind of a man has he become? Will he do us proud once in office?"

Dirk, of course, had nothing at stake and little to have to get back to Princeton for, so Cameron couldn't fault him for sleeping soundly through the ordeal.

A tiny family inn had allowed the college boys to sleep on couches in the lobby until a room opened at dawn, when a crew of emergency workers checked out. Cameron spent most of his time pacing and calling around, trying to see if there was a chance of his getting to the airport in time for his flight to Tucson. No go.

When the clock finally slid past when a miracle might have allowed him to make it, Cameron tried to sleep, putting off the dreaded call to his family. He finally dozed fitfully for a few hours, until awakened by a harsh sun. Unfortunately, while the snow had stopped, the sun melted only enough snow and ice to cause the roads to be closed when the temperature plummeted yet again. Even snowplows were having trouble gaining purchase on the road.

Cameron and Dirk were stuck.

"Your mother is going to be terribly disappointed, Cameron," his father said on the phone.

"Well, I am too, Dad. I don't see what else I could have done."

"Maybe you should have come out here instead of going to Boston."

"Well, sure, in hindsight that would have been the right thing to do. But Mom wanted me to go, and I would have missed out on the job opportunity of a lifetime."

He told his father all about it, was set back by a less-than-enthusiastic response, and asked to talk to his mother.

"You can't right now, Cam. She's having a bad day."

"What does that mean?"

"Sleeps on and off. Can't eat. Isn't coherent. The doc thinks we ought to get her to the hospital, but she puts up such a fuss when we try. . . ."

"She's getting worse?"

"What? Where you been, boy? 'Course she's getting worse. That's what cancer does. It kills you in the end."

"Well, I know that, Dad. I'm just saying, is it imminent or—?"

"I don't know what *imminent* means, but I think you'd better still get out here as soon as you can."

"Dad, I'm broke. My ticket was nonrefundable. My car is probably shot. I don't even know how I'm going to get back to school."

"Well, you'd better think of something, Cameron. Your mother wants to see you."

Nicolae had to hand it to Fortunato, who proved right about Tismaneanu and the debate challenge. The excuses for not engaging in yet another made the incumbent look like a loser.

"Nothing is served by these wastes of time," Tismaneanu said. "I should think that Mr. Carpathia would have more important things to do than invest his energies in criticizing everything I have tried to do for the people of Romania. For instance, he could apply himself to pulling his vast empire out of a deep hole of debt. Should he go bankrupt due to a reckless investment in an American technological scheme, the taxpayers will have to foot the bill. Avoiding that, it seems to me, would be a more worthy use of his time."

Nicolae's camp fired back immediately with a challenge to prove that Carpathian Trading carried even one cent of debt.

Tismaneanu bit and bit hard, announcing that an examination of the public record at Intercontinental Bank would bear out his charges.

Within an hour, press releases blanketed Bucharest, announcing that Intercontinental had confirmed that "Nicolae Carpathia and Carpathian International Trading are customers in good standing with this financial institution, and neither the man nor his company carries any debt. Rather, much of Mr. Carpathia's holdings are invested here."

That, virtually, was the end of Tismaneanu and his candidacy. For all practical purposes, he was finished.

He would never recover, and it was clear Nicolae
Carpathia would be swept into office.

———

Cameron sat dejectedly in Dirk Burton's dorm room as
his friend ran his car towing and repair bills through the
calculator. "Here's the happy total," Dirk said, ripping
off the paper and holding it in front of Cameron's nose.

"Yech. I don't know how I'm even going to get to Tucson over spring break."

"Why not go for an advance from the *Globe*?"

Now there was an idea. Cameron had never been one
to beg. That would be a hard phone call. But after he
took one from his brother, he was more willing to try
Dirk's idea.

He was alone in his own room late that night when
Jeff called. "Do you not get it or what?" Jeff said.

"Of course I get it. What do you want me to do?"

"Get out here! How hard is that to understand? Do
you have no priorities?"

"You got a magic wand, Jeff? I'm hopelessly in debt
here."

"Beg, borrow, steal, do something. Mom is dying.
She's in intensive care, asking for you."

"Thanks for that guilt trip."

"I thought you ought to know. It's not pretty, Cam.
You know you're her favorite, and—"

"Don't start with that again, Jeff. Come on."

"I'm okay with it. I just wish you'd live up to it. Earn

it. All I've done is stayed here and done whatever I could
for the family, for the business. And what do I get? Taken
for granted. You're out there doing your own thing, finding yourself, chasing your dream, and going busted picking up some award. And who is she asking for?"

"I'm sorry about that, Jeff. I'm sure she appreciates
everything you've done. She just—"

"You don't get it, Cam. After all this time you really
don't. I don't really care. I'm doing what I think is right.
The point is, if she wants to see you before she dies, I
want her to see you before she dies. Get here somehow,
would you?"

"I'll do my best."

The next morning, hands shaking, Cameron placed
a call to Dizzy Rowland.

"How good to hear from you, son. Got a story for
us?"

"No. I wish."

"Then what can I do for you?"

"Well, I was sort of hoping you had a story for me."

"You're the guy we'll come to if anything breaks there
that ought to be in the *Globe*. You may have a better
handle on that than we do."

"How about a human-interest story?"

"Well, sure. That's your strength, and we would have
to count on you to ferret that out. There's not much hard
news out of Princeton that Boston readers can't get elsewhere. So, yeah, some drama, human interest, pathos.
Got something in mind?"

"How about a college student who can't get home to

see his dying mother because he's out of money and his car died?"

Rowland was silent a moment. "That could work. Handled delicately, of course. Not too sentimental. Just straightforward. Maybe covers how the kid finally makes the trip happen. Friends kick in, that kind of thing."

"I could shoot it to you on spec?"

"Sure. We'll take a look."

"Um . . . here's the hard question."

"Shoot."

"Any way I could get an advance on it?"

"On a spec piece? What if we don't take it?"

"Then I'd owe you."

"You short, Cameron? You need money?"

"Yeah."

"It's highly unusual, but if it's for a good cause, I might be able to work something out. Just this once, you know. We're not a bank."

"I know. But, see, I'm the subject of the story."

Rowland sighed long and loud. "Why didn't you say so, son? Just tell me how much you need. And don't exploit that story unless there's really something there. Tell me where to send the money."

TWENTY-ONE

"I'M STARVING to death spiritually," Irene said.

Jackie sat with her in the park, watching Raymie and Brianna on the monkey bars. "You can imagine how that makes me feel, Irene. I'm sorry."

"Oh no, Jackie! What I get from you every week is fabulous. I'm learning so much, and—I hope—growing. But it's not enough. I try to do the daily stuff—the reading, the studying, the praying—but I wish I could be involved in a church where I could be used. And where I could soak up real Bible teaching and preaching every Sunday."

"You're always welcome at New Hope, Irene."

"I know. And the day may come when I'm ready to put it forcefully to Rayford. Right now everything in our marriage is how he wants it. There's no real give-and-take. I mean, he's a good provider and a great dad. The kids worship him. And if he'd just give me an iota of consideration, I'd be more than happy to let the rest of my life revolve around him. Something tells me, though, that he's got the wrong idea of what it means to be the head of the household."

"Hey," Jackie said, "even Christian men often miss that. Dooley and I had to work through that early in our marriage. He was raised in a church where they taught that the man being the head of the home meant that he made all the decisions. We went where he wanted to go, ate what he wanted to eat—even *when* he wanted to eat. Anytime there was a disagreement, he won. I felt like a failure. I resented him, believed I was falling out of love with him."

"You guys are so great together now—unless that's just for show."

"No, it's good now. He was really transformed."

"How? What happened?"

"He got under some solid Bible teaching. Pastor Billings is a very wise man. And he has a long-term marriage to a woman who is plainly still head over heels in love with him, and vice versa."

"How'd he manage that?"

"He must practice what he preaches, hmm?"

"What *does* he say about the head-of-the-home business?"

Jackie called Brianna over and wiped her nose, then sent her back to the jungle gym. "He warns husbands that their spiritual responsibility is a grave task with huge accountability. He tells them they will have to answer for their wives' spiritual health someday. And boy does he poke holes in the idea that being given spiritual authority means you get your own way all the time. He says that role should be employed only when a husband and wife come to loggerheads over some important issue. Otherwise, he says, you should submit to each other and put the other ahead of yourself.

"The best part was when he was teaching that how a man treats his wife is like an investment. The more you put in, the more you'll get out. Treat her right, love her, honor her, and you will eventually get the same in return. Consult her, take her counsel, and love her as Christ loved the church. Thinking spiritual headship means you get everything your way is a far cry from being willing to die for your bride. I'm telling you, Irene, Dooley was never the same after he learned all that. And neither was our marriage."

Irene had to look away to hide her tears. How long had it been since she had felt cherished by Rayford? And this business about a spouse being an investment . . . what if she invested in Rayford, hoping for the dividends she needed? How could he cherish her if she didn't prove she cherished him?

"Good news, Jeff," Cameron said. He told his brother about the advance from the *Globe* and how it would allow him to come home over spring break after all. "So let Mom know, okay? And if she's up to talking, let me know and I'll call her. All right? . . . Jeff? You there? Hello?"

"I'm here."

"Did you hear me?"

"I heard you."

"And?"

"You know, Cameron, it's at times like these when I don't envy you in the least. Everybody feels sorry for me because I'm the older brother but you're the star."

"Jeff."

"You're the hotshot Ivy Leaguer, gone off to find your fame and fortune, and I'm just a blue-collar dolt here, driving truck."

"Stop it, Jeff. What on earth has set you off now?"

"That you still don't get it! I don't know how else to say it, Cam. For a smart guy, you ain't too bright, are ya? If you've got the means to get out here, why aren't you on a plane? I'll pick you up at the airport."

"Jeff, there's no way I can come right now. I missed my holiday window with the car trouble and the blizzard and all. I'm swamped here with classes, projects, the school paper, my job, all kinds of—"

"Do you want to see your mother before she dies?"

"Well, of course. I—"

"Trust me. She'll be in the ground two months by the time your spring break rolls around."

"Seriously?"

"Hello!"

"It's imminent, then."

"It's day to day, Cam. Now I don't want to have this conversation again. The only thing keeping Mom alive is her thinking you're going to be here anytime."

"All right, listen, I've got an exam tomorrow afternoon and a big deadline late the next morning. I'll get a flight that evening. I won't be able to stay long, but—"

"You're not even here yet and you're already heading back."

Cameron caught a glimpse of himself in the mirror, running his hand through his hair. And he saw himself in Jeff's comments. He didn't like what he saw in either reflection.

"Yeah," he said. "Sorry. See you soon."

———————

The Steele family sat together at dinner for one of the few times that happened each month.

Chloe had a gleam in her green eyes and used both hands to push her blonde hair behind her ears. "Ready for my surprise?" she said.

Irene looked up. "You have a surprise?"

"No, I just said that for my health."

Chloe was smiling, but Irene was struck anew by the quickness and acerbic wit of the twelve-year-old. Often, when she was sarcastic like that, she wasn't kidding.

"What is it, Chlo'?" Rayford said.

Chloe lifted her plate and slid out her report card, handing it first to her dad—which cut Irene.

"Wow," he said softly. "That's great, but it's hardly a surprise."

"It will be to Mom. She thinks I'm going to hell."

"What? I never said that."

"But you do. I know you do." Disconcertingly, Chloe was still smiling.

Rayford passed the report card to Irene. "Straight A's," she said, "and all these teacher comments. 'Great attitude.' 'Impressive participation.' 'A leader.' 'A joy to have in class.' That's wonderful, honey. Congratulations. Great work."

"Thanks. Now how do we celebrate?"

"I don't know," Irene said. "Your favorite dessert tomorrow night?"

Raymie hollered with his mouth full, "Dessert!"

"C'mon, Mom!" Chloe said. "I'm not five. A whole quarter's worth of hard work and perfect grades ought to be worth more than your chocolate-chip cookies. Though they are the best."

"Cookies!" Raymie shouted. "The best!"

"What did you have in mind?" Rayford said.

Chloe chuckled. "You know what Mom says every year when we ask what she wants for her birthday? 'Nothing but obedience and a little respect.'"

Even Irene had to laugh. "I do say that, don't I?"

Chloe nodded. "I want something like that."

"Obedience?"

"Ha! No, I wouldn't dream of anything like that. But a little respect would be nice."

"I respect you, Chloe," Irene said. "I love you. You know that."

"I know you love me, Mom. Respect is another story."

When did this baby girl become so grown up? so articulate? so cold? Irene worried about where this conversation was going and the impact it might have on Raymie. For now he seemed to be ignoring it, except when some-one mentioned cookies. "Keeping in mind that little pitchers have big ears," Irene said, "what do I need to do to prove that I respect you?"

"You say that all the time about pitchers and big ears, Mom. What does it even mean?"

"The handles on a pitcher are also called ears, Chloe. It's just an expression that means to be careful what you say in front of little ones who hear everything."

"Whatever."

"So," Irene said, "what is it you're driving at?"

"I just think I'm old enough to start making some of my own decisions, that's all."

"Well, your grades prove you can be mature and responsible, though I disagree that you're old enough to make adult decisions. I'm still the mother. You're still the kid."

"How well I know."

"Come on, Irene," Rayford said. "You don't even know what she wants yet."

"No, but I'll bet you do." Irene hoped she was wrong, but she could tell by Rayford's look—not to mention Chloe's—that she had scored. These two had been talk-ing behind her back. Rayford had probably coached Chloe on how to manipulate her mother with a good report card.

"All right," she said. "Spill it. What's this report card going to cost me?"

"Respect," Chloe said. "I told you."

"Quit stalling. What do you mean in practical terms? What decisions do you think should be yours alone?"

"What I do with my Sundays."

Irene tried to bite her tongue. She wanted to explode, to accuse Rayford of conspiring, to blurt that Sunday school and church were not up for discussion. Praying silently for wisdom and restraint, she forced herself to take another bite. Why was this being-like-Jesus thing so hard? Impossible, so far, she concluded.

"So much for respect, huh?" Chloe said.

"Watch yourself, young lady," Irene said.

"At least let me out of Sunday school! I'll sit through church with you, but those dumb stories! And those kids are so stupid!"

The truth was, of course, that Irene found Dr. Bohrer's sermons just as bad. It wasn't the classes or the services; it was the church. Well, as long as Rayford and Chloe were conniving to outsmart her, Irene felt free to bring out her big guns.

"All right," she said, "I'll make a deal with you. You try a new church with me, one I think we'll both like. Give it a month and attend Sunday school and church without complaining. And then I'll let you decide whether you want to keep going."

"No, no," Rayford said. "You're not dragging my daughter to that Holy Roller church."

"Rafe! She's my daughter too. And that's no Holy—"

"Daddy! This sounds fair. I'll be a good sport about it. I can't imagine it being any different, but I could give it a few weeks if I really get to decide after that."

"I don't like it," Rayford said. "That means I'd have to go too."

Now you're thinking, Irene mused.

TWENTY-TWO

THE PRESSING-THE-FLESH part of the campaign was upon Nicolae, and he was pleasantly surprised to discover how much he enjoyed it. He had always been a private person, and the idea of camping out at a bus or train station or outside a factory at the end of the workday—just to introduce himself to the people—at first repulsed him.

He liked it when people came to him and he could grant—or choose not to grant—audiences. But Leon insisted that a man could not hope to sway the masses without proving he was one of them.

"But I am not," Nicolae said.

"Of course you're not. And instinctively the people know that. That's why it's so important for you to—in essence—prove that you don't mind condescending to their level. But you must sell it, Nicolae. No running to the limo as soon as you're free. No sharing a *gustare* with them at their snack bar and then being seen half an hour later at a nice bistro. Look them in the eye, listen, shake hands warmly. Mean it."

"Or pretend to."

"Of course."

"Are you saying we do not use my cars to get to these places?"

"We might do better to use mine," Leon said. "It's big and roomy and perhaps more appropriate."

Fortunato's car proved to be a black SUV, which attracted little attention. Nicolae began by setting up outside the gate of an ironworks factory. As the men and women emerged, sooty and greasy and clearly exhausted, Nicolae stood by a large sign and thrust out his hand to every passerby. "Hi, my name is Nicolae Carpathia, and I am running for Parliament."

Many ignored him, which was a novel experience that enraged him. But he left his smile plastered on and kept trying. Many, especially women, said, "I know who you are. I see you on TV." More than half wished him luck and told him they were voting for him. Others said they were supporters of Tismaneanu, but oddly, they were always quick to shake his hand.

"Ever work a day in your life?" a man asked, staring Nicolae in the eye. A few others heard the question and gathered around. That brought more, asking what was up. When the question was whispered to them, they summoned more.

This was more like it. Nicolae was offended by the question, but he loved an audience, and this was the time to practice his newly manufactured humility. "Thank you for asking," he said. "That is a fair question I am happy to answer.

"It may surprise you to know that I was raised by a single mother and that I was expected to do my part around the house and the farm. Yes, I was raised in the country, and I have mucked out my share of stalls. I was always a good student with a mind for business, so I took a risk, put up my own money, and built a company on my own.

"I daresay I do not work as physically hard as you do, and that makes me admire what you do. But I put in long days and provide jobs and salaries and benefits for a lot of people. I want to see change and reform in my homeland, as I am sure you do. I hope I can count on your votes."

Nicolae walked away to warm applause and a deep, hungry feeling. He liked communicating with groups. He wanted to do it again. Next stop was a rail station, where people seemed in even more of a hurry to keep moving. But the experience was the same. He would meet and greet those who took the time—some acknowledging him, some not; many recognizing him, a few not. And then someone would ask a hard question, people would gather, and Nicolae would hold forth.

Back in the car and heading home, he told Leon, "We need to make these appearances more efficient. The one-on-one hand shaking is good and will look fine in the paper and on the news. But things really start to happen when I am challenged and can defend myself."

"What are you suggesting?"

"That we plant such questions, get them in the air immediately upon my arrival. That way we can lose the waste of time and awkwardness of meeting and greeting everyone individually and can rather get on with the pitch."

"Brilliant," Leon said. "You were born for this."

———

Cameron Williams was waiting at the gate for his flight to Tucson when he took a call from his brother, Jeff.

"When's your return flight again?" Jeff said.

"Day after tomorrow."

"Got time to get that changed before you board?"

"If I had to. Why?"

"Funeral's the day after tomorrow. You'll need at least another day out here."

"Jeff! Are you saying . . . ?"

"About an hour ago. I don't mean to lay this all on you, Cameron, but she was asking for you right up to the end."

Cameron swore. "I didn't need to hear that."

"Yeah, you did. You should have been here."

"Okay, all right, I know! I'm on my way."

"A day late and—"

"Don't say it, Jeff, all right?"

The flight was uneventful but seemed longer than ever. Cameron had no appetite, and though weary from having rushed to clear the decks before leaving, he found he was unable to doze. Of course his mother was on his mind the whole way.

They'd long had a strange relationship. As a teenager he had discovered that she would believe anything he said and so began a pattern of telling her whatever she needed or wanted to hear. She trusted him, admired him, believed in him, and he had shamelessly taken advantage of that.

Cameron had not been a bad kid. Typical. Did his partying and carousing, but mostly he had been a conscientious student and insatiably curious young journalist. Having decided early what he wanted to be when he grew up, he seemed more mature than his friends, especially to teachers, authorities, adults of all stripes.

He had worked for his father too, enough to know he didn't want to stay in gas and oil the rest of his life. And of course that—and many other differences—caused a rift between him and his brother.

Cameron didn't look forward to that confrontation. He had been wrong; that was all. He had found it hard to believe his mother was at death's door, especially since he had never seen her that way. She had long been over-weight and was showing her age, but she was otherwise robust and energetic, a doer. She had always loved the next new thing. Even imagining her in the hospital was hard for Cameron.

And now she was gone. Guilty? Of course he was. But he was also pragmatic. Cameron had not contributed to her death, and he was not going to beat himself up over it. He might appear to, so his relatives wouldn't feel the need to punish him, but beyond feeling bad that he had not given his mother the pleasure of his company during her darkest hours, he didn't know what else he could or should have done.

Jeff didn't so much as shake Cameron's hand, let alone embrace him when he picked him up at the airport.

"How's Dad doing?" Cameron said as they carried his bags to the car.

"He knew it was coming, but it's still hard. It'll be good to have friends and family here." That, Cameron decided, was as close as Jeff was going to get to saying that it was good to have him there.

Cameron was relieved to discover that Sharon and the kids were waiting in the car. His sister-in-law greeted him warmly and expressed her sympathy. Jeff was stonier than ever as he drove. Cameron tried small talk but was rebuffed with one-word answers at every turn.

Finally Cameron turned to face him. "Why don't you just say what you have to say and get it over with?"

Jeff continued to study the road, but he said, "Maybe I just will. I thought you'd never ask. I'm mad, Cameron, as mad at you as I've ever been. You've always been your own person, not caring about anyone else. But this is the epitome. Dad and I tried a million different ways to impress on you how important it was that you get out here before it was too late, and what happens? You get here too late."

"I'm sorry, Jeff. I don't know what else to say."

"You're sorry. That's easy to say now. And Mom can't hear you."

"All right. You going to let me up now?"

Jeff just shook his head.

"Don't hold back if there's more," Cameron said. "I don't need this the whole time I'm here."

"Yeah, whatever's most convenient for you, Cam. You just let me know."

Cameron wanted to slug his brother, knowing full well Jeff probably wanted to smack him too. Maybe that would get it out of their systems. Maybe they ought to come to blows at the funeral and let the whole family see it.

From behind him Sharon put a hand on his shoulder, and Cameron was stunned at the effect it had on him. She didn't say a word, but he felt she was communicating sympathy, forgiveness, a caution to keep his temper, all that. He looked forward to getting a moment with her sometime over the next few days.

———

To Irene's abject disappointment, Rayford traded assignments with someone and had to fly Sunday. She was convinced that he worked hard to do that on purpose, but it didn't deter her from taking Chloe and Raymie to New Hope.

She hadn't even told Jackie she was coming, and the look on her friend's face alone was worth the trip. Jackie immediately introduced her to Pastor Vernon Billings, a dapper, genial man in his mid- to late fifties. Irene was struck by how accessible he was to everybody. New Hope was, of course, much smaller than her church, but still she wasn't used to a senior pastor who mingled with the congregation like this.

Irene felt bad that Raymie appeared petrified of the new place and people, but he was brave and didn't cry. She assured him he would have a good time and that if he behaved she and Chloe and he would go out for chicken after church.

Chloe was in full slouch-and-scowl mode, though she did make the effort to be cordial to Jackie. Irene asked if she wanted help finding her Sunday school class. Chloe said, "Boy, I don't know, Mom. You think I'll ever be able to find it in this huge complex? You want to hold my hand too and introduce me to my teacher?"

"All right, just get going."

"You're not going to pin my name to my shirt?"

"Go on!"

All Irene wanted was a more personal, genuine experience with God, one that matched her new relationship with Him. She had determined to not let whatever she discovered at New Hope reflect poorly on her church. But she couldn't help it.

The first thing she noticed, after the humanity of the pastor, was how many people welcomed her, asked her name, and said they were glad she was there. She thought it interesting that none asked about her husband or family. Maybe they had learned to avoid embarrassing divorcees or widows and to wait to learn about the family situations of newcomers.

The service proved much more informal than any she had ever attended. This church sang hymns similar to those she was used to, but they seemed more robust and energetic. She thought Rayford would like it, but who knew? Maybe he would find it all a little too overt.

The pastoral prayer was different too. Informal. Not written and read. But it was the sermon that really moved Irene. No homilies. No lofty pronouncements. No performing. Pastor Billings merely pointed people to the passage he was going to speak on, and all over the sanctuary came the rustling of onionskin pages.

Irene quickly located 1John 2:12-14:

I write to you, little children,
　Because your sins are forgiven you for His name's sake.
I write to you, fathers,
　Because you have known Him who is from the beginning.
I write to you, young men,
　Because you have overcome the wicked one.
I write to you, little children,
　Because you have known the Father.
I have written to you, fathers,
　Because you have known Him who is from the beginning.
I have written to you, young men,
　Because you are strong, and the word of God abides in you,
And you have overcome the wicked one.

Now that was one confusing passage. Irene couldn't help but wonder why she had never heard it before in all her years in church. Probably because it was obscure and would take some explanation. It wasn't one of the majestic, beautiful passages that just sounded good to the ear from the get-go.

She couldn't wait to hear what Pastor Billings had to say about it.

TWENTY-THREE

WITH RELATIVES IN from all over the Southwest for the funeral, Cameron found himself having to face them all the day before. One by one and in groups and families they descended upon his childhood home.

He had never felt so much like a foreigner. Cameron had no idea whether his imagination was in overdrive or if he was really able to read everyone's thoughts by their expressions, tones, mannerisms, and body language.

An aunt seemed to assume that he was so grateful to be home and away from the strange and exotic East Coast that he might even consider transferring to the University of Arizona. "They have a writing program, don't they?"

"A journalism course? Oh, I'm sure. But I've just a few months until graduation at Princeton, and then . . ."

"Yes, I heard about the position at the big paper. The *Boston Sun* or some such."

"The *Globe*."

"Um-hm. And you have to wonder if those Boston Brahmans have ever even heard of Tucson."

"Believe me they have. And I'll try to represent us well there."

Others were so overly sympathetic that Cameron read in them a belief that he felt terribly guilty for having been unable to see his mother before she died. An elderly cousin clucked that he must forgive himself. "I know you would have been here if you could," she said.

Still others were plain in their judgment of him. An uncle quizzed him about how it came to be that he was late. "And you couldn't borrow some money, get an emergency fare, prevail on a friend to get you out here somehow?"

"I did everything I could, sir. And as it was, I just missed seeing her."

"Didn't you know how bad off she was?"

"Dad and Jeff tried to tell me, but maybe I just didn't want to accept it."

"Well, you should have been here."

"Were *you* here?" Cameron said. "Did you see her?"

"Well . . . ah . . . no, no. But we knew it was going to be soon. Anyway, Cammy, she's your mother."

Yeah, I got that.

Cameron was impressed with his father and worried about him at the same time. His parents had not had the best of marriages, but they had gotten along and spent nearly thirty years together. He'd seen the pictures of them in their courting days, when both were young and

thin and obviously putting their best feet forward. They
also looked dreamily in love in some pictures, something
he couldn't remember seeing in person. They were not
physically or verbally affectionate, but they were nice
enough to each other.

Cameron was sure his dad would be panicky and feel
lost without her for a while. But he was being the consummate host, thanking every person individually for
coming and saying just the right things. He was fine, he
said. It was hard, though he had known it was coming.
He felt a little numb, had done his crying in private and
was sure more was to come. But for now he wanted to
remember her the way she was before the cancer over-
took her.

Most impressive to Cameron, however, was Sharon,
Jeff's wife. While Jeff was distant and quiet—and most
gave him his space—Sharon assigned him to look after
their son and daughter, apparently to occupy him.
Cameron was only guessing, but it appeared Sharon
didn't want Jeff moping around, saying angry things,
casting aspersions on his little brother.

It was obvious from Jeff's demeanor that he meant to
play up Cameron's slothfulness until he could wring no
more benefit from it. The attention had always seemed to
be on Cameron, but here was a way to step into the spotlight. Jeff was a sympathetic character, the rock-steady
stay-at-home guy.

With the funeral planned for midmorning the next day,
guests and relatives began abandoning the house for
their hotels early in the evening. Jeff took his kids home

to put them to bed while Sharon stayed to help her father-in-law clean up. Cameron tried to get his father to just sit, but he insisted on keeping busy. Between the three of them, the place was tidied in way less time than Cameron would have predicted.

When his father allowed himself to be talked into going to bed early, Sharon started making noises about getting home. And though she grabbed her coat and headed toward the door, she paused and sat in the living room, looking up at Cameron.

"How are you doing, Cam, really?"

"I'm all right. I should have been here, but there's nothing I can do about it now."

"Jeff will get over it," Sharon said. "I think his anger is misplaced. There are other things going on there. You're just a convenient target."

Cameron snorted. "I always have been. Why should that change now?"

"He really loves you, Cam."

Cameron waved her off.

"I'm serious. He does. He doesn't talk a lot about it. There's jealousy there, sure. And self-righteousness. But a wife can tell. He talks about you a lot. Wonders. Worries. Cares."

"You don't say."

"I do say. You know how I can tell what he really thinks of you? By what he tells other people. A person can't talk to him for five minutes without his bringing up your name and what you're up to."

"I'm surprised."

"Don't be. He always wanted to leave Tucson too, you know. Just felt obligated to stay, especially when you went."

"So, again, it's my fault."

"I didn't mean it that way. Maybe when your father is gone Jeff can sell the business and do what he wants wherever he wants."

"What and where would that be?"

"You don't know?"

"He doesn't talk to me, Sharon. He hardly ever has, even when we were kids."

"But surely you know of his love for horses and ranching."

"Yeah. It was his favorite thing to do as a kid: spend time on a ranch, roping, herding cattle, rodeoing. What're you saying? He'd become a rancher?"

She nodded. "Probably in Texas."

"Well, more power to him. Whatever makes him happy."

"That's my motto," Sharon said. "The kids make him happy, I think. I'm not sure I do anymore."

Cameron was curious, as always, but he wasn't sure he wanted to get into this. In fact, he was pretty sure he didn't. But Sharon seemed to settle back on the couch, as if warming to the topic and hoping Cameron would pursue it.

"So, big day tomorrow, huh?" he said. "I suppose you've got a lot of work to do at the funeral too. It's great how you helped out here. Like you were a daughter instead of a daughter-in-law."

Sharon smiled but couldn't hide the fatigue around her eyes. "Listen, Cam, when I married in, I bought in for the whole ride. Like it or not, I'm family now."

"Oh, don't get me wrong. I like that you're family."

"Do you?"

"Of course."

"Well, that's sweet of you to say. I'm not sure it's a sentiment widely shared."

Where was this going? Cameron was struck by the fact that if he had been talking to someone else, someone not related, he would be dying to follow every rabbit trail, pursue every question, get to the bottom of the vagaries of every relationship. This was just too close to home. He no more wanted to know why Sharon felt unwelcome than he wanted to know why she worried she didn't make Jeff happy anymore.

As he was to find out, both insecurities were rooted in the same fear. "People are put off by my faith," she said.

Cameron knew that, but how was he supposed to respond? "They are?" he said.

She nodded. "I take it all a little too seriously, I guess. Or so they think. It seems to me that if we all believe in God and go to church, it ought to be the most important thing in our lives. Or am I missing something? What do you think, Cam?"

He shrugged. "Each to his own, I guess. Some people are more into religion than others."

"I'm not talking about religion, Cameron. I'm talking about Jesus."

And she wondered why people were put off? How

many people went around talking about Jesus? God was one thing. Even Christ was a little more theoretical. But talking about Jesus like you were on a first-name basis with the guy—the real guy—from the Bible? Cameron didn't want to say so, but there was something a little brassy, a little in-your-face about that. He admired that Sharon was courageous enough to be plainspoken, but it should come as no surprise to her that it made some uncomfortable. People like him.

"Um-hm," was all he could muster, smiling.

"How about you, Cam? Where are you in all this?"

So there it was. If she was going to put it to him like that, he would be honest; that was for sure. "Have to admit I'm probably where Jeff is," he said. "He and I ran from our church as soon as we were old enough to talk my parents into it. They were disappointed, but they didn't make a big deal out of it. I respected them for that. They kept going and they invited us to special events. Sometimes we would go. But I gotta tell ya, Sharon, if the church we grew up in is what God is all about, He's boring. And I mean *boring*."

"Well, that church is *not* representative; I can tell you that. And that's the problem. At least you and Jeff were honest and on the right track getting out of there. Your mistake—forgive me for being so blunt—was that you thought all churches were the same. So once you were out of that church, you were out altogether. Am I right, or are you attending somewhere there in New Jersey?"

He shook his head. "Too busy. With work and school and . . ."

She looked him dead in the eye. "It's not about busyness, Cameron. You just said so yourself. You got turned off to church or you'd find one."

"Truth hurts," he said.

"Yeah, but it's less painful than lying to yourself."

It was kind of her to refer to his as the lesser sin of denial than actually lying to her, which was what he had done. Sharon might tend toward the obnoxious, but she wasn't afraid of the truth.

He shrugged. "Guilty as charged."

She stood. "I'd better get going. But can I give you my pitch?"

"Your pitch?"

"My sales job. As long as everybody in this family has me pigeonholed as the devout lunatic, I might as well get some mileage out of it. Here it is, Cameron. I love you and care about you as if you were my own brother. Your church was a poor representation of God and Jesus and all They are about. God loves you. He sent Jesus to die for your sins. He wants to hear from you, to make you His child, and to see you interacting with Him in a church that knows what that's all about. Think about it. You don't have to answer to me. I know better than that. But, if nothing else, now you know why the family sees me the way they do, and you've got your own story you can tell behind my back."

Cameron stood and embraced her. "Sharon," he said, "I will never do that. I appreciate your being so honest and forthright. And caring."

TWENTY-FOUR

THERE HAD BEEN NOTHING flashy or dramatic about Pastor Vernon Billings. He simply had a natural, down-home way about him, knew how to keep his audience's attention, and put his emphasis on the message and not on himself. He actually seemed to be keeping Chloe's attention too, no small feat. Irene couldn't wait to find out what she had thought of her first Sunday school class at the new church.

Pastor Billings's message was straightforward and informative. He made the Scripture so clear that Irene felt as if she were drinking fresh water. And it wasn't an easy passage to explain; at least she didn't think it was.

His bottom line was that the apostle John was writing about two families: the family of God and the family of Satan. Christians were forgiven and pulled out of Satan's family, so they were now part of God's family. They were not to love Satan or his family or the world that is controlled by him.

But what was all that business in John's letter about little children, fathers, and young men? The pastor explained that the Greek word translated "little children" in verse 12 was actually different from the word translated the same way in verse 13. The first word, he said, referred to offspring of any age, while the second reference was literally to little children. According to the pastor, John repeated his message to hammer home the point of the believer's belonging to the family of God.

As for the references to fathers, young men, and little children, Pastor Billings explained that these signified different stages of spiritual maturity. Could Irene ever relate to that! She so wanted to grow and become mature in her faith. But she believed she was stagnating. How she would love to make New Hope her church.

The truly spiritual person—the fathers, the pastor said—was spiritually mature because he had come to know God in His fullness. He referred to Philippians 3:10: "That I may know Him and the power of His resurrection, and the fellowship of His sufferings, being conformed to His death."

Pastor Billings further explained that the second stage of spiritual maturity—the young men—was made up of those who may not yet know God in the power of His resurrection and the fellowship of His sufferings, but who did know sound doctrine. They had read and been taught and had an arsenal to help them stand against the deceit of the devil.

That's where Irene had thought she was, or was at least getting there with Jackie's help. Now she wasn't so sure.

Finally the pastor explained that the earliest stage of spiritual maturity for the believer—the little children—comprised those who had only the most rudimentary knowledge of God and needed to grow the most. Irene feared the rest of her family was not even at that door yet and were thus vulnerable to the falsehood and deception the evil one tried to foist upon people.

Irene's head and heart were so full when she and Jackie went to retrieve their kids that she hardly knew where to begin.

"Enjoy that?" Jackie said lightly.

"Enjoy?" Irene said. "Jackie, I should be further along as a believer. I'm getting a lot from you and from the Bible and from praying, but it doesn't show in my life."

"I think it does."

"C'mon, Jackie. I want to be myself around you, but of course I always try to put my best foot forward. I have to live this in front of Rayford. My whole point is to try to reach him, but everything I say and do turns him away. I can't blame him. It's as if I can't help myself. I'm doing the opposite of what I want to do. I love him. I care about him. I want to win him, bring him to Christ. But if I'm the example of Jesus to him, I'm failing."

To Jackie's credit, she didn't argue. Without a word, Jackie's mere sympathetic look spoke volumes. Irene knew she was right, that she had to examine herself, make a wholesale change in her approach.

Cameron had what he could only call a nearly out-of-body experience at his mother's funeral. The service was so formal, so by-the-book, and full of so many platitudes and empty speeches that he found himself imagining her washing her hands of the whole thing.

She would rather people be honest and tell the truth about her. When the eulogies began and old friends and relatives made their way to the microphone, things livened up a bit. People laughed and cried and told stories of the real Mrs. Williams.

Cameron had decided not to participate but nearly changed his mind, particularly when Jeff spoke.

He was remarkably articulate and heartfelt and told stories of interactions between his mother and him that Cameron had never heard before.

Strangely, Sharon sat weeping through the entire service, unable to be consoled, apparently unable to even look up. Cameron could only imagine what upset her so. Yes, she had been close to his mother. But it was also common knowledge that the women had been honest with each other. That was one thing he could say of his mother: she met straightforwardness with the same.

Much as his mother accepted and, yes, loved her only daughter-in-law, she had never hidden that she did not appreciate Sharon's take on religion. Sharon was too critical, too judgmental, couldn't leave well enough alone. Cameron's mother had always contended that one's religion was as private as one's politics and that it was impolite to probe either.

That had never stopped Sharon. She had invited her
in-laws to her own church, and they had gone more than
once—mostly to the grandkids' programs. But Sharon
couldn't just leave it at that. She would quiz them later,
ask them if their church believed the same way hers did.
Could a person become born again at their church?
What did they think about the pastor's invitation to
"give your life to the Lord"?

Jeff had been at first bemused and would regale
Cameron with stories of how their father would jump
through any hoop to avoid commitment or confrontation. He would answer all such questions with, "Yes,
that was nice. Very impressive."

But Cameron's mother? No. Honest to a fault, as his
father always said. "That rubbed me the wrong way,"
she would say. "Implying that I'm not as good a person
or a Christian if I haven't been saved just the way the
preacher says."

"You thought he was talking to you, Mom?" Sharon
said.

"He was talking to all the outsiders and making
us feel more that way. It was rude. Get us in there to
take pictures of our precious grandbabies and then hit
us over the head with the Bible, implying we don't
stack up."

Sharon had not given up. She raised the subject again
and again until finally her mother-in-law had told her
enough was enough. "I get it, all right? I get it. Is this not
my own decision?"

Jeff reported that his wife had said yes, of course it was.

"All right, I'll tell you, Sharon," their mother said. "I think it's fine for you, and I'll take my chances staying with what makes me comfortable." When Sharon got into making sure "you're not comfortable now but burning in hell later," that was nearly the end of the relationship. They barely spoke for more than six months.

And yet when Cameron's mother was struggling with cancer, who was the first person she wanted to see? Who was the one who spent hours at her bedside, attending to her every—and Jeff emphasized *every*—need? Sharon, of course. The women developed a bond breakable only by death, but there was no indication that Mrs. Williams had ever received Christ.

Perhaps that's why Sharon was so distraught now. She missed her friend, but maybe she feared the woman was in hell. Sharon's agony carried to the gravesite and to yet one more reception at the house. She did her duty, serving and playing hostess, but tears streamed and her face was crimson. The more people embraced her and tried to console her, the more she seemed to suffer.

Cameron's dad was the enigma. The man seemed to have run out of energy. He appeared so tired at the house later that people on every side urged him to get a nap. He refused. It wasn't like him to abandon a houseful of guests, regardless of the circumstance. But by the end of the afternoon, he sat, clearly trying to keep his eyes open as dozens came by to express their condolences once more and say their good-byes.

Cameron's own emotions were complicated. He was flooded with memories of his childhood relationship with his mother, when he had idolized her and she had been the object of his make-believe games. How many times had he rescued her from the enemy, saved her from a burning building, pulled her off railroad tracks with the locomotive bearing down?

It was not lost on him that he had somehow pushed from his mind memories of deceiving her when he was a teenager. Had she ever been the wiser? It didn't seem so. Her love and devotion to him never seemed to abate. That left Cameron feeling sleazy, and part of him wished he could have confessed it all to her so they could share a laugh and he would feel forgiven.

Why did preadolescents have to be so maddeningly unpredictable? Irene would have bet Chloe had a million complaints for the ride home from church and would start her case about how she was giving this test a fair shot but it wasn't going to turn out the way her mother wanted.

Raymie was quiet and nodding off, and Chloe was largely silent. If there was anything as bad as arguing with an unreasonable daughter, it was dragging opinions out of her one syllable at a time. Irene refused to do it.

It wasn't that Chloe was wholly silent. In fact, she said things Irene was tempted to latch on to. Irene knew better than to yield, of course, because just about the time she concluded she had won over her daughter, Chloe would disappoint her with a unilateral decision.

Chloe sat in the passenger seat, pleasant enough, but hardly forthcoming. Irene glanced at her a few times, resisting the urge to say, "So . . . ?"

As Irene pulled into the drive-through chicken place, Chloe said, "At least these kids are more real than the ones at our church."

"More real?"

"Well, they're nerdier and a little out of it, but they seem—I don't know—sorta genuine about it. Know what I mean?"

"Not really."

"Maybe they're faking it, like we all do at our church, but—"

"Not all of us fake it, Chloe."

"I was talking about the kids, Mom. Except for a couple, we've even given up pretending anymore. But there the kids sure seemed to know a lot about the lesson and all that. And you know when the teacher prayed out loud, she asked kids to pray too, if they wanted to."

"Did you?"

"Are you kidding? I wouldn't do that with people I know, let alone a bunch of strangers. But some kids did. And they sounded like they pray a lot."

"That impressed you?"

"I guess. Not sure I want to be that into it, you know, but I don't think they're faking it. Far as I can tell anyway."

"What was the lesson about?"

"Same as the sermon, which was kind of an interesting idea. I don't know if I get it all, but it makes sense to do it that way, don't you think? Like they did it on purpose. They ever do anything in our church on purpose?"

Irene stopped herself from saying anything disparaging about her church. Just when it seemed Chloe was about to concede that the new place wasn't so bad, she asked her mother to remind her how long this experiment was supposed to last and wasn't her father expected to have to go too.

"I'm not your father's mother," Irene said. "I'm asking you to give it a fair shot, and then I'm going to ask you to keep going, even if you would rather not."

"I knew it!" Chloe said, waking Raymie just in time for him to smell the chicken and want some. "You're not going to respect my decision at all!"

"The fact is, Chloe, I'm scared. I want you to know that I love you and I do respect you, but I want the best for you. I would never forgive myself if I let you badger me out of having you in church every Sunday. What kind of a mother would I be?"

"One who treats her daughter like a human being and not a possession."

"That's not fair."

"Don't talk to me about fair, Mom. You're not being fair at all. I'll do my part, uphold my end of the bargain, but you have to uphold yours too. This was supposed to be my decision."

"I was hoping yours would be a decision I could support."

"So it's my choice as long as I choose the way you want me to."

"You make me sound pretty unbending, Chloe."

"Am I wrong?"

"Please withhold judgment for a few weeks."

"That's not going to be easy, Mom."

"I know, but do it for me."

"Everything I do is for you. I wish you'd do something for me once."

Someday, Irene knew, Chloe would have a child of her own and—hopefully—she would come to her senses and regret that remark. In the meantime, Irene would do all she knew how to do for her beloved daughter. She would pray for her with all her being, hoping God would change her mind and eventually her heart.

TWENTY-FIVE

"I AM WORRIED about the women, Nicolae," Viv Ivins said. "And I am not the only one."

Carpathia folded his hands and leaned back in his office chair. "The women? I have told you: they are mere dalliances. I seriously have no interest in any of them."

"That's my point, beloved. I don't care what you do for recreation, but you must be discreet. The election is close. And others are nervous—"

"That is another thing!" Nicolae said, letting his chair return upright. "Do not talk to me about others or about your not being the only one concerned! If someone has an issue with me, he should say so to my face. Now who are we talking about?"

"I don't know if I should speak for—"

"Aunt Viv! *You* raised the issue. *You* said you were not the only one. Now who?"

"They have your best interests at heart, Nicolae. They

should not be in trouble for caring about you and your future."

"I appreciate that, Viv, but what does it say about their concern for me and their loyalty to me if they are running around behind my back, talking to you and who knows who else about my—?"

"I have no evidence of that."

"Then what? What are they saying? And who are they so I can put their minds at ease?"

Viv studied her shoes, and Nicolae could tell she would cave if he just waited her out. "Tristan," she said softly.

"My night-shift driver? Tell me you are not serious! Get him in here."

"He is, of course, sleeping right now, Nicolae. I can ask him to come to work a few minutes early this evening. But, please, you must know he is among your most loyal staff and a great admirer of—"

"He will get a chance to affirm that soon. And explain himself, of course."

It became clear to Irene that Rayford and Chloe had once again conspired against her. They wouldn't admit it, of course, and she didn't have hard evidence. But suddenly Chloe decided that despite whatever was good or interesting or unique about New Hope, she would stay with their old church, as long as Irene was insisting that she continue to attend.

"That's where I'm going too," Rayford said, and Irene

realized she was caught. What was it about New Hope that so threatened Rayford? He was essentially saying that he would back her insistence that Chloe stay in church a few more years—against her will—and that he would even attend more frequently, as long as they stayed at their regular church.

"We'd like it if you went with us," Rayford said.

"Oh, *we* would, would we?" Irene didn't want to sound so shrewish, and if she could just count a beat or two before responding, maybe she could be more civil. But if Rayford's comment wasn't evidence of collusion, Irene didn't know what was. Well, she wasn't about to split up her family over which church they attended, desperate as she was to move to New Hope. Maddeningly, she had succeeded on some level. Rayford might attend more, and Chloe would reluctantly go every Sunday—at least for a while—as long as it was at this nonthreatening country club of a church. Well, Irene would just have to continue using Jackie as her lifeline to real spiritual growth. She would recommit herself to daily Bible reading and prayer, and she would throw herself into the weekly sessions with Jackie like never before. If she couldn't personally sit under the teaching of Vernon Billings, getting his input secondhand would have to do.

But what abut Raymie? Soon he would be old enough to understand that he, too, needed Jesus. It would be up to her—which she assumed was the way it should be anyway—to lead him to faith. He certainly wasn't going to be guided toward a real experience with Christ in a church that never emphasized that.

One thing was sure: though Irene had no idea how long it would be before Chloe dropped out altogether—and while Irene would fight that to the end—that would signal her time to switch churches. She was not about to wither and die on the vine when she knew she belonged somewhere like New Hope.

———

Cameron Williams was finding it hard to concentrate on finishing at Princeton. He knew he could coast to graduation with a great grade point average and lots of attention, but his enthusiasm was fading for campus activities, the school paper, his class work, all that. The job at the *Globe* loomed, and he could hardly wait.

That news had gotten around in his circles, and he was suddenly *the* celebrated young journalist on campus. His very personal piece about attending his mother's funeral and how he felt about missing seeing her alive became the piece the *Globe* used to introduce their soon-coming new reporter.

Cameron had not been aware that he was an emotional writer, and he didn't try to affect a certain tone just for effect. But even Dizzy Rowland told him he was impressed by how Cameron had used simple, straightforward language to tell a story with universal impact. "You didn't manufacture emotion, son. You elicited it from the reader."

"You know, sir," Cameron had said, "I hardly think about that—when I'm writing I mean."

"What *do* you think about?"

Cameron shook his head and squinted, trying to conjure the feelings and emotions that went into his craft. For a man who planned to make his living with words, he was having a hard time articulating his own thoughts.

"I guess I'd have to say I'm consumed with curiosity," he said. "I have so many questions, and I assume the reader does too. I'm his agent, asking what he would ask, trying to find out every detail he would want to know—and maybe a few he hasn't thought of. When I'm focused on putting a piece together, I'm desperate to include every cogent detail and leave out anything that slows it down or detracts."

"You're not thinking about avoiding clichés or forcing the emotion?"

Cameron shook his head. "Comes naturally, I guess."

"Intuitive."

"I hope so."

"It's a gift, Cameron."

The *Globe* also assigned Cameron to interview a Boston native who had accepted a department chairmanship at Princeton, and Cameron somehow managed to turn it into more than a simple news story. And he had covered the story of a Massachusetts family who had seen their three adopted Asian children graduate from Ivy League schools, marry, start successful businesses, and move to New Jersey.

All Cameron wanted was to get out of school and get to Boston so he could do this every day.

Nicolae liked Tristan and had almost since the day he hired him nearly two years before. The young man was quiet and industrious, and when he did speak, he was complimentary of his boss. Carpathia knew he himself was above being impressed by flattery, but anyone, he concluded, liked to be respected.

He decided to host Tristan in the living room rather than the office, which might have been more intimidating. Nicolae wanted to coax as much information as he could from the young driver. But when Tristan entered, wearing his black chauffeur's uniform and carrying his cap, he looked wan and wary.

"Sit there, please," Nicolae said, pointing to an easy chair across from the divan where he sat. "Ms. Ivins tells me you have a concern you would like to share with me."

"Oh yes, sir. I feel bad that I confided in her and did not come directly to you."

"By all means, be assured I prefer the latter."

"Yes, sir. And I assure you I have not shared my concerns with anyone else."

"Then there is no need for you to be *speriat*. I would be most concerned and would not mind your being nervous if you were spreading things about me among the staff and especially anyone outside."

"Oh no, of course not."

"So, what is on your mind, Tristan?"

"Ms. Ivins did not tell you?"

"As a matter of fact, she did. And she shares your

worries, as you probably know. But I want to hear from you. In your own words."

Tristan worked his cap in both hands and looked past Nicolae. "First off, I realize it is none of my business."

"I am none of your business, Tristan? That is *ridicol*, absurd! Not only am I your business, I *want* to be your business. How many times have I told the staff that to be successful you all must take a certain degree of owner-ship in me and in the company?"

Tristan nodded. "Many times, yes, I understand."

"So, out with it. What?"

"I don't begrudge you your guests."

"The women who visit me nearly every night."

"Yes. I wish I had them lining up at my door."

"I am sure you have little problem in that regard, Tristan."

"Well, let's just say my home is not as busy as yours is."

"It is merely recreation, my friend. No one is com-pelled to visit me."

"Oh, I understand. And I doubt most people would personally have any trouble with it. But there is a reason you send me to pick up these women and return them, and that it is always after dark."

"Of course. Discretion."

"Which means it is important I keep this confidential. From your enemies particularly."

"Of course."

"That is what I worry about, Mr. Carpathia. I can only imagine what Mr. Tismaneanu might do with such information."

"A point well-taken and one of the reasons I use someone as trusted as you to carry out this duty. Do you have any suspicion that he or his people might be aware of this?"

"Actually, I do."

That Nicolae had not expected. He leaned forward expectantly, his stare begging for details.

"I know a man who works for Tismaneanu," Tristan said. "Well, knowing him is probably overstating it. He is an acquaintance. A friend of a friend."

"Yes, and what does this man do for Emil?"

"I don't even know that. I know he is not educated and is a bit of a *delincvent*, so I—"

"What would a criminal be doing in Tismaneanu's employ?"

"—doubt he is in any position of trust or authority. Probably works on the grounds. Perhaps his boss asked anyone there if they knew anyone here."

"Perhaps. And so he contacted you."

"Yes, with a strange question and a request. He wanted to know if I wanted to make some extra money—innocent money, he called it. I assured him I was well paid and not looking for more work. He said it would be no more work. Only that when I deliver guests to you late at night and leave with them before dawn, I should stop under the light in the circular drive rather than under the covered portico at the entrance. He said no one would be the wiser and that for this I could expect a few hundred in cash for less than one week's work. Of course it would have been no work.

It would have required only that I walk your guests an extra twenty-five feet or so."

Nicolae gazed at the ceiling, then closed his eyes. "He wants them illuminated, does he?"

"Apparently. And call me *prost*, but I do not understand why."

"I would never call you stupid, Tristan. But surely you can guess why."

"But I have looked from every angle out there, and I cannot see where anyone could mount a camera."

"With modern technology, Tristan, they could be a long way away. Illumination is the key. The alternative, of course, is to follow you to where you pick up these guests and drop them off, and perhaps the lighting is better there."

"But a photo of their getting out and getting back in right here at your own residence, that is clearly what Tismaneanu is after. Do you suppose he means to ruin you with this? sell photographs to the newspapers?"

Nicolae stood and shrugged. "That might be beneath even old Emil," he said. "But it would not surprise me if an emissary of his came and showed me pictures, trying to exact some concession on my part."

"Concession?"

"Get me to pull out of the race at this late stage. Something like that."

"We must not let that happen! You will win unless this gets out. We need you in Parliament."

"Do not give it another thought, Tristan. Thank you for telling me, and remember what to do in the future."

"Tell only you."

"Good man. Now I am about to make some arrangements for tomorrow night, and I may want you to accede to your acquaintance's wishes."

"But I already refused him."

"Can you not change your mind? tell yourself there could be little harm in this and that you could always use a few more dollars?"

"Maybe. If you wish."

"I will let you know. I have some work to do first."

TWENTY-SIX

A CALL FROM SHARON, Jeff's wife? Something had to be wrong. Cameron called her back as soon as he could get to the privacy of his own room.

"Jeff's talking about leaving again."

"Leaving? For where?"

"Anywhere but here."

"Well, does he have a buyer for the business? Dad can't—"

"He's not leaving Tucson or the business, Cameron. He's talking about leaving me, us."

"He wouldn't. With the kids there? I mean, he wouldn't leave you either, would he? And why, anyway?"

"He did before, Cam. You remember."

"Yeah, but that was different. You didn't have kids and you were both young. He just didn't know how to be a husband yet."

"You know why he left."

"Yeah. But you're different now, aren't you, Sharon?"

"Less strident, you mean?"

"I guess."

"I hope so. But since your mother died, Jeff's been on edge. I've never made him go to church with me, and I've tried not to nag him about going. But he senses the tension. I go and take the kids, of course. He has to feel bad, especially when he has nothing else to do, no excuses. He doesn't play golf or bowl or play poker, you know. I couldn't tell you if he's even got friends. When he's not working he likes to just sit around, read the paper, watch television. And I don't begrudge him that. I don't. And while I wish he'd come back to God, back to the church, I know it's his decision alone. But I don't want to lose him. Can you talk to him, Cameron?"

"Me?"

"Who else?"

"I'm the kid brother, Sharon. Remember? He may be proud of me, but he doesn't want me to know that. I doubt he looks up to me. And I've never dated anyone more than three times in a row, let alone been married. Who am I to counsel him?"

He could hear her breathing, and he knew she knew he was right. But she was without options. Cameron's father was sure not up to confronting Jeff. "How's Dad doing anyway?"

"Ah, he's constantly underfoot. He had been phasing out of the business, you know, especially during your mother's last few months. But he needs something to do now, and both Jeff and I urged him to come back. We shouldn't have. We had in mind that he would help out in the shop, keep an eye on the mechanics, that kind of thing."

"Didn't work?"

"Not at all. Jeff had to quit filling in and driving routes, because when he's away, Dad thinks he should take over. Everything goes back to the way it was when he was in charge, and everybody's frustrated."

"I'm sorry."

"But that's not the issue, Cam. I can't lose Jeff. Frustrating as he is, I love him and want him around. The kids need him. He's a good dad."

"You told anybody else about this?"

"No."

"Then he's going to know where I heard it."

"That's all right."

"I'll talk to him, Sharon, but I'm not optimistic."

―――――――

Leon Fortunato was giddy over his assignment. "I'll wear my best suit," he said.

"No, just do this by phone, Leon," Nicolae said. "You cannot risk being seen with her."

"Of course."

"And be quick. This could be crucial."

Leon called Luciana Tismaneanu, Emil's grown daughter, who, the society pages had recently announced, was engaged and would be married shortly after the parliamentary election.

Leon identified himself and asked if Luciana was aware of her father's relationship with Mr. Carpathia.

"Only that they are running for the same office, sir. I know they have said inflammatory things about one another, but Father assures me that's just politics and that he harbors no personal animosity."

"That is wonderful to hear, Miss Tismaneanu. I assure you the sentiment goes both ways. In fact, Mr. Carpathia greatly admires your father and considers him a friend."

"A friend? I was not aware they knew each other that well."

"Getting more acquainted every day," Leon said. "And close enough to know that your father's birthday is on the horizon."

"Yes, a week from tomorrow," Luciana said. "We're planning a private family gathering."

"How wonderful. Now I am wondering if I could consult with you about something in total confidence."

"Well, sure, I guess."

"Mr. Carpathia is determined to keep this election on the highest moral ground possible and to call a moratorium on the mudslinging."

"Father will be overjoyed to hear that and will, I'm sure, comply reciprocally."

"Mr. Carpathia wishes to remain friends with your father, wholly apart from the results of the election."

"I suppose it's no surprise to you, Mr. Fortunato, that early polling shows a victory is unlikely for my father.

He still has high hopes, of course, and is planning to announce some new initiatives. But he is a realist, a pragmatist. He is only disappointed, I believe, because he sincerely thought one more term in the Parliament would set him up to run for the upper house and eventually the presidency."

"That's very interesting, Miss Tismaneanu, because the truth is that the only hesitation Mr. Carpathia has about winning this election is that he hopes it does not damage your father's potential for a run for head of state."

There was a brief silence on the other end of the phone. Finally Miss Tismaneanu said, "Are you serious? Mr. Carpathia thinks my father is presidential material?"

"You would be surprised at the esteem in which Mr. Carpathia holds your father."

"I *am* surprised."

"Prepare to be more so. We are fully aware that what I am about to propose could look like a cheap political trick, but I assure you it is not. Mr. Carpathia would like to hold a surprise birthday reception for your father, a small gathering here in his home for just your family and close associates and a few guests on this side. Mr. Carpathia would pledge absolute confidentiality so that he would gain no political or media benefit. He merely wishes to do this as a token of his admiration for a worthy opponent."

"I am stunned," she said. "And father would be too."

"The point is," Leon said, "we would have to work very hard to surprise him, would we not?"

"Very."

"That is where you come in. Mr. Carpathia would appreciate it very much if he could meet with you privately soon to go over plans for the evening and to strategize with you about the best way to get your father here for the surprise."

"Nicolae Carpathia wants to meet with me?"

"Very much. This would be at your convenience, would have to be totally confidential, of course, and he would be prepared to have you picked up and delivered back to your residence."

"I live downtown in the apartment where my fiancé and I will be living after our wedding."

"No problem. Are you willing and able? We're looking at very late some evening within the next few days."

The second time Hattie Durham asked Rayford for a ride home, he suggested she just count on him from then on.

"Are you sure, Captain? It's a lot to ask."

"I don't mind. It's not that far out of the way, and I'm sure your roommate will enjoy the break."

"Yeah. She's out of town for a few days and my car's on the fritz again."

Rayford couldn't tell whether Hattie was telling him this to explain her predicament or if she just wanted him to know she was home alone. He wasn't about to suggest anything, but he had to admit to himself that he would be flattered if she asked him to come up. He told himself he would decline, but he was disappointed when she didn't ask.

To cover himself, he told Irene of his offer to Hattie.

"That's nice," she said, "as long as she's not in love with you."

Rayford snorted. "That'll be the day. I'm nearly old enough to be her father. And, hey, would it bother you so much if she *was* in love with me?"

Irene laughed. "Of course. But it wouldn't surprise me. I can't be the only woman in Illinois with good taste."

That stabbed Rayford. All he had put her through, how cold he had become, how formal their marriage was . . . and she was still saying nice things. He wished he deserved that.

———

Cameron was on the phone with Jeff.

"So she told you, huh?"

"Yup."

"And, what, she wants you, of all people, to talk me out of this?"

"Shows how desperate she is, Jeff. You remember when you left her the last time, you didn't behave."

"I know. I left and then gave her reason to not take me back."

"But she did. And why?"

"I know, Cam. She was a better person than I was. Probably still is."

"Then don't be stupid. What are you doing? Why do you want out?"

"Because she's got it all together, man. I hate my job. I hate what Dad's doing. I don't hate you, but I should."

"Then go ahead and hate me."

"I don't, Cam, but I don't like you sticking your nose into my marriage either."

"You think I like it? She called me, Jeff."

"I probably won't leave anyway. I don't know how I'd explain it to the kids."

"Easy. Just tell them their mother is a better person than you and that you're an idiot who doesn't know how good he has it."

"All right already, Cam. I said I probably wouldn't do it."

"Well, could you do me a favor and give me the credit if you stay? I could use the brownie points with your wife."

"Why? She tell you she thinks you're lost too?"

"Not in so many words," Cameron said.

"No," Jeff said, "but we get the point, don't we? You realize how hard it is to live with a saint?"

"I can't imagine. Especially when you're the opposite."

About thirty people showed up to the surprise party for Emil Tismaneanu, and it was clear to Nicolae that the man was truly stunned. He seemed to paste on a grateful smile for his family, who had all been involved somehow in the ruse. But his eyes conveyed something else altogether when he looked at Nicolae.

When they finally had occasion to be apart from the others for a moment, Tismaneanu said, "I need a minute with you when it's convenient."

"Even this evening?" Nicolae said.

"If possible."

"Shall we steal away right now? retire to my office?"

"Let me cover my tracks," Emil said. He went and spoke briefly with his wife, then his chief of staff, then a man who appeared to be part of his security detail. The man handed him a manila envelope, and Emil returned to Carpathia.

"All set? Follow me."

In his office Carpathia sat at a small conference table directly across from his rival. "I hope this was a pleasant surprise, Emil."

"Oh, please let's cut the *bălegar*, Carpathia. I don't trust you for a second."

"I assure you the press knows nothing of this, sir, and I plan to keep it that way. I will not exploit this for my political gain."

"What then? There has to be something in this for you."

"Just your presence and friendship."

"You make me sick."

"Emil, please. I am extending an olive branch here."

"Well, let me show you what I am extending." Tismaneanu slid the envelope across the table.

Nicolae eagerly slit it open. "Why, look at that!"

he said, beaming. "That looks like my place. And my car. And my driver. But who is the young lady? She looks so familiar. Fetching, do you not agree?"

Tismaneanu sat stonily, staring at Carpathia.

"Tell me, Emil, if you do not think she is more than *atrăgător*?" He turned the picture right side up for Tismaneanu.

But the older man would not look. "It does not surprise me that you entertain attractive women, Carpathia. It might surprise the voters, however."

Carpathia feigned his most curious look. "The voters? I do not understand, Emil. What are you saying?"

"I'm saying that if you do not pull out of the race within forty-eight hours, that photograph goes to the media."

"But, Emil, surely you know I have the same shots. My entrance is thoroughly blanketed by security cameras twenty-four hours a day."

"So?"

"Perhaps my shots are clearer? Perhaps mine will make it obvious who the young lady is. She does look familiar; does she not?"

He tapped the picture, and Tismaneanu finally looked at it. Carpathia basked in the gradual recognition that came over the man's face. He stood, pale and shaking. "I'll kill you, Carpathia," he said.

Nicolae stood and turned to reach for two buttons on the wall. One silently summoned his security staff. The other started a microchip recorder playback with Emil Tismaneanu's threat in high fidelity.

"Someone *is* going to shockingly withdraw from this race," Nicolae said. "I wonder which of us it will be."

Emil lunged for him, just as Nicolae's bodyguards burst through the door to pull the older man away.

TWENTY-SEVEN

CAMERON FRANKLY WASN'T SURE how serious he was about Janet. He had dated her exclusively a half-dozen times and found himself thinking about her frequently. Was he in love? How would he know? Enamored perhaps. She was fun and funny and attractive and, of course, smart. Best of all, she seemed genuinely interested in his thoughts and plans and dreams.

He had stumbled only once with her, and he chalked it up to naïveté. He hoped she did too. They had gone out on her birthday, and his gift, a jade necklace, was, she said, "Beautiful. But, Cameron, I can't accept it."

"What? Why?"

"It's a bit much for where we are in our relationship. We're just getting to know each other. Really, I wouldn't feel comfortable accepting this or wearing it."

"For real?"

"I'm sorry."

He shrugged and accepted it back, then felt more than awkward the rest of the night. The following weekend Janet accepted a Friday night date with him but passed on Saturday night because she had another date. Cameron didn't know why that rocked him so. He figured that if he was seeing only her, the sentiment would be reciprocal.

He asked around, and a few buddies told him it was time to make a move, make his intentions clear. "That's all she's waiting for, Cameron," one said. "Some expression of commitment."

He reminded his friend about the necklace.

"But you've dated a few times since. Tell her where you stand. Find out where her head is."

That seemed straightforward enough. So on Friday night he asked if she was free Sunday afternoon. The way she looked at him and smiled when she said yes gave him the confidence he needed. He practiced his speech. "Thought we'd just enjoy a picnic at the preserve," he said.

"Sounds perfect," she said.

Cameron was uncommonly nervous Sunday morning. Though Janet offered to prepare the picnic lunch, he insisted on bringing it from a deli. They enjoyed a long walk in the woods and spread a blanket in a clearing, where they sat and talked and ate.

"I like spending time with you," he said.

"Me too," she said.

"In fact," Cameron said, "I've been thinking that I'd like to suggest taking this friendship to another level."

She smiled. "Meaning?"

"Make it exclusive. Try that out. Pursue a real relationship. See what comes of it."

"Hmm."

"Is that a yes or a no, Janet?"

She was still smiling. "It was a *hmm*, Cameron."

"Meaning?"

"Meaning I'm thinking."

He knew enough to fall silent. It was a full hour later, however, when she finally got back to the subject. They had picked up the blanket and tidied the area and were heading back to his car. She took his hand, but somehow he knew there was no hidden or implied meaning in that. In fact, he sensed it might be a sympathy bone she was tossing his way.

"I'm going to have to say no, Cameron. I'm sorry."

"Really? Why? I'm doing something wrong? Or there's someone else you're more interested in?"

"Actually, no on both counts. I like my freedom, like to get to know different guys. But no one else I'm seeing holds a candle to you."

"That's nice. So . . . ?"

They put the stuff in the car; then Janet leaned back against it and reached for Cameron's hands. "Someday I want to be the love of someone's life," she said.

"But not mine?"

"That might be nice, Cameron, but it's not going to happen."

"How do you know? That's why I'm suggesting we give this thing a chance."

She shook her head. "Listen, I'm not expecting you to be head over heels for me, but—"

"And I've been honest with you, Janet. I can't say I'm in love yet. I just want to see if it might come to that if we gave each other more time and attention."

"I'm saying no, Cameron."

"So you've decided we could never fall in love."

"I could. You couldn't."

"You're deciding for me?"

She chuckled. "I know you better than you know yourself." He began to pull away, but she held on to his hands. "Hear me, Cameron. You're a wonderful, talented person with a lot to offer. And you are in love already."

"Sorry?"

"You're in love with your career."

"I don't even have a career yet."

"Of course you do. You're further along toward your career goals than anyone else I know at Princeton. You're already working for the *Globe*. In a few months that will be full-time, and you'll be on your way. That'll probably be just a stepping-stone to bigger and better things. You'll probably wind up on television, one of those international correspondents reporting from Tel Aviv, Bonn, Rome—you name it."

Cameron cocked his head. "I could live with that."

"I couldn't."

"You couldn't?"

"No. Cameron, I wish I could hold a mirror to you when you're talking about journalism. I'd be surprised if you ever love anything like you love that. You get a far-away look, a gleam in your eye. You rhapsodize about it. Whoever winds up with you will compete with that mistress all her life."

"That bad, eh?"

"That bad. I wouldn't even want to try to talk you out of it. I wish I was as consumed by someone or something—anything—as that."

"You don't think I could change, could examine myself and work on—"

"That's just it, Cameron. I wouldn't want you to. You take the purest joy in this pursuit of yours, and I would do you a disservice to ask you to sublimate it to me. But you would be doing me a disservice to try to concentrate on me while pursuing your true love."

Cameron let go of her hands and thrust his into his pockets. "Wow," he said. "I could sure use someone like you in my life."

"I know you could. But it's not going to be me. I hope you understand, and I hope I haven't hurt you."

"I think I understand. Thanks . . . I think."

She cupped his face in her hands and kissed him lightly on the lips. "Thanks for asking, anyway."

Irene was fascinated by Chloe's development. Blonde and green-eyed, she was suddenly gangly—all arms and legs.

She wore braces and glasses that would soon give way
to contacts, then laser surgery. But she was also suddenly
on the phone to her girlfriends all the time and fero-
ciously protective of her privacy. She stopped talking
the moment Irene came within earshot. She would scowl
and scold and whisper and turn away.

Irene found this frustrating, of course, and felt shut
out more than ever. But it also amused her. Here was
this frisky colt, all angular and awkward and clumsy,
suddenly aware of fashion. No matter what Chloe wore,
she still looked like a newborn animal trying to get its
legs under itself. But apparently that didn't stop the boys
from seeing her potential.

That was what Chloe was talking about with her girlfriends. Constantly. Irene heard enough to know that.

Also strange was the sudden change in Chloe's attitude
about going to church. Irene was naturally suspicious.
Rayford had all but completely stopped attending, except
for the occasional off-golf-season Sunday when he couldn't
arrange to fly somewhere. But Chloe was up early on Sundays, trying on outfits, spending inordinate amounts of
time in the bathroom, and emerging eager to go.

She wore the latest fashions and accessories, but it
was all Irene could do to keep a straight face, watching
the gawky preteen try to look hip and cool.

When Chloe went from whining and complaining
about having to go to church at all to where she started
attending Sunday school and church and young people's
activities, Irene knew something was up. That something,
of course, turned out to be *someone*. Bobby.

Every time his name was mentioned, Chloe blushed. And when he began sitting next to her during the morning service, Irene saw the dreaminess in their eyes. Ah, first love. Or at least first crush. It was fun to watch and not hard to see what they saw in each other. His hair had a pair of cowlicks competing for wildness. He was shorter than Chloe, and he also wore braces and glasses.

Around each other, both were extremely quiet. They couldn't hide that their fingers were touching under the hymnal and that they played footsie during prayer time. Irene wanted to caution Chloe about boys, but it wasn't like they were dating. They probably hardly even spoke.

Bobby seemed harmless enough, and when Irene figured out that he came from an old church family, her mind was at ease. Whatever or whoever was getting her daughter to church every Sunday was fine with her.

———

Nicolae had never seen Reiche Planchette so clearly shaken. His lips looked thin and pale, and his eyes darted. He had insisted on a meeting with the senior cabinet of Carpathian Trading: Nicolae, Leon, Viv, and himself.

"I was threatened," he said. "We were all threatened."

"By whom?" Nicolae said evenly.

"He didn't give me a name, but it was clear whom he represented."

"Start from the beginning," Nicolae said.

"Okay, well, you know I enjoy a late-afternoon aperitif."

"At The Longshoreman, yes."

"Well, apparently I've been seen there."

"Only by everyone in Bucharest at one time or another," Nicolae said.

"I was at the bar when a man approached and asked if I would join him for a moment at his table. I said, 'Do I know you?' and he said, 'No, but I know you. I ask for only a minute of your time.' Needless to say, I was curious. I took my drink to his table, which was in a secluded area. He didn't look like a thug. Most pleasant looking and sounding, actually."

"Get to the point, Reiche, please," Nicolae said.

"Sorry. He leaned forward and whispered, 'You and your boss and the other two members of your inner circle and their loved ones are in danger.' I'm paraphrasing, of course, but—"

"I would not expect you to remember every word, Reiche."

"Thank you, but I will never forget the import of what he said. I said, 'In danger of what?' and he said, 'In danger for your very lives.' He said 'your *very* lives,' almost like out of Shakespeare. I said, 'Why?' and he said, 'I think you know.'"

"You'd have been proud of me, Nicolae. I said, 'I don't know, so if you have a serious message for me, you had better try being more clear.'"

"Good job," Nicolae said, working to contain a laugh.

"Well, he got more clear. He said, 'Unless I can assure my boss he doesn't have to drop out of this race, one of you or a loved one is going to die. You have twenty-four hours.'"

"Tell me," Nicolae said, "that he was stupid enough to say he would meet you again at the same place. I will have him taken down right there if he does."

"No. He had quite specific instructions for you."

"For me?"

"You are to say something during your next speech, which if I am not mistaken is set for tomorrow morning—"

"Right."

"—about your esteemed opponent, and you are to use those exact words. You are to admit that you would endorse him as a candidate for the presidency and look forward to the day when you might actually be able to do that. Then you are to indicate that you are considering—just considering—actually dropping out of the race and that you will let the public know within another day or two."

"Dropping out of the race with just days to go," Nicolae said, grinning.

"Just considering it."

"Do not be mad, Reiche. If I told the press and the public I was even thinking about something like that, it would end the race for me. Who would vote for someone so wishy-washy?"

"Exactly," Leon said. "Anyway, we do not fear Emil Tismaneanu and his thugs."

"Fear?" Nicolae said. "I will meet aggression with aggression."

"I fear them," Viv said. "I am not eager to be in danger."

"Then lie low for a while, Viv. And, Reiche, after tomorrow's speech, I would avoid The Longshoreman."

"What are you saying?"

"If you have to ask that, Reiche, you might even consider not going anywhere for a few days."

"Well, I'm assuming you're not going to accede to their wishes then?"

"Not allow my opponent to write my speeches, you mean? No, Reiche, I am not going to accede to their wishes. In fact, they are going to accede to mine, which I made clear to Emil when he was here."

"So it's come to this?" Reiche said, looking suddenly weary.

"Yes!" Leon said. And he looked energized.

TWENTY-EIGHT

RAYFORD HAD NEVER been called on the carpet per se, so he was pretty sure this summons to Earl Halliday's office was something other than that. And when he saw Earl's smile, he was relieved.

"I don't know if it was all the coverage you got for that safe landing in L.A. or your background in ROTC," Earl said, "but the brass at the CIA and the Defense Department want to talk with you."

"Think it has anything to do with my being on the reserve list for *Air Force One* and *Two*?"

"No idea, but you can bet they know about that. They probably have a record of every traffic ticket you ever got too, and if you got caught chewing gum in school."

"Kids still get in trouble for that, Earl?"

"How would I know? Showing my age. Anyway, I'm changing your next assignment so you'll fly into Reagan, and you'll have plenty of time to meet with those boys. They made it clear it would be super classified, confidential, and all that, but you gotta promise me, Ray. Promise you'll remember every word."

"Yeah, I forgot. You love all this cloak-and-dagger stuff."

"Don't you?"

"Sure. But who knows what this is about?"

"Not me," Earl said.

"Let me see the crew list for the original pattern."

Earl produced it from his computer, and Rayford scanned it. He would have to call Hattie and tell her she'd need another way home.

Nicolae's morning speech was scheduled for a One World rally at the University of Romania at Bucharest. For some reason the students there, particularly those belonging to liberal cause clubs, had turned on their old favorite, Emil Tismaneanu, and decided he was now too establishment. They had to be aware that Nicolae Carpathia was every bit as much a materialist and capitalist as Tismaneanu, but he was also young—not much older than they—and had charm and energy unmatched by other politicos in their memory.

Besides, Carpathia rarely spoke of business and commerce. He spoke of the poor, the oppressed, the disenfranchised. He spoke of opening Romania to the rest of the world—a message that would go down easily at a rally for globalism.

Nicolae mounted the podium to enthusiastic applause and assumed the students and faculty had seen the latest polls that showed him ahead by nearly ten points. He suspected their motives. Had he been trailing by that much, would that many have shown up, and would they be so enthusiastic if they thought they had thrown in with a loser?

Nicolae felt upbeat and stayed on point. He said what the education crowd wanted to hear, then waxed eloquent on globalism and the need to de-emphasize national borders. He was interrupted time and again by cheering and applause.

"This is where my opponent and I disagree," he said. "Do I esteem my opponent? No, I do not."

Wild applause.

"But I will say that Emil Tismaneanu happens to be a close personal friend and, I hope, long will be, even after I defeat him. And I will beat him with your help! Does it come as a surprise to you that he and I are friends? Would it shock you to know I recently hosted a dinner party in his honor? I wonder if the favor will be reciprocated when I am looking for a place to celebrate victory.

"But I tease my friend because we disagree on fundamentals. A sincere man? Yes, he is. One who loves his country? Certainly. But therein lies the rub. He would enclose us, strengthen our borders, keep us from being cosmopolitan. There is a reason Emil Tismaneanu is a successful businessman. He does not like to share the wealth."

And so there it was. Nicolae had not only not used

the code language prescribed in the threat, but he had also used the opposite. And he had broken his promise to not use the surprise party for political gain. But there was more. Nicolae had sunk in the knife. It was time to twist it.

"I shall leave to my other-than-esteemed opponent the explanation of why his campaign is flagging and why it would not surprise me in the least if he opted out of the race, even at this late date. He actually broached that subject with me recently, and one of his representatives discussed his dropping out with one of my staff members only yesterday. I do not know about you, but I would prefer a man in the Parliament committed to a long-term future, a man who knows his own mind, a man other than wishy-washy about his own future. But that is just me. I am not the one looking at poll figures showing an all-but-hopeless cause."

Nicolae left the platform to cheering and a standing ovation, having left the ball squarely in Emil Tismaneanu's court.

"Class elections this time of the year?" Irene said.

Chloe nodded, smiling through her complex braces. "It's for next school year, but they're doing it now. I'm running for president of the seventh-grade class."

"Really? And what do you feel are your chances?"

Chloe looked suddenly crestfallen. "You don't think I can win."

"I didn't say that. Of course you can win. I just wonder how confident you are."

"Totally, Mom. In fact, the only other person I know for sure is running is a football player. He's like the male version of the dumb blonde."

"Careful. You're blonde too."

"I don't mean literally, Mom. His hair is brown. But he's a jock, beginning and end."

"Is he popular?"

"'Course. But this isn't a popularity contest. This is about issues."

"Don't kid yourself. Every election is a popularity contest."

"Mom! Why do you have to throw a wet blanket on everything?"

"Oh no, I'm not. I just want you to be pragmatic, practical."

"You don't think I'm popular."

"I know you must be."

"Then why would you say that? You don't know anything about me!"

Nicolae settled into the expansive backseat of Leon Fortunato's monstrous black SUV. As his driver pulled into traffic, Leon smiled.

"You like that speech, Leon?" Carpathia said.

"Loved it. There's Tismaneanu's answer to his strong-arm tactics. If he had any doubt or question, he doesn't now."

Nicolae laid his head back. "I just hope I gave him a reason to do something that will give me a reason to respond."

"I have little doubt," Leon said.

After a day filled with appearances, press conferences, and meetings, they were finally headed home when Leon took a call. "Slow down, Viv. What do we know for sure?"

"Give me that phone, Leon," Nicolae said, pulling it from Fortunato's fingers. "What is the problem, Viv?"

"You wanted Reiche to lie low, and after what I heard on the news this morning, that was wise counsel."

"And so?"

"He refused my offer of a drink here. He's on his way out."

"Surely not to The Longshoreman."

"No. He said something about the *Biserică Strană*."

"The Church Pew! Does he not know where that is?"

"Where is it?"

"In Tismaneanu's neighborhood. Reiche must be suicidal. Call him and tell him to get back to the compound immediately. I need to see him."

"I'm sorry to hear that, Captain," Hattie said. "I was going to thank you for your kindnesses lately by offering you a late dinner at my place."

Rayford hesitated. Since it wasn't going to happen anyway, he could say what he wanted without fear of repercussion. "Oh! My loss. Well, maybe another time, but of course dinner is totally unnecessary."

"I know."

"It's my pleasure to run you home," Rayford said.

"The pleasure is all mine."

———

Leon's driver was pulling into the Carpathia estate by the time Nicolae took another call from Viv.

"I'm getting no answer at Reiche's number," she said. "Nicolae, I'm scared."

"Best not to worry about things over which we have no control. I believe you taught me that, Aunt Viv."

"Why does Reiche have to go out every day? Why can't he just enjoy something from your liquor cabinet?"

"Precisely. He happens to be a bright man, a spiritual man, without a lick of common sense."

"Someone's pulling in right now."

"It is us, Viv."

"I so wish he would pull in right behind you. He will be back soon, won't he?"

"We can hope," Nicolae said. But privately he wished for the worst. He was dead serious in his desire to have a reason to retaliate. And if he had to pick one dispensable member of his inner circle, it was Reiche. Fortunato was irreplaceable. Viv was weak but genuinely cared for him. Reiche had always been a sycophant and always would be.

"Keep trying his phone, Viv," Nicolae said once they were inside and he saw how distraught she was. It would give her something to do.

But with each failed attempt to reach him, she became more and more distressed. "I'm going to call the bar itself," she said.

"Put it on speaker," Leon said. "We may have to go down there."

The number rang. Then, "Hello. We're closed."

"Closed? But . . ."

"We've had an incident here. This is a crime scene."

"What happened? Who was—?"

Click.

TWENTY-NINE

RAYFORD HAD LITTLE EXPERIENCE—beyond meeting the president of Pan-Con—with high-level meetings, especially in Washington. He decided he could quickly get used to the hospitality.

His CIA contact asked if he wanted to be flown in a military jet or first-class commercial, or if he preferred his usual free ride on Pan-Con.

"Actually, Pan-Con has arranged for me to fly myself, along with a few hundred guests, but I don't guess they're invited to our meeting."

No laughter. No response. Okay, so no sense of humor.

"Seriously, they have scheduled me with a long enough layover to easily accommodate your schedule."

"You'll be in your Pan-Con uniform then?"

"Correct, though I could bring a change of clothes if a suit would be more appropriate."

"Your uniform will be fine, Captain. We'll have military personnel here as well, so you'll fit right in."

Rayford thought of another funny line but decided not to try it. He also wasn't sure his rather austere Pan-Con getup would fit in with a top-brass military uniform, especially worn by someone decorated enough to have reached that level.

"Two men in their early thirties, looking almost like twins, both with short dark hair, will await you at the end of the Jetway. They won't be holding any signs, but they have your picture and will recognize you."

"No trading code phrases then, I guess," Rayford said, wincing when he was again met by silence.

Finally he heard a sigh, then detected actual mirth. "If that disappoints you, Captain, I can have one of them tell you he has the yo-yo. Then you can respond, 'I have the string.'"

"No!" Rayford said, howling. "But I'm sure glad to know you've run into rubes like me before."

"Every day," the man said. "And I'm sure you know that the people you are meeting with are not likely to have time or interest in frivolity."

"Roger that. And I thank you for indulging me. I'm finished now."

"Not a problem, Captain. I won't see you here, but I wish you all the best and thank you for your time."

Nicolae was grateful that Leon's SUV windows were tinted black and no one could see in. Leon's driver raced them toward The Church Pew bar, but they were held a block and a half away due to all the emergency vehicles. Nicolae slid out of sight when Leon lowered his window and asked passersby what was going on.

"Rumors say it was a gang-type hit," a man said.

"Really?"

"Yeah. Some guy took six .22 slugs to the back of the head. Quick and easy. Down and out. Of course, the throwaway gun is still there and nobody saw a thing. That will be the end of this one."

"Any idea who the guy is?"

The looker-on shook his head. "Somebody said they're about to haul him out of there though."

"Roll up your window, Leon," Nicolae whispered. "Then walk down there and see if you can confirm who it is."

Irene was intrigued by Rayford's summons to Washington. "And you have no idea what they want?"

He shook his head. "I can't imagine, though I suppose Earl is on the right track. He's guessing something to do with terrorism and how it affects flights, pilots, flight decks, that kind of thing."

"Well, take pictures and remember everything," she said.

"Um, I don't think you're allowed to do that in CIA headquarters. Anyway, wouldn't it look a little touristy?"

"I wouldn't mind being a tourist."

"You want to come along, Irene? I'd love that."

Irene was touched. He sounded like he meant it. "Are you serious?"

"You wouldn't be able to be in the meeting, of course. But you might be able to tour the headquarters. And if not that, there are plenty of things in Washington to see. You know downtown D.C. is less than ten miles away."

"Don't tempt me."

"You ought to come."

"But, Rayford, how much time would I get with you? You're piloting both ways, and when we're there, you're in a meeting I can't attend. I'd just be tagging along. Anyway, I promised Jackie I'd go to this meeting with her."

"What meeting? Where?"

"New Hope," Irene said softly. She didn't want to set him off, but it was apparently too late. He went from wishing she would come along with him to Washington to now wanting to badger her anew about this.

"All right, what's the meeting?"

"It's preplanning for VBS."

"VBS? What's that?"

"Vacation Bible School. It's like Sunday school every day for a week during the summer. For kids of all ages. I want Raymie to go."

"At New Hope, of course."

She wanted to say, "Obviously. Our church wouldn't host anything like that." But she caught herself and merely nodded.

Rayford shook his head and sighed. "You want us to

do more together and here's your chance. But no. You'll be at New Hope planning Summer Bible Camp."

"Vacation Bible School."

"Whatever."

"Rafe, if you'd only try New Hope, you'd enjoy going to church again." She didn't want to fight. She simply wanted to show him how earnest she was.

"I doubt it," he said.

"I've finally figured out the difference between New Hope and our church."

"Do tell."

"Truth."

"Truth?"

"Exactly. Our church dances around the truth. We sing, we read a few verses, Pastor Bohrer doesn't so much preach—and he never teaches—as much as he just shares thoughts. Like a homily. Listening to him is like reading those inspirational books full of partly true but mostly made-up stories of long-lost kitties finding their way home, orphans teaching some curmudgeon a life lesson, an elderly woman—"

"Yeah, yeah, I get it, okay?"

But Irene was on a roll, feeling confident, tired of backing down when Rayford acted bored. Her new resolve had been lost somewhere in the conversation. "I can tell from what I'm learning from Jackie that New Hope is about truth. The real truth. Hard truth. If the Bible says it, they ferret out the meaning and figure it out. You know what the Bible says about truth?"

"No, I don't. But I have a feeling you're about to tell me."

"John 8:32 says, 'You shall know the truth, and the truth shall make you free.' You know who said that?"

"I don't know. Let me guess. Since you said it was in John, I'm going to take a stab at, oh, John?"

"No. Jesus."

"Well, there you go. How'd you know that verse, by the way?"

"I know a lot of verses."

"You've got it bad, Irene."

"No. I've got it good. In the Psalms, David says he has hidden God's word in his heart so he won't sin. That's what I want to do. That's why I try to memorize a lot of verses."

"Oh, please. Well, more power to you. Just leave me out of it."

Irene sat on the arm of the couch. "You know what, Rafe? I can handle arguing and going back and forth about this stuff, but that really hurt. For you to tell me to just leave you out of it cuts me deeper than I'm sure you even meant to."

Rayford looked stunned. "Well, you're right about that, Irene. I didn't mean to cut you at all. I wasn't thinking about you. I was thinking about me. I don't want to be part of this; that's all. If that hurts you, I'm sorry."

"You know what makes me sorry? That you know yourself so well and still don't want to do anything about it."

"I know myself so well?"

"You said it yourself. You weren't thinking about me. You were thinking about you."

When Rayford left the room without another word, Irene slowly shut her eyes. If he never came to the truth, she decided, it would be her own fault. Her and her big mouth.

When the SUV was secure again and Leon was hustling down the crowded street, Nicolae sat up and peered toward the tavern. "Sure enough," he said to the driver, "emergency medical personnel are wheeling out a gurney. Look at those people jostling for position to see what they can see."

"Yeah," the driver said. "Sort of like what we're doing."

Presently Leon jogged back and climbed into the car, where he sat huffing and puffing from the effort. "Whew!" he said. "His head and face were covered, but it was Planchette all right."

"Really," Nicolae said, signaling the driver to close the soundproof window between the front and back seats.

"I'm so sorry," Leon said as the driver pulled away.

"Do not be sorry," Nicolae said. "This is all the instigation I need."

"But he was your friend," Leon said.

"Hardly. Listen to me, Leon. You can do the work Reiche was doing and do it better. He has just served me the best way ever."

Leon looked amazed. "You are one cold man, Nicolae Carpathia. I believe you're more ruthless and heartless than I."

Nicolae grinned at him, and Leon shook his hand.

———

As he had been told, Rayford found the CIA operatives awaiting him at the end of the Jetway at Reagan International. They looked somber but proved cordial and accommodating. They asked if he wanted to do any sightseeing or needed anything before proceeding to headquarters.

"I'd rather just get to the meeting, if you don't mind."

"We've been assigned to give you a walking tour of headquarters. By the time we're through, everyone will be assembled. They're actually having this meeting in the auditorium."

"Seriously? How many will be there?"

"Well, they won't fill six hundred and fifty seats," one said, laughing. "No, there'll be fewer than ten. I believe they just want to be sure the meeting is under the radar."

"Have to worry about that even at the CIA, huh?"

"You have no idea."

———

"Nicolae, you can't be serious," Leon said. They were in Carpathia's home office. "You don't retaliate for a foot soldier's death by taking out the general."

"You do not?"

"No."

"You may not. But I do. I will never be conventional, Leon. Now do you have access to the personnel I need, or do you not?"

"Of course I do. I just want you to think about this. You have not even informed Ms. Ivins that her old friend and mentor is gone, and now you want to assassinate a leading political figure?"

"Does it matter in what order these things are accomplished? If you believe it is so crucial to let Aunt Viv know what has happened, get her in here."

The operatives pulled into the CIA complex and began the tour from the car. They told Rayford of the nearly two hundred and sixty acres and two and a half million square feet of building space. They walked him from the original precast concrete building to the newer steel-and-glass addition, now decades old, and showed him the twin six-story towers and the four-story core building.

Rayford was most impressed that the entire complex looked like a college campus. And he found it interesting to finally see for himself the massive seal of the CIA embedded in the main lobby floor.

Most stunning, however, was something that made him stop and stare. He was aware of the two men glancing at each other, but he couldn't take his eyes from the etching in the wall. If ever he had the haunting feeling that someone was trying to tell him something, it was now.

The etching read, "'And ye shall know the truth and the truth shall make you free.' John VIII:XXXII."

THIRTY

Viv was shaking when she sat down. "Something's happened to Reiche," she said. "I know it has. When you came back and went straight in here, what else could I think?"

"You thought correctly, Aunt Viv," Nicolae said. "He was murdered."

"Oh no! Oh no, no, no."

"Do not worry, Viv. We shall exact revenge, and at the highest level."

"No, no, no!"

"You are not hearing me, Auntie. We will make Tismaneanu regret this, and we will lock up the election."

Viv scowled at him, tears streaming. "Have you no heart whatsoever? How does whatever you are planning bring back my dear friend, my teacher?"

Nicolae looked at Leon, then back at Viv. "Are you

not an adult?" he said. "Bring back your dear friend?
When have you ever known of someone coming back
from the dead? There will be no returning of Reiche
Planchette. The sooner you accept that, the better. Now
we must make the best of it, and the best is what will
come of that which it gives us license to do."

"Is that all you ever think of, Nicolae? What will best
serve you?"

He was nonplussed. What else was a person to think
of? "What is best for me will be best for Romania. And
Europe. And the world."

"Your ego knows no bounds!" she said, sobbing.

"Be careful, Aunt Viv. Remember to whom you are
speaking."

She sat shaking her head.

"Say something, Leon," Nicolae said. "I cannot console a crazy woman."

"I'm no crazy woman! I'm grieving! Can't you see that?"

Leon rose and moved to her side, kneeling and putting
a hand on her shoulder. "I am so, so sorry for your loss,
Ms. Ivins. Reiche Planchette was a true friend and a loyal
employee, and I know how much you thought of each
other. Nothing I say or do can make this better, but just
know that I am sympathetic and that I care."

Nicolae was stunned to see the change in Viv. She
wiped her face and began to nod. Then she whispered,
"Thank you very much, Mr. Fortunato, for those kind
words. I will want to be heavily involved in Mr. Planchette's memorial service, inviting his many friends and
relatives, of course."

"Of course." Leon turned to Nicolae. "I should think Ms. Ivins would be the perfect choice for that task, Mr. Carpathia. Do you not agree?"

"Hmm?" Nicolae said, looking up from taking notes. "Just a moment. '. . . just know that I am sympathetic and that I care.' That was good, Leon. Very good. Now, what was it?"

"I'm advising that you take Ms. Ivins up on her offer to handle Mr. Planchette's memorial service."

"Oh, well, yes, certainly. And, Viv, to show my sympathy and care, I am guessing you will feel a whole lot better once Emil Tismaneanu is dead."

Viv stood and stared at Nicolae, then left the room.

When she was gone, he shrugged. "Leon, there are some people in the world you simply cannot please."

The CIA operatives led Rayford to several sculptures and other objects of art in the main building, on the grounds, and on a couple of different floors. Finally they walked him through a tunnel to the dome-shaped auditorium connected to the original building.

"What are the big plaster rings?" Rayford said, looking up and pointing at the inside of the dome.

"Partly for looks, partly for sound," one said, and Rayford was impressed with the acoustics. "But look at this."

The operative pushed a button and a projection screen rose from the floor. "We'll leave that up," he said, "as the meeting facilitator wants to use it today."

A side door opened and three men in suits and three more in military uniforms entered. The meeting facilitator introduced himself as Jack Graham and quickly introduced the others, and Rayford was suddenly lost in the sea of names and titles. Only Graham was CIA. Two were from the Defense Department, and the three in uniform were on various task forces under the Joint Chiefs of Staff.

All greeted Rayford formally by name, shaking his hand and thanking him for coming. Graham led everyone to the first two rows of seats, and he faced them, his knees on the lowered seat of a chair in the front row. Rayford realized his initial hosts had disappeared.

"We have a problem," Graham began, "and, Captain Steele, we're hoping you might be able to shed a little light. We understand your military experience is limited and that you are not an expert in munitions or antiterrorism."

"I can confirm that," Rayford said.

"You are here as a representative of every commercial pilot in this country. We're looking to you less for technical expertise than for a gut-level reaction of how you think your colleagues might respond to our dilemma. An old problem has resurfaced, and it could be a disaster if we don't nip it."

"May I counsel you, Nicolae?" Leon said.

"Do you not always?"

"Yes, but I don't want to be critical, and I certainly

don't want to offend. I simply want you to be the best leader possible. I have hitched my wagon to your star."

"You have what?"

"Emerson."

"Who? The poet?"

"Never mind. I want to serve you long and well, Nicolae. Your attempts at humility are coming along, and I have seen you sway masses with the new approach."

"It is not easy, Leon. As you know—"

"Yes, you have little to be humble about. But your lack of compassion and empathy is nearly inhuman."

"Maybe I am not human. Have you ever considered that?"

"As a matter of fact, I have. But the truth is you were the product of sperm and egg, born of a woman fertilized by a man."

"Two men."

"Very well. At the very most you were the first but will not be the last of a hybrid generation. A case can be made that you are wholly human."

"And so?"

"And so you must act like it. Telling your aunt that one of her dearest friends died a horrible death, just as she had dreaded, and then acting surprised at her shock and grief . . . that is simply not normal human behavior. Did you feel nothing for her?"

"No."

"At least you're honest."

"Or at least straightforward. You asked."

"I did. And now I am saying that you must at least

affect an attitude of empathy, the ability to put yourself in another's shoes."

"You saw me taking notes; did you not?"

"Yes, what was that about, Nicolae?"

"I am not totally unaware, Leon. I recognized that you scored with that little act of yours, and I do not mind telling you I plan to appropriate it next time."

"It wasn't an act."

"It was not? You genuinely care about a woman you barely know? a woman who would just as soon you were not here with such a high level of access to me?"

"Yes, and I can even empathize with her on that score. At first I was jealous of and resented Reiche. Then it became clear you were less than enamored with him and his contribution, so I was put at ease."

"You do not feel the same about Aunt Viv?"

"Jealous of her? Threatened? No. She is a woman. You clearly relegate women to secondary status, a rare proclivity I happen to admire in this day and age. She brings to the table unique strengths and gifts, and I for one am glad I don't have to contribute in the same ways."

"You like being my top adviser."

"Exactly."

"See?" Nicolae said. "As I said, I am not totally unaware. Now are we finished with this little life lesson? Can we get to planning the demise of my opponent?"

———

"You're here, Captain Steele, because some of us have been impressed with how you carry out your job,

including when you're under pressure, in crisis, or deal-
ing with the press. Correct us if we're wrong, but we'd
like to think you have the ability to remain confidential
and discreet."

"I'd like to think so too."

"Our problem is a resurfacing of shoulder-fired missiles on the black market."

"Capable of taking down commercial aircraft,"
Rayford said, "particularly on takeoff or landing."

"Exactly. You responded to that as if you've given it
some thought."

"It's discussed among pilots, sure. We're all jumpy.
Even with the occasional air marshal on board and the
increased security—double-thick doors, sophisticated
locking systems, new secret procedures—we all know
there are no guarantees anymore."

One of the military men said, "Would you say a personally fired missile, ground to air, is highest on a pilot's
anxiety list?"

Rayford cocked his head. "Well, on the one hand,
there's never been—to our knowledge—such an attack
in our airspace. Unless you know something I don't."

"We have suspected some, but without hard evidence,
there has been no sense alarming the public."

"Or the pilots," Rayford said.

"Precisely. The problem, Captain, is that there have
been more of these types of weapons turning up in the
usually suspected black-market centers around the
world. A few have been sold to undercover buyers, and
a limited number more have been confiscated in raids

and stings. But we're worried about further proliferation. The sheer numbers we're hearing about make full containment unlikely and an attack or attacks almost inevitable."

Rayford shook his head. "Wasn't expecting to hear that today. I daresay I'll feel different in the cockpit on the way home. If you're wondering whether this will impact the thinking of pilots, yes. But I don't guess you brought me here to have me confirm the obvious."

"No," Graham said. "What we'd really like is to bounce some of our strategic initiatives off you, ways we would hope to counteract these weapons. See what you think of the cost and complexity and give us your best guess as to the response of your colleagues."

"Yes," another military man said. "We'd prefer to tell the rank-and-file pilots the problem and our solution at the same time. The fix is not cheap. Not that it would cost the pilot a cent."

"Except that if passenger fares go up strictly to offset this cost—which I imagine will be in the billions—my colleagues and I are unlikely to get appropriate raises for a while."

The men nodded.

"Not to mention," Rayford continued, "that if your proposed cure has anything to do with somehow arming commercial aircraft, then we're no longer commercial, are we? We're military pilots again. Flying fighters that are heavy, sluggish, and slow."

"You've read our minds, Captain. But we frankly see no alternative. You know Israel has long equipped certain civilian planes with missile-warning systems. And Jordan is now the leader in that technology."

Rayford nodded. "And don't some of those pilots also have the capability of firing flares or other incendiary devices to try to lead a heat-seeking missile off target?"

The men looked at each other, and Rayford hoped he detected their favor at his knowing something about this. "The bigger problem," one said, "is that we would have to arm all of this country's more than eight thousand aircraft. That would run us in the neighborhood of nearly 15 billion dollars, plus more than 2 billion a year to maintain a system we've proved with B-52s will work, but . . ."

Rayford pressed his lips together. "And you wonder what I think my pilot brothers and sisters will think of the ethics and safety related to that?"

THIRTY-ONE

Jack Graham produced a device from his pocket and pointed it toward the giant screen behind him. Up came the image of a young, smooth-faced Middle Easterner in combat boots, khaki shorts, a blousy military shirt, and a turban.

He looked to be in his early twenties with dark skin, black eyes, and black hair peeking from under his head-dress. The eyes told a story, Rayford thought. Here was one intelligent, thoughtful, knowing man.

"Abdullah Ababneh," Jack Graham said. "A Jorda-nian fighter pilot and friend of the United States. An enemy of terrorists. Ababneh is a relative newlywed, married less than three years, father of two—a male tod-dler and female infant. Muslim.

"He attended Mu'tah University in Karak, the military wing. Expert in munitions and arms. Intelligence off the charts. When I say he is a friend of the U.S., I am vastly understating it. He is a student of America, so enamored with us and committed to us that he insists on speaking English almost all the time. His mates began to call him Smith or Smitty because they said he was more American than Jordanian—despite his thick accent. He loves the moniker and uses it exclusively now.

"Captain Steele, we would like you to meet him. We see value in ties with countries that share our view of terrorist threats and are willing to cooperate in fighting them. We have enough diplomats and contacts from high levels of government and military. What we would like is an informal relationship based on common ground . . . like aviation. Are you willing?"

Rayford didn't know what to think. Willing to do what? Meet a Jordanian fighter pilot? Sure. Why not? But where? When? And for what purpose? He asked all these questions.

"We would fly you to Jordan. You spend a day or two getting acquainted. Share ideas, strategy, and report back to us for debriefing."

"Remind me again," Rayford said. "Why me?"

With the diminutive Jordanian's visage bearing down on them, Graham sat facing Rayford. "Ababneh—or I should say Smith—has a lot to offer in the way of ideas, according to his superiors. He knows a lot, thinks things through, and is far and away their best pilot. The trouble is, he's quiet and apparently painfully shy. He's best in one-on-one situations when he has learned to trust someone. He suddenly becomes a fount of information.

"They have put him in uncomfortable situations with dignitaries, diplomats, and the like. He clams up. We don't want you to fake or manufacture anything. We just want to see if you can become his friend. And while that may take some time, you understand that terrorism is not on anyone else's calendar or clock. If this guy has as much to offer as we think he does, we need to start mining it. Are you willing? And if so, when can you go?"

———————————

Two days before the Romanian parliamentary elections, Emil Tismaneanu, his wife, his driver, and a bodyguard were killed when their automobile exploded upon ignition.

Nicolae stood in his office, watching the coverage on his wall-mounted TV screen. He thrust his fists before him and shouted, "Yes!" quivering with the thrill of it.

The phones began ringing, so he ran for the shower, then changed into his most sedate, most expensive suit. Within half an hour the press filled his driveway, and he instructed Leon Fortunato to inform them that he would have a statement in ten minutes but would take no questions.

Exactly ten minutes later he emerged alone and strode to a makeshift dais containing nearly a dozen microphones. He looked out into a sea of cameras. With a somber expression and tone, his throat sounding constricted with grief, he leaned toward the microphones.

"I have a message for the people of Romania and

specifically the citizens of Bucharest. Our nation has suffered a great loss today, and I have lost a dear friend. Naturally I call upon our government and every appropriate
agency to mount a thorough investigation and to bring to
justice the cowards who perpetrated this heinous act.

"This has been a most difficult campaign, because
though Emil and I—" here Carpathia paused and bit his
lip, seemingly struggling to go on—"disagreed over the
most trivial political matters, we were like brothers.
Many do not know that each had pledged to the other
his full support, regardless of who won, and we would
have been laboring together for the good of the citi-
zenry—the winner in the House of Parliament, the loser
behind the scenes.

"While recent polls showed I was favored, I was quite
sincere in my pledge to support my most esteemed opponent" —there it was for the astute—"should he ever run
for the presidency.

"And now, while I am in no official capacity with the
power to effect this, I am calling upon the government of
Romania to postpone this election, to give another representative of Emil's views the time to mount a campaign.
Should this prove impossible, I pledge here and now, in
honor of my dear friend, to withdraw from the race and
allow the people to select their own representative.

"In my abject grief, I have lost the impetus to remain in
the race. So if the election cannot be postponed, I hereby
withdraw and urge the populace to write in their own
candidates. I promise to support the will of the people.

"I have respectfully requested no questions at this time

and ask that the press and the public honor a brief season of solitude and contemplation as I mourn my own
loss. Thank you."

Irene was irate and determined not to let it show, but she
was not succeeding. She wanted to scream, to throw
things, to demand that Rayford change his mind. "That
is the first time you've had that many days off in two
years, and you were going to take us to Disney World."

"I know, Irene. But when your country asks you to do
something, don't you think it's your duty—?"

"Your duty is here, with these kids. We need you,
Rafe. We need time with you. Don't you see the family
drifting apart the way you and I have? I need this too.
Surely there are other people qualified for this task."

"There may be, but they chose me, and I'm honored."

"I'm honored *for* you, Rayford, but if they really think
you're indispensable to this task, let them work with
Pan-Con on giving you the time to do this. You shouldn't
have to use your own vacation days."

"I told them I'd go, and I told them when."

Leon was waiting in Nicolae's office when Nicolae
returned. Carpathia was still wearing his mask of grief
until he shut the door behind him. Then the two
embraced, slapped hands, and giggled.

"That!" Leon said, shaking his head. "That was genius."

"Did they buy it?"

"Did they? *I* almost bought it!" And they dissolved into laughter again. "Let's watch the coverage," Leon added.

On every channel pundits talked about the tragedy and the poignant response on the part of the favorite in the election. Already veteran newspeople were editorializing that the election should not be postponed, that Carpathia should not withdraw, that the country needed him now as never before.

"Get out a press release immediately, Leon," Nicolae said. "Reaffirm that I am resolute in my decision to withdraw. Not shirking, just mourning and committed to the will of the people."

Nicolae sat on the floor, flipping channels, drinking in the accolades while Leon sat at Nicolae's desk, crafting and transmitting the release to the media. Nicolae was amused when Fortunato finished and came to join him on the floor, his thick body straining to get comfortable in his suit.

They sat watching until interrupted by urgent knocking. "Nicolae?" Viv called through the door. "I must speak with you."

Nicolae nodded to Leon, who struggled to his feet and opened the door.

Viv looked past him to Nicolae. "Luciana Tismaneanu is on her way over here, insisting on speaking with you."

"Fine," Nicolae said. "Leon, this will be the true test.

Be sure she is alone, and walk her through the metal
detectors hidden in the pillars of the south portico.
If she brings her fiancé, make him wait for her. Tell
him I am not up to seeing anyone else, especially
someone I have not met. Oh, Leon, if I can win her
over . . ."

"Have you been looking forward to our vacation, kids?"
Rayford said at dinner.

"'Course," Chloe said. "I haven't been to Disney
World since I was Raymie's age."

"Disney!" Raymie shouted. "Mickey!"

When Rayford hit them with the news that they
weren't going, it was clear Raymie didn't understand.
Irene jumped in with an alternative, promising she would
take him to the local Kiddieland Park, where he loved to
ride the train and the merry-go-round. He was soon
crowing about that while Rayford studied Chloe for her
true reaction.

She shrugged. "I wanted to go, but this is pretty neat.
The government wants you to do this?"

He nodded. "Problem is, it's classified. So no one can
know."

"I can't tell my friends? What am I supposed to say
about not going to Disney?"

"Blame it on me," Rayford said. "Just don't be specific. My schedule changed, I got pressed into duty, it
couldn't be helped."

Nicolae Carpathia, in the same natty suit he had worn before the cameras, sat at his desk with his face in his hands. His suit jacket was draped over the back of his chair, his tie was loose, and his top shirt button was open.

As Luciana Tismaneanu was ushered in, he stood quickly, brushing tears from his face and wiping his hands on his trousers. He staggered toward the young woman. "Oh, Miss Tismaneanu! I am so, so sorry for your loss. You have my deepest—"

Luciana rebuffed his embrace and stiffened. "You can stop with the *piesă de teatru*," she said.

"Oh, miss!" Nicolae said, fresh tears streaming. "This is no act. These are not histrionics. I am devastated, and I can only imagine your pain. Such a great man and, I assume, a great father."

"My parents were not perfect, Mr. Carpathia. But they were my parents, and we loved each other."

"Please, sit. Please."

"My fiancé is waiting. I will not take much of your time."

"Take all you need, dear. I have no higher priority."

She sat. "Tell me it isn't true, sir. Tell me you didn't use me, photograph me, just to get at my father."

"What?" Nicolae sounded as genuinely at a loss as was possible.

"My father's people say you lured me here under the pretense of planning my father's surprise party, only to be able to show him a picture of me visiting you late at night. The implications are abominable, and—"

"Never! Never, never, never. The sad fact is, Miss Tismaneanu—and had you not raised this horrific charge I would never have shared this with you—but it was your father who showed *me* your picture. The photograph was shot by his people. They were trying to dig dirt on me, claiming that I had lady friends visiting me every night. Nothing could be further from the truth, of course, but the night they chose to try to document this, they did not realize I had a legitimate visitor and that it was you."

"I don't believe you."

"Luciana, listen to me. Why would I need to photograph you? My security cameras run twenty-four hours a day. Plus, by the time your father recognized you in the photo, he knew why you had been here. Whoever is planting these suspicions in your mind is not a friend. Why can they not simply let you grieve without making you angry and spurring you to put some blame where it does not belong?

"If I had done this, if I had been behind any of these tragic events, why would I be withdrawing from the race? What is in it for me? I am deeply wounded, first by the loss of my friend, your father, and second that someone has misled you so."

THIRTY-TWO

RAYFORD WAS CLOSE to the seniority needed to fly international hold patterns for Pan-Con, so he enjoyed being jetted to Jordan aboard a supersonic transport by the U.S. Air Force. Rocketing across the Atlantic in the middle of the night, he imagined maintaining a 747 from continent to continent.

He found it propitious that Abdullah "Smitty" Ababneh was away on assignment when he arrived, as Rayford was able to sleep off the jet lag at the beautiful Four Seasons (compliments of the U.S. government) and get acquainted with Amman by walking around. He visited the Roman Amphitheater and The Citadel but passed on the Eagle Distillery. That would only make him thirsty for things he shouldn't imbibe. Rayford had found himself less and less careful with his drinking when off duty, so he inwardly pronounced this entire trip on duty.

He had little doubt he was being closely watched, if not followed. The feds had to have been fairly impressed with his résumé and record to entrust him with a diplomatic effort like this, but they would also likely want to make sure he kept his nose clean and didn't embarrass them.

Rayford felt that, short of being awarded those international routes, he had pretty much reached the pinnacle of his profession. To have caught the attention of the government and to be on at least the long list for piloting the president or vice president—all that was gratifying. He needed new goals and dreams, and he wasn't about to scotch them all with, well, scotch.

Rayford was scheduled to meet Abdullah and his superiors for lunch at the Al Matar Air Base in Amman-Marka. He was transported there from his hotel via a Royal Jordanian Air Force jeep with a driver who understood very little English. Rayford couldn't make that compute, sending a monolingual man for an American. He was evaluating everything, trying to gauge whether his hosts were excited to have him here or were trying to tell him—in passive-aggressive ways like this—either that he was unwelcome or they were suspicious. The worst-case scenario, in his mind, would be the Jordanians feeling in any way pressured to host him.

Those fears were immediately dispelled, however, when Rayford was ushered to a small private eating area within the commons at the air base. There five men immediately stood, smiling and seemingly eager to meet him. He recognized Abdullah from his photo, and as the men were introduced in order of rank, Ababneh was last.

It was plain, though, that Abdullah was a favorite among these men. Whenever he had the floor or anyone said anything about him, the others looked at him and beamed. It was as if he was the life of the party, and Rayford had to wonder if it could be real—his reputation for shyness and being a man of few words.

He was quiet with Rayford there; that was for sure. The men, all of whom spoke passable English, had many questions for Rayford, many of them personal. The commanding officer remarked on the similarities between Rayford and Smitty. "I assume you understand why we call him Mr. Smith?"

"I've heard."

They all laughed, and Abdullah, if Rayford could read a change in his dark face, appeared to redden.

"It is because he is so much a fan of the United States that he wants to be an American. Some of us believe he really is and is here in disguise."

"Your own Yankee spy, eh?" Rayford said, and the men laughed.

"Yes, and like you he married a woman too good for him. And they have both a son and a daughter."

The commander asked Rayford to sit next to Abdullah. "He will be your guide and interpreter," he said.

"But you all speak English so well," Rayford said.

"My apologies. I meant he will interpret our customs and practices. I was under the impression that this is your first visit to Jordan."

"True."

"Then Abdullah is well equipped to inform you of what is going on. We customarily have our main meal at midday, which I understand is not true where you are from."

"Right. Our main meal is usually in the evening."

"We have prepared for you a feast. In fact, we have brought in many helpers to cook and to help serve."

"I'm honored," Rayford said.

"It is our pleasure."

Abdullah's eyes lit up, and finally he spoke. "It is my assignment to take you up for some loops and rolls in the F-16 immediately after you have eaten."

"I sat with her fiancé until she returned," Leon said. "She appeared less agitated than when she arrived. Did you win her over?"

"I do not know," Nicolae said. "And frankly, I do not care. I mean, I would like to assume she will think twice before talking poorly about me behind my back, but she is no threat. She has no platform. She will be seen as the wounded daughter, the grieving offspring, the betrothed who must naturally put off her wedding until an appropriate time after the funeral. I should attend both, should I not?"

"The funeral and the wedding? The first, of course. For the wedding you would need an invitation, and unless you charmed her, I do not foresee that."

"You see, Leon, you are shortsighted."

"What? Why? You think she will invite you?"

"No! I would be shocked. But what will she or her people do if I show up? Ban me? Usher me out? It would be a scandal. I will bring a nice gift, enjoy the revelry, toast the bride and groom."

Fortunato gazed at him with seeming admiration. "I do not know where you come up with these plans," he said. "But you are unique."

"We will enjoy the *mansaf*," Abdullah said. "It is not only my favorite; it is nearly everyone's favorite. It proves I really am Jordanian by blood. But please, call me Smitty."

Hors d'oeuvres, which Abdullah called *Mazza*, began the meal and consisted of a variety of hot and cold treats that could have served as a meal in themselves. Then came salads and mounds of bread to be eaten dry or dipped in one of many sauces. The aroma alone intoxicated Rayford, but Abdullah assured him they had just begun.

When it came time for the main dish, Rayford had never seen so much rice. It was delivered in heaping, steaming bowls. The *mansaf* proved to be lamb seasoned with herbs and light spices, cooked in yogurt and eaten with the rice. Rayford had wondered if he would find the cuisine too exotic. This he would never forget.

The bread alone would have filled him, and the rice proved overkill. Still there were dessert pastries to come, and when he finally finished with those—including *bak-lava* and *katayeff*—the heavy scent of coffee wafted from the kitchen.

"There is another smell I don't detect in American coffee," Rayford said.

Abdullah smiled. "Cardamom seeds. You will enjoy."

The coffee was poured from long-handled copper pots, and Rayford was struck that only a few drops went into each cup. He made the mistake of slugging it down as if it were a sample. The men laughed when it hit his system and woke him. His cup was refilled every time he took a sip, but he soon noticed that when the others had had enough, they tipped their empty cups from side to side. Once he had done that, the repouring stopped. Rayford didn't know whether it was the cardamom or caffeine, but something had brought his senses to life.

Rayford found himself in delightful pain and knew his hosts had to feel the same. They all sat back and patted their bellies as they chatted. All save for Abdullah. The shortest and lithest of them, he had eaten a lot, but nowhere near the quantities Rayford and the others had packed away.

As the table was being cleared, a high-whining cry came from loudspeakers around the base, and the men quickly sat up. "It is time for the midday *Salaah*," Abdullah said. "You are not expected to participate, of course, and I have been given permission to merely explain it to you."

"The *Salaah*?" Rayford said.

"Our Muslim ritual of prayer. We do it five times a

290

day, and when we can, we are to first bathe and then get to a mosque. People in unusual occupations—like ours—who are not able to get to the mosque are free to perform the ritual wherever they can."

The other men hurried off to the washroom, then returned and pulled mats from a corner and knelt before a window, facing Mecca.

"What you just heard, Captain Steele, was the *ezan*, which is called out by the *muezzin*, commanding us to pray."

"It sounds like a long song," Rayford said. "What is he saying?"

"He says four times, 'Allah is most great.' Then twice, 'I bear witness that there is no god but Allah.' Then twice, 'I bear witness that Muhammad is the messenger of Allah.' Then twice, 'Come to prayer.' And twice more, 'Come to the good.' Finally, twice, 'Allah is most great.'

"During the predawn call the *muezzin* adds twice, 'Prayer is better than sleep.'" Abdullah whispered, "Frankly, Captain, there are mornings when I am not so sure."

As Rayford watched, the men stood on their mats with their hands to their ears; then they folded their hands right over left on their chests. They bowed and placed their hands on their knees, then stood upright again. They then prostrated themselves fully on the ground, sitting up and then repeating the ritual. All during this the men murmured phrases in praise of Allah. Finally, sitting again, each passed a greeting to one another.

Abdullah interpreted this, "'Peace on you and the

mercy of Allah.' Some say the worshiper is greeting fellow Muslims, but others say he is speaking to an angel on each shoulder who records his good and bad deeds."

Rayford did not know why, but this all hit him as terribly ritualistic and depressing. In many ways it reminded him of his own feeble attempts at religion: the obligation to go to church when he could and guilt when he found excuses not to.

Abdullah confirmed Rayford's suspicion. "This fixed ritual is so rigid that in our religion there is no departure from it. The devout practitioner performs it five times a day, cleansing himself and getting to the mosque whenever possible to do it with the rest of the congregation."

"And they bathe before each time?"

Abdullah nodded. "It is called ablution, and when possible it includes washing face, hands, feet, and sometimes the whole body."

"Really?"

"Oh yes. If you are in a state of ceremonial impurity, the holy book requires you to fully bathe."

"What if you do not have access to water?"

"Then you are to use sand and earth."

"And this is five times a day?"

Abdullah nodded. "And that is not all. There are many other prayers and rituals, but the five per day are the minimum requirement. There is the early morning prayer, which may be offered anytime between dawn and two hours later. The noon prayer may be offered anytime after the sun begins to decline. The third prayer begins soon after the middle of the afternoon. Calendars tell the time of each prayer, but otherwise one must resort to his best judgment.

"The sunset prayer begins after sunset and extends till the glow in the horizon disappears. The evening prayer time then continues till before the dawn."

"What is the point of all this, if you don't mind my asking?"

Abdullah shrugged. "The devout Muslim believes he is making his entire day spiritual, from beginning to end and in between. He combines his religion with his life and believes he is building his morals on strong foundations. He believes he is making his whole life a spiritual exercise."

"What about you, Abdullah? Do you have to make up for missing this one?"

"Please. I prefer Smith or Smitty. And yes, if I were pious, I would be owing a double prayer now." He whispered, "I am ashamed to say I am not so pious. The ablution alone is filled with many requirements and also many ways in which it can be nullified. If you are wondering whether I fear for my mortal soul . . . yes. I was raised Muslim and am steeped in the tradition. But an impersonal, demanding god holds less and less appeal as I get older."

This, Rayford decided, was something he and Abdullah were going to have to discuss. It was far afield from the mission of his trip, but these were universal issues with which he could identify. To him it didn't matter what your religion was, but too many demands took all the joy out of it.

THIRTY-THREE

CAMERON WILLIAMS SAT in the academic dean's office at Princeton, feeling sheepish and telling himself it would be the last time in his life. He had felt sheepish when he had been rejected by the girl he hoped to fall in love with. And he had felt sheepish when scolded for arriving just in time for his own mother's funeral.

But Dirk Burton had been working on him, bucking him up, reminding him who he was and what he had to offer. "Hold your head high, man. You're somebody already. You need confidence to do what you do and do it so well. Believe me, when I'm on the Exchange, I'll be hanged if I care what the Brits think of Welshmen. I know as much as they do and I'm going to compete at their level. You can show deference to the veterans at the *Globe*, but go in there with confidence."

That wasn't Cameron's problem now. He had brought

this crisis on himself by letting his schoolwork slide. He could graduate if he did nothing more, but his GPA would roll off the table, and he would not be able—as Dirk had urged him—to hold his head high.

"I will not be recommending you for all the awards and prizes due you at graduation, Mr. Williams," the dean said, "if you rest on your laurels and your outside activities. All your professors are concerned that you are behind in your final self-study projects. No, it won't cost you your hotshot new job—congratulations, by the way—and it may not amount to a hill of beans once you're a celebrated journalist. Who knows, maybe some-day you'll be back here as Alumnus of the Year, speaking at graduation, winning an honorary doctorate. How will you feel if you have to admit you coasted through your last lap here?"

"Not well."

"Of course not. Not to belabor this, I say as I belabor it a bit more, but imagine yourself at the *Globe* in a few years and your prodigious talent wins you some plum job somewhere else. Do you just drop everything at the *Globe*? Do you give them notice and mail in your assign-ments until you move on? Of course you don't. Have some pride, Mr. Williams. Make me proud. Make this institution proud. Do yourself proud. Will you do that?"

Fortunately for Rayford, Abdullah had been kidding about aerial acrobatics so soon after the noon meal.

Rayford enjoyed watching the younger man in and around the multimillion-dollar flying machines. Abdullah opened and closed hatches and flipped switches and checked settings as if he had manufactured the craft himself. Here was a man who seemed born to fly these machines.

There were no loops, dives, or rolls, but Abdullah did seem to enjoy making a two-seater F-16 scream as he showed Rayford his country from the air. For a quiet man he carried on a surprisingly constant stream of chatter as he pointed out the eastern plains by the Jordan River, the Great Rift Valley to the west, and Lake Tiberius, "which you know as the Sea of Galilee." He pointed out an area he said was seven hundred feet below sea level, and "of course, the Dead Sea, thirteen hundred feet below sea level and the lowest point on Earth."

Abdullah also overflew the King Hussein Air College in Mafraq and the Muwaffaq Salti Air Base, "so you don't have to say you came all this way and didn't at least see them from above."

After they landed and spent time in the pilots' lounge talking about anything and everything other than what Rayford had been sent to talk about, the tinny clarion call again blared from the loudspeakers, calling the faithful to prayer.

Abdullah pointedly ignored it. "What do you suppose Jordan is known for?" he said.

"Sand, heat, olive oil, and petroleum products," Rayford said. "But I'm just guessing."

"You guess what everyone from the West guesses.

They assume we are all Bedouins, wearing sandals and living in tents. Would it surprise you to know that we also export soap, cigarettes, cement, phosphate, food, paper, glass, drugs, and even textiles?"

"Yes, it would."

"I knew it would. I love America, but I am jealous for the reputation of my own country."

"Admirable. But talk to me about the Muslim thing, Smitty. You are Muslim, but you are not, what did you call it? Devout?"

"Pious."

"Does that mean you don't believe? Or don't accept the requirements?"

"I suppose," Abdullah said. "I know myself too well. I do too many things that disqualify me from being known as a true Muslim. There is too high a cost to come out and renounce, so I let people believe what they want to believe about me. If I am around during prayers, I bow to Mecca. I don't make an issue of it."

"But when you can get out of it . . . ?"

"I get out of it."

"You sound like me." Rayford didn't know why he felt so free to talk about such personal matters with a perfect stranger, but here he was, thousands of miles from home, spilling his guts.

Abdullah said, "There is also the matter of how I— what is your word for it?—*supplement* my income."

"And how is that?"

"First, we are not here to report on each other to our superiors, are we?"

"Not on this subject," Rayford said. "Hardly."

"I buy and sell, shall we say, outside normal trade routes."

Rayford raised an eyebrow. "You're a black marketer?"

Abdullah crossed his arms and smiled shyly. "That makes it sound romantic. It is actually quite labor intensive and dangerous."

"Illegal."

"Obviously," Abdullah said. "But for a member of the air force, doubly so. Despite that many of my customers are colleagues. Is there anything you need or want, by the way?"

"Maybe. What do you have?"

"Did you wonder, Captain, why I was able to so quickly rattle off the many goods produced here?"

Rayford nodded. "As a matter of fact . . ."

"I have not seen you smoke since you arrived. Are you not a smoker?"

Rayford shook his head.

"Neither am I," Abdullah said. "But I used to be, and I have tried cigarettes from all over the world. None compare with ours. They would make excellent gifts for your smoking friends."

"How much?"

"About triple what you would pay in the States, but of course you can't get ours there."

"Will I have trouble getting them into my country?"

"They are contraband. Will you be searched upon boarding or deplaning?"

"I wasn't on the way."

"Then you are unlikely to be on the way back. If you are, you may tell them these were given to you as gifts, but you would protect me by not saying it was I who gave the gift."

Rayford decided lying was no worse than buying contraband on the black market. And who knew what other exotic gifts he might find through this source? Once he started flying to Europe, Jordan wasn't so awfully far away. Abdullah Smith could prove a valuable contact.

Meanwhile, they had better talk business and make this trip worthwhile.

Not only was Nicolae Carpathia never officially considered a suspect in the assassination of Emil Tismaneanu, but he also became the object of public sympathy over the loss of his dear friend. Small pockets of suspicion were obliterated when he made good on his pledge to withdraw from the race, going so far as paying the fees and filing the paperwork to make it legal.

Nicolae seeded the murder investigation with a huge infusion of funds, so that the force empowered to look into the matter became known as the Carpathia Commission. Despite the stony stare from Tismaneanu's daughter and the look of apprehension on the face of her fiancé, Carpathia not only attended the funeral, but he also spoke briefly—"brilliantly," according to the press—eulogizing his former opponent to the point that editorials all over Europe lauded him as a model for the politics of the future.

The day after the funeral Carpathia was elected to the lower house of the Romanian parliament, garnering more than 80 percent of the votes as a write-in candidate. His competition proved to be dozens of dilettantes and pretenders whose friends wrote them in on a lark.

Leon Fortunato took credit for the write-in idea, having employed dozens of lackeys to spread the notion to reporters, commentators, and columnists, many of whom claimed the idea as their own. Support for the idea had swept Bucharest, and the polls had reflected the change immediately.

With the death of Tismaneanu and Carpathia's withdrawal, the polls had been hopelessly skewed, but by the time of the election they accurately predicted a landslide for Nicolae vastly beyond what had been forecast when both candidates were on the ballot.

An obsequious Carpathia, eyes cast down, stepped before press microphones when the actual polls closed and, with a quavery voice, announced, "I said I would not run. I did not say I would not serve. I am overwhelmed. I am humbled. And I hereby accede to the wishes of the people and pledge to give this my all in the memory of my friend."

Several days later the new member of Parliament was an uninvited guest at Luciana Tismaneanu's wedding. Leon choreographed a quiet, understated arrival. "No fanfare," he said. "We are simply dropped off at a side entrance and slip into a back pew. No escorts, no sirens."

"But a lot of press, no?" Nicolae said.

"Of course. What is the point otherwise?"

When Leon's driver pulled into an alleyway beside the church, the way was besieged by reporters and photographers, each having thought they were scooping the others. Someone had confided in each that the faint third- or fourth-generation copy of Carpathia's itinerary, outlining his arrival time and location, was something no one else was privy to.

Carpathia made a great show of trying to simply hurry into the *biserică*, only to pause at the door because of the press of media personnel. He sighed and sadly said, "Ladies and gentlemen, I respectfully aver that this is not the time or place for this. Please allow me to simply celebrate with the daughter of my late friend and not detract in any way from her day."

Such a humble display was trumpeted in every newspaper and on every television station. It was garnished with another tidbit: "Private sources tell us that Mr. Carpathia's wedding gift is a trust fund that will fully cover the education of the new couple's offspring. While the bride stands to inherit vast business interests, there is some speculation that legal issues and falling profits may find these less than beneficial to her. No word as yet as to her response to Mr. Carpathia's largesse."

Meeting Abdullah's delicate young wife, Yasmine, and their small boy and girl was a treat for Rayford, as was enjoying another delicious meal—though much lighter evening fare—in their home.

Rayford was intrigued by the formal interaction between Abdullah and his wife. She was quiet and servile, handling the household and meal preparation and serving details. She appeared to nearly panic when Rayford offered to help, but Abdullah rescued her with a raised hand and a shake of the head, which told Rayford he would be violating some cultural domestic code.

Yasmine also tended to the children, though Abdullah seemed smitten by them too. When the meal was over and the children were in bed, Yasmine disappeared as the men sat and talked.

"Your wife is lovely," Rayford said.

"I worry about her," Abdullah said. "When first I began to let it show that I was not as devout a Muslim as I had led her to believe—ignoring the calls to prayer and so forth—I saw sadness and bewilderment on her face. But what troubled me even more was that she soon followed my example."

"Have you discussed it?"

Abdullah held his index finger and thumb a half inch apart. "Only a little. She is frightened by the whole prospect of whether Allah might be disappointed or angry with her, but she shares my feeling that our religion has become too impersonal and rigid. And while she is not what I would call a modern woman and hardly a feminist, neither does she feel honored or respected in the Islam system."

Rayford returned home via Washington, D.C., where
he was debriefed by his CIA and Defense Department
contacts.

"We heard the two of you hit it off," Jack Graham said.

"That's fair. He's an impressive young man."

Abdullah's ideas for defending against terrorist attacks
were understandably military in nature: teaching pilots
evasive maneuvers, equipping jetliners with defensive
weapons, and increasing cockpit and cabin security measures—all of which would merely add to the already
astronomical projected costs that attended this new
threat. But Graham and his associates assured Rayford
that they believed the connection with Jordan—and
Abdullah Ababneh in particular—was worth the time
and effort.

For Rayford personally it certainly had been. By the
time he had assessed the black-market goods Abdullah
offered, he had added several hundred dollars' worth
of treasures from Arabia to his luggage. To his knowledge neither Abdullah's superiors nor his own were
aware of any of this. Rayford would be careful not to
resell any of the booty in the U.S., so that if he was
questioned about it, he could rightly say they were
all gifts.

Several of the items from the black market—though
Rayford did not, of course, describe them that way—
were met with enthusiasm by his own family. Irene
seemed to love a supply of velvet material. Raymie
enjoyed a collection of small animals carved from olive
wood. And Rayford was stunned at Chloe's response to

an embroidered rug, which she immediately put to use in her room.

"I had no idea you'd like this," he said, sitting on her bed.

Chloe sat at her computer desk. "It's beautiful," she said. "And it's from you."

"Your mother told me about the election," he said. "I'm sorry."

She shrugged. "The kids want a dumb jock; they got one. At least it was close."

"Don't be defeated by one defeat."

"That's sorta like what the principal said in his letter to all the losers. Something about losing a battle doesn't mean you've lost the war."

"There'll be more elections."

Chloe shook her head. "I've had enough of politics. I couldn't take another disappointment like this. The worst part is, Mom was right. It was a popularity contest, and I'm not popular."

"C'mon," Rayford said. "You said it was close."

"Not close enough. And you know, Dad, there are more girls than boys in our class. Let's face it: we live in a male-dominated society. Even the girls vote for the boys."

Rayford was struck by the contrast between his smart, articulate daughter and Yasmine Ababneh. Was he raising an activist? a feminist? He had the feeling Chloe would do him proud one day.

THIRTY-FOUR

CAMERON WILLIAMS GOT HIMSELF IN GEAR, finished well at Princeton, and graduated with honors, awards, and acclaim. He hit Boston like a road sweep of the Yankees and immediately made enemies on the staff of the *Globe*.

Fortunately, according to Dizzy Rowland, this was assessed by the brass as "largely jealousy. Anything that interrupts the status quo threatens the old-timers. And when a young guy comes in and does well, noses get bent out of joint. I would, however, urge you, Cameron, to lie low. Let others praise you. And throw out a few compliments. Don't be criticizing colleagues or offering suggestions. Just do your job and let the readership assess you."

It was good counsel but hard to keep. Cameron was alarmed at the laziness on the part of other reporters. They shirked, they cheated, they counted on secondary sources. They would spend a whole day doing nothing, then finally interview someone late and try to make a feature of it. Cameron didn't understand that. He loved his job, read everything he could get his hands on, looked for stories. He used the phone and the computer and a lot of shoe leather and tire tread, blanketing the Back Bay. He had his regular assignments, but at least every other day he submitted a human-interest story too, a feature, even a few opinion pieces. He was, in short, working full-time fulfilling his regular duties while also acting as a freelance writer with a wealth of ideas.

"You're working over and above the call of duty," Dizzy said. "If you'd rather do this stuff on your own time, we can pay you freelance rates."

"I don't mind doing it on work time, unless you see it as a conflict," Cameron said.

"So far it hasn't been."

"Anyway, I've seen newspaper freelance rates. I'd rather use my own time to sell elsewhere."

And he did. Cameron's social life was virtually nil, except for a young woman he'd met at the mailboxes in his building. They went to dinner and a movie a few times, but twice he was late and another time he had to cancel. He shouldn't have been surprised, he told himself, but he was, when she finally gave him the same speech he had heard at Princeton. He was in love with his career and didn't have time for a relationship, and any woman who pursued him would have to compete with journalism as his mistress.

Cameron let that depress him for about half a day until he serendipitously ran into a jockey at a bar, a young Mexican hoping to make the grade at Suffolk Downs, the thoroughbred horse-racing track in East Boston, a mile past Logan Airport.

Enrique Reyes of Mexico City had made a name for himself at tracks in his homeland and had ventured north to conquer American racing. He had shone at Southern tracks but decided he would not get his real break until he made it at the big tracks in New York. Boston was on the way, and so he had settled in, trying to catch the eye of trainers and owners in New York.

The going had been rough so far for the rider, but Cameron saw a bit of himself in Enrique. Something in his eyes made it plain he would not be denied, and Cameron decided to chronicle a week in the life of a jockey. He did not consult his superiors about it; he merely turned in a small feature, then wrote the series on his own time.

Cameron knew he was on to something when Dizzy Rowland asked to see him off-site after hours. "I'm getting heat for not talking to you through your immediate supervisor," Rowland said. "And frankly, that's fair counsel. I keep telling you how to avoid making others jealous, yet I contribute to it by parading you up here during the day."

When they finally got together, Rowland came right to the point. "Let me tell you what I like best about the jockey feature. It was your infusion of yourself into the piece."

"Seriously? I worried about that. It wasn't a column, and I didn't want to be intrusive."

"Intrusive? You just mentioned that you got to the track on the Blue Line. Genius. That's how our readers get there, Cameron. It would have been easy for you to drive and let the *Globe* pay for mileage and parking. But no. Your telling about the characters on the train, how some share their hints and others jealously guard theirs while reading the scratch sheets . . . great, great stuff."

"Thanks." Cameron told Rowland of his plan for the weeklong feature.

"Can't wait to see it. And if it's as good as this first piece, maybe I'll show it to my friend at *Sports Illustrated*."

"Seriously?"

"Of course."

"Because, sir, it will be better. It's coming along well and starting to look like something special—if I do say so myself."

Cameron had to deal with the guilt of knowing his career turned on a propitious tragedy that thrust his name into the national spotlight. Rowland kept telling him that it was his instincts and skill and energy that put him in the position in the first place, but for weeks, Cameron could not be consoled. He feared his stature had benefited from the pain of another.

Cameron's weeklong series on Enrique Reyes had proved immediately popular, and Dizzy Rowland's *Sports Illustrated* contact was impressed too. While he initially passed on rerunning the feature, he set up an appointment to have Cameron visit in New York and talk about other assignments. Before Cameron could go, however, tragedy struck at the racetrack and changed Enrique's and Cameron's lives overnight.

Enrique had been having a good week, on pace to win more than he had in any previous week of the season. In a match race in the middle of the afternoon Enrique found himself settled in third place along the rail, mounted on a promising filly. The favorite was leading, but Enrique would tell Cameron later that he sensed fatigue in the stallion and believed he could steal the race if he could get past the number-two horse and stay on the rail.

Coming around the far turn, the number-two horse broke down and tossed its rider directly into the face of Enrique's filly. The filly crashed into the rail, and Enrique was thrown, cartwheeling toward the infield. His foot caught briefly in the rail, and though he landed on his head and was knocked out, the only serious damage was to his leg.

And it was serious enough to cost him his career.

Cameron's feature went from one about the hopes and dreams of an immigrant rider to what happens when a leg and a dream are shattered. Enrique's leg had to be amputated just below the hip, and though he made bold pronouncements about one day riding with a prosthetic, it would never happen.

The Enrique Fund, initiated by the *Globe*, brought in hundreds of thousands of dollars—not enough to defray the real costs of his care but enough to get him back to Mexico City, where he was eventually able to start a training facility for young jockeys.

Sports Illustrated assigned Cameron a fresh feature on the story, then used a shorter version in *Time* magazine. Suddenly Cameron was known to all the newsweeklies and other high-paying magazine markets, and he began to make as much money—and noise—after hours as he did on the job.

He had been at the *Globe* less than a year when it was learned that his Enrique coverage had been nominated for a Pulitzer Prize as a distinguished example of local reporting of breaking news—already his second such nomination. The *Globe* also had nominations in other categories, including one for the paper itself in the public service category—the only noncash category. Winners of the other categories would be awarded cash prizes, while the paper that won the Public Service prize would receive a gold medal.

Late in May Cameron traveled to New York City with Dizzy Rowland and a half dozen others from the *Globe* for the Pulitzer Prize luncheon at the beautiful and ancient Low Library on the Morningside Heights campus of Columbia University. There Cameron became the only reporter to win for the *Globe* that year, pocketing a check for $15,000. The *Globe* also won the Public Service gold medal for its series on security issues at Logan Airport.

On the way back to Boston, Dizzy Rowland chatted privately with Cameron. "I'm sure it is not lost on you, son, that you are the youngest and most celebrated new employee the *Globe* has ever had. Now is the time for you to buckle down, recommit yourself to excellence and industriousness, which is what got you where you are today."

Cameron nodded, wondering where this was going. He certainly hoped he had not given the impression that he thought he had arrived and would begin taking liberties as a man of privilege.

"If you haven't already, you will soon start hearing from many other prestigious periodicals, and many will turn your head. We don't want to lose you. I want to offer you a thrice-weekly column, which we will also syndicate. You will see your income double or triple almost immediately. And you will still be free to pursue any features or reportage you care to."

Cameron, still reeling from the fact that much of this was due to the disaster that befell Enrique Reyes, simply said, "I accept, Mr. Rowland. And thank you."

He did not share with his boss that he had already heard from several other publishers, wanting to talk with him about exciting new opportunities, including big raises. But he felt obligated to the *Globe*, which had been the first paper to recognize his potential.

And anyway, there was only one other periodical he wanted to work for. But he had not yet heard from *Global Weekly*.

THIRTY-FIVE

WITH THEIR KIDS now in school most of the day, Irene and Jackie had more freedom and enjoyed doing things together several times a week. Both were antiquers and junk shoppers, and one day they came upon an item that especially intrigued Irene.

They were at a suburban flea market in an otherwise abandoned warehouse, and Irene had found a stack of paintings leaning against a wall. She began idly picking through them, noting that they were simply cheap copies of famous paintings in gaudy frames and that the twenty-dollar asking price would likely be covering only the frame.

She flipped past the *Mona Lisa*, *Dante's Inferno*, Whistler's *Portrait of the Painter's Mother*, some Picassos, two Vincent van Goghs, and even a Rembrandt. Looking slightly out of place but captivating her nonetheless were Warner Sallman's *Head of Christ*, as well as his *Christ at Heart's Door.*

The latter stopped Irene and she stood studying it. She was surprised when Jackie said something behind her, so lost was she in the image. Jackie commented on the kitschy look of the frame, but Irene had already decided on it. "I will replace the rococo," she said. "But tell me about the painting."

Later, as Irene carted her cheap treasure to the car, she was strangely excited. She had just the spot for it, though Rayford might be horrified. That was all right too. It was also her home, and if he still forbade her from going to the church of her choice, he couldn't tell her how to decorate.

With more than an hour before she picked up Raymie, Irene stopped in a frame-it-yourself shop and traded the sprayed-gold-foil frame for half the price of a simple dark wood. She hurried home, hung it over the couch, stood admiring it for a while, then headed for the school.

Now in his late thirties and enjoying seniority at Pan-Con, Rayford was finally flying the international patterns he had coveted. The only downside was that his one diversion—which had never materialized into anything actually adulterous . . . yet—was Hattie Durham, and she was still on domestic routes. He knew her goal was to hold international trips as well so she could get back to flying with him occasionally. But she was still only in her early twenties.

The hard part of international flying, of course, was jet lag and fatigue from flying through so many time zones. Regulations called for Rayford to get eight hours' sleep during the twenty-four hours preceding the end of his flight duty. That he found a bit of a complicator. The flying was tense, mentally straining work, but he enjoyed variety in his life. So when Rayford had downtime, he didn't waste it in a hotel room. He was out and about, sightseeing, and visiting his various contacts—many introduced to him by Abdullah Smith. Rayford had black-market contacts all over Europe and the Middle East and a decent little side business in the States.

Besides the intriguing aspect of raising children and trying to remain civil in a marriage that had become boring, black marketeering provided the only real rush in Rayford's life. He missed the kids when he was gone, and sometimes he even missed Irene. But he had to admit he enjoying leaving more than returning. There was more to do on the road.

Rayford was at the top of his profession, occasionally still consulting with the government, and enjoying the looks he got when he strode through airports in his dress blues, stretching his six-foot-four frame as tall as he could. On the other hand, there were days when he wondered if this would be the extent of his life. He had reached all his goals, though he would love to finally get to fly the president's 747 at least once.

It was raining when Irene finally pulled into the driveway with Raymie, now eight. He was disappointed that he couldn't play outside, especially given that she didn't let him play on the computer or watch television until after dinner. But she gave him a snack and then found him roaming the house, looking for something to do.

A few minutes later he called out to her from the living room.

She found him riding the back of the couch like a horse. "What have I told you about riding that couch?" she said.

"That it's okay because we need a new one," Raymie said, grinning. His head was inches from the new painting. "What is this anyway?"

"What does it look like?"

"Jesus. And He's at somebody's house. But whose? Zacchaeus's? I thought Jesus found him in a tree."

One thing that could be said for Raymie's being in Sunday school every week, even at Irene's less-than-ideal church, was that he had heard every Bible story and knew them all. "I don't know this story," he said.

Irene sat on the couch and looked up at him. "It's not from a Bible story," she said. "It's actually symbolic. Know what that means?"

He shook his head.

"*Symbolic* means it shows something that means something else."

"So, what does the picture mean?"

"That door Jesus is knocking on, that is like the door

to a person's heart. Jesus wants to come into our hearts, into our lives."

Raymie sat staring at the painting. "There's no door-knob," he said.

"Hmm?"

"How's He gonna open the door with no handle on it?"

"What do you think, Raymie?"

"There has to be a handle on the inside. Somebody's gonna hafta let Him in."

"That's right. Jesus won't push His way into our lives. We have to decide to invite Him in. Just a minute. I want to read you something."

Irene hurried upstairs to her bedroom and brought down her well-marked Bible. She turned to Revelation 3:20 and said, "Listen, Raymie, to what Jesus says: 'Look! I stand at the door and knock. If you hear my voice and open the door, I will come in.' Know what, Raymie? I asked Jesus into my heart."

"Was He knocking?"

She chuckled. "I think He was."

Irene was sorely tempted to push Raymie, to ask him if he wanted to do the same. But he was at an age where he would have jumped off a bridge if she had suggested it.

"So He's inside you, Mom? in your heart?"

"It's like I told you. That's symbolic. That's how I say it, but it just means that His Spirit lives in me. Of course I don't have Jesus Himself inside my body."

"How did you get Him in your heart?"

"I just prayed and told Him that was what I wanted."

"And how do you know He came in? Can you feel Him?"

"In a way I can. I know He's with me all the time."

"*Humph*. Mom, you want to be the bad guy and I'll be the sheriff? You run out into the kitchen and I'll try to shoot you from my horse."

Irene wanted to say no. She wanted to ask Raymie how he could have such a short attention span. How could he not see how important this was? that this was everything compared to the nothing of his imaginary games? She'd rather say no and tell him she was busy, then leave him alone so he could think about what they had discussed. But would he? For all she knew he would use the Sallman painting as a target.

"Okay," she said, "but you get only two shots."

Irene leaped off the couch and was nearly around the corner before she heard the surprised boy make a shooting sound. "Missed me!" she called out, and the sound came again. Irene made a big show of being hit, bumping the wall, sliding to the floor. "I'm gut shot!" she said. "Not gonna make it."

Raymie laughed and climbed down, running to her. "Gotcha," he said. "Good thing you got Jesus in your heart."

———

While keeping his distance from the dirty work, Nicolae Carpathia succeeded in killing what little was left of the late Emil Tismaneanu's business by letting Leon Fortunato and Jonathan Stonagal do their magic behind the scenes. Stonagal made sure Tismaneanu Tech defaulted on its payments to Corona Technologies in Louisiana, and suddenly Carpathian Trading had the inside track on both of Corona's cutting-edge products.

Sales multiplied exponentially, and it wasn't long before Nicolae had paid off Stonagal and was far and away the wealthiest, most successful businessman in Europe. *Forbes* magazine already listed him among the top 10 percent of the richest people in the world, and Stonagal himself teased that Nicolae might one day topple him from his perch as number one. Carpathia had laughed heartily at this, as he held less than 5 percent of what Stonagal owned, but inside he was not amused.

Surpassing Stonagal's wealth was just one of his many goals. In fact, with the memory of his visitation from the spirit world still fresh in his mind, he would always consider virtually owning the world an entitlement. And he wanted more than to own it. He wanted to rule it.

———

Chloe arrived home from her after-school activities early and went straight to her room as usual.

Irene knocked lightly on her bedroom door.

"Busy!" Chloe called out.

"Doing what?" Irene said. "You just got here. Can't a mother at least get a greeting?"

"Hi, Mom! Bye, Mom!"

"Chloe, please. Can't I see my own daughter a little at the end of the day?"

"I'm on the phone."

"I want to talk to you when you're off. I'll be in the kitchen."

"Fine!"

Cameron Williams had been a staff writer at *Global Weekly* just less than a year, and he had a new nickname: Buck. Because he was constantly bucking tradition and protocol. The youngest writer on the staff, Cameron thought nothing of trying to scoop even his own colleagues.

"You think this is a newspaper," one of them said at a staff meeting, "where we're all out to beat each other? It doesn't work that way in New York, sonny boy. We work together."

"Calling me sonny boy doesn't sound like us working together, all due respect. And the fact is, you'd better hustle, because if you don't I *will* beat you. Make no mistake; I'm more interested in scooping the other newsmagazines, but if you get left in the dust too, whose fault is that?"

"Okay, people," Senior Executive Editor Steve Plank said, raising a hand. "Down to business. We've selected President Fitzhugh as our Newsmaker of the Year, and I want Williams to do the cover piece."

"You've got to be kidding! He's all of, what, twenty-five years old, and you're giving him—"

"Twenty-six," Cameron said.

"So I was off by a year. He's still too young to—"

"Seems your facts are often just slightly off," Cameron said.

"Now, Buck," Plank said, making the others laugh. And the nickname stuck. "All right, everybody, no more bickering. We do have to work together on this. I don't expect Buck, er, Cameron to do all the reporting too, so let's supplement his one-on-one interview with everything you can dig up, and—"

"One-on-one? We've never interviewed a sitting president one-on-one."

"Well, I misspoke," Plank said. "Of course I'll be there, as will Bailey."

"Stanton *Bailey* will be there?" Cameron said.

"Well, duh," someone else said. "He's only the publisher."

"I know who he is," Cameron said. "But, I mean, wow!"

"You and Bailey will be there and Buck Rogers here gets to do the interview?"

"That's enough," Plank said, reddening. "I'm still in charge here, so you can quit challenging my decisions if you like your jobs."

A few snickered.

"You think I'm kidding, just push me some more."

Silence.

"That's better. Buck here has earned this assignment,

and you don't have to agree with it. But the fact is some of you others *didn't* earn it. If you had, you'd be there. You can make all you want of the youngest guy in the room getting the cover piece, but if you'd like to have an assignment like that, you'd better get off your tails and start hustling."

Later, in Plank's office, he said, "Buck, it's a good thing I like you. You're driving these people nuts."

"Seems like it. But I don't get it. I thought working hard was what journalism was all about. This is the only job I ever wanted, and I want to do more than just keep it. I want to excel at it."

"You're already doing that, Buck."

"You gonna be calling me that from now on?"

"I don't know. Probably. I like it. But anyway, lay off the others. The best revenge is success. You want to get their goats? Keep beating them, but don't say a word about it. Don't lord it over them. You'll frustrate them no end."

"And that's okay with you?"

"Maybe it'll make 'em work harder."

THIRTY-SIX

IRENE WAITED for Chloe until she grew mad, then finally
marched up the stairs to demand an audience. Chloe had
had her driver's license a few months, and her new sense
of freedom and independence had seemed to help her
turn a corner in her relationship with Irene. And not for
the better.

Chloe drove herself to and from church, arriving late
and slipping out early. And especially when Rayford was
away, she had become more lax about her curfew, letting
it slide twenty to thirty minutes. Irene was going to
threaten to take away her keys and ground her after one
more offense.

But when she got to the top of the stairs, she overheard Chloe and Raymie.

"Don't open my door without knocking, Raymie."

"Sorry. I just wanted to tell ya somethin'."

"What?"

"I got Jesus in my heart."

"You what?"

"I prayed and asked Jesus into my heart."

Irene stopped, holding her breath.

"Well, that's good, I guess, huh?"

"'Course it's good," Raymie said. "What do you think? You got Jesus in your heart?"

Irene had to exhale and made herself dizzy trying to be quiet.

"No, I don't, Raymie. But I'm glad you do."

She is?

"Good for you," Chloe said.

How sweet, Irene thought. Chloe could have been cold, mean, challenging. She had been so to her little brother more times than Irene cared to remember. Was it possible she somehow realized the import of this? Or did she simply not know how to respond?

"You should get Jesus in your heart too, Chloe," Raymie said. "Then He's with you all the time, and when you die you go to heaven."

"That's nice."

"So, will ya?"

"I'll think about it, okay?"

"You ought to think about it soon, because—"

"Don't bug me about it, or I *won't* think about it, okay?"

"But I'm just worried—"

"Don't worry about me."

"Okay. See ya."

Raymie ran out and bounded down the stairs, holler-
ing hello to his mother as he went. Irene reached Chloe's
door just as she was shutting it. She saw her mother,
looked right into her eyes, and shut the door.

"Chloe!" Irene said.

"What?"

"I need a minute."

"Busy!"

"No, you're not! Now open this door or you're going
nowhere tonight."

Chloe opened the door and headed to her bed with her
back to Irene. "What?" she said.

"Can't you just take a minute for me?"

"Yes! What?"

"I just wanted to say that I appreciated how you
reacted to Raymie."

"You were listening?"

"I didn't mean to. I was coming to see you and heard
him in here."

"Okay, so?"

"So I appreciate your not poking holes in his news."

"Well, I should have. What are you brainwashing him
about now?"

"It's not brainwashing, Chloe. It's what I believe. And
now it's what Raymie believes."

"Well, it's not what I believe, and he's too young to
know what he believes. What's the matter with you,
Mom, force-feeding that stuff to an eight-year-old?"

"Will you remember who you're talking to, young
lady?"

"Will *you?*"

Irene cautioned Chloe about her curfew and warned her of losing her freedom.

Chloe fell silent and merely nodded. Perhaps she was getting the point that her mother still held that card: the car keys. And she was going to the library this evening with her friends.

"Your father gets home late tonight, so you'll want me to be able to tell him you were in on time."

"Fine."

———

Few things thrilled Nicolae more than reading about himself in the paper or hearing about himself on television. Normally the popularity polls were limited to the top leadership positions in the country, but he had become so popular with the people and with his colleagues—political allies and foes alike—that the polling organization had expanded its research to include him.

While the president and prime minister were nearly in a dead heat with popularity figures just points over 50 percent, Carpathia was judged popular with nearly 70 percent of the populace. That necessitated his winning over even opponents, of course, and his plan was to persuade everybody that he was the real thing.

In his race for a second term in the lower house, he had pulled out his pacifist strategy. And with Romanians tired of skirmishes and civil wars resulting in the deaths of many of their young men and women, not to mention threatened invasions by Bulgaria and Ukraine, his timing was perfect. Leon Fortunato had counseled him through a diatribe about pacifism that had captured the imagination of the masses.

In the weeks before the election his opponent made the mistake of adopting the opposite view and insisting on debating Carpathia. By the week before the election the polls showed Nicolae so far ahead that even members of the other party were publicly calling for their man to withdraw. Despite an outcry from the party faithful, demanding to know who would carry the flag for their values, opinion polls showed Carpathia expected to win by the largest margin in the history of a contested race, just a few points under what he won with following the death of Emil Tismaneanu.

Carpathia's opponent did not withdraw, but he eschewed the final debate, removed all advertising to keep from chasing bad money with good, and virtually disappeared from the news. Rumor had it that he voted in absentia and would not even be in Bucharest on election day. That proved true when he was unavailable for comment following a defeat that bore out the polls.

Pundits claimed that Carpathia could have run for the top office in the nation and won in a walk. And they suggested that that should be his next race.

Irene was sitting up at 11:30 PM, an hour past Chloe's curfew and half an hour before Rayford was expected home. She had called Chloe's phone four times, the last time at 11:20, threatening to call the police if she didn't get a call back in ten minutes. She was frantic, praying, and about to make that call when the phone rang and the caller ID showed it was Chloe.

"Where are you?"

"Just finished having a tire changed, Mom. Sorry. Directly home after that."

"Why didn't you call me?"

"Sorry. I got so busy trying to find someone to help; then I left my phone in the car. It won't happen again. I'm fine."

No way Irene would be able to sleep. She just wanted to hug her daughter. The girl infuriated her, and because of the hint of a slur in Chloe's voice, Irene wasn't entirely sure she believed her. But above all that, Chloe was still her daughter, and Irene was relieved beyond measure to know she was all right. It would be good to be up when Rayford returned too.

Irene was satisfied with her decision to leave Rayford out of this crisis until he got home. She knew he had to be on the ground and likely headed away from O'Hare, but there was no sense troubling him when he could do nothing. When she saw a car pull into the driveway, moving a little too quickly, she thought it might be him. It wasn't like Rayford to pull in fast, but he did always seem eager to get to bed when he had been gone a long time and got back this late.

Irene jumped when she heard a thud and a crash, including glass breaking. She raced outside to find Chloe painfully stepping from her car and swearing. She had smashed her right headlight into the corner of the garage, and her mouth was bloody from banging her lips on the steering wheel.

"Were you not even wearing a seat belt?" Irene said, reaching to embrace her. "Chloe!"

"Thanks for caring that I'm okay!" Chloe spat, running past Irene and into the house.

Irene smelled liquor on her breath. "Chloe!"

She had left the car running and even in gear. Irene debated following her to prove she cared more about her than the car, but she couldn't leave it that way. She carefully backed up and parked it in the garage.

Irene decided she had better attempt to talk to Chloe, but as she mounted the stairs she heard, "Don't come up here! I'm fine! Just leave me alone!"

"What are you doing about your mouth?"

"Don't worry. I won't get blood on your precious carpet!"

"I'm not worried about the carpet, honey. I'm worried about you."

"I told you I'm fine; now leave me alone!"

"Chloe, have you been drinking? Were you driving drunk?"

Irene couldn't tell whether it was the bathroom door or Chloe's bedroom door, but something slammed so loud it shook the house. And woke Raymie.

"What's goin' on?" he whined from the top of the stairs.

"Nothing," Irene whispered from the landing. "Everything's okay now. Go back to bed."

She went back outside. While she was in the driveway sweeping the glass, Rayford pulled in. She greeted him with a kiss, but she couldn't hide her fear and anger, and of course he saw the damage.

"All right," he said, "I'll bite."

Abdullah Ababneh was up early as usual and getting ready to go to the airfield. Yasmine had breakfast cooking. The kids were sleeping, but something was wrong. Yasmine would not maintain eye contact with Abdullah.

"Are you all right?" he said.

"I am fine," she said evenly.

"Do you need to talk with me about something? something I have done or not done? something I have forgotten?"

"No," she said, but he was struck that she appeared as sad and downcast as he had ever seen her.

"I can call and go in late if we need to talk," he said.

"Perhaps later," she said. "Not now."

"But there is something then?"

"There is something, but I am not prepared to discuss it."

"Am I in trouble?"

She smiled but her eyes still showed dread. "No, Abdullah," she said. "It's nothing like that."

"Are you in trouble then?" He said it to elicit a smile, but her hesitation made something stab in the pit of his stomach.

She shook her head. "Later, please."

"When?"

"When I am ready."

"This evening?"

She stopped her work and faced him. "When I am ready, Abdullah. Now please, stop pressing me."

"I just want to know and to help."

"I know."

"Call me if you need me to come home."

Suddenly she was crying, but as he approached her, she waved him off. "Please, just eat and go."

"I didn't mean to make you sad," he said.

She shook her head. "Frankly, it touches me that you seem to care so much."

THIRTY-SEVEN

THIS WAS THE LAST THING Rayford needed after a long day of flying. His heavy had sat more than an hour on the runway at Heathrow due to weather and traffic before the long flight home, so passengers and crew had grown testy.

One thing was sure: Chloe was his daughter. Yes, even more than she was Irene's. Who knew why? The father-daughter thing? Temperaments? Competition? From what Irene said, it was clear that only Rayford would be able to talk to her, and who knew if even that would work?

"Go to bed, Irene."

"I won't sleep till I hear how it went."

"If you're awake when I come in, I'll tell you."

"I will be. Trust me."

They climbed the steps together, Rayford peeling off to

Chloe's bathroom, where he stood outside the closed door. "I'm home," he said.

"Hi, Dad," he heard, and she sounded resigned.

"Can we talk when you're ready?"

"Yeah. Wait for me in my room."

Rayford stretched out on her bed. A mistake. He nearly dozed. But he knew she dreaded facing him. The last thing he wanted was for her to find him sleeping. He sat up and scanned the room. Pin neat. Just the way he liked to live. Her walls were covered with academic and citizenship and extracurricular awards.

Rayford moved back to the bathroom. "You 'bout ready, hon?" he said.

"Can't get this lip to stop bleeding," she said.

"I'll get some ice."

When he got back upstairs Chloe was sitting on her bed with a bloody washcloth over her mouth. He sat next to her and handed her a plastic sandwich bag full of crushed ice.

"Thanks. Sorry, Dad."

"For what?"

"The garage. The car."

"How about lying to your mother?"

"I didn't lie to her! I just didn't answer my phone."

"You said you had a flat tire. Your spare hasn't been touched."

"Oh, yeah, that. Okay, sorry for lying to Mom too."

"You'll have to tell her that."

Chloe scowled and nodded.

"What else are you sorry for?"

She shrugged. "I think that's it."

"So you were where you said you were going to be tonight?"

She nodded. "I was at the library. Have a couple of books to prove it."

"How long were you there?"

"The whole time."

Rayford shook his head and stood quickly. "You're about to really tick me off, Chloe."

"*What?*"

"You think I don't know the library closes at nine? And you think I can't smell alcohol on your breath even over all that mouthwash you used? And you think I don't know you're a better driver than one who bashes into the garage when you're sober?"

That did it and Chloe broke down. "I'm sorry, Dad. For all of it."

"What were you drinking and where did you get it?"

"Dad, don't make me get anyone else in trouble. I was at Sherry's and she raided the refrigerator and her dad's liquor cabinet."

"Are you sick or just drunk?"

"Just tipsy, I think. Guess I'll know in a while, won't I?"

"You're impaired; I'll tell you that. You want the speech now or in the morning?"

"I want the sentence first."

"You're sure?"

She nodded miserably.

"You're going to apologize to your mother, and you're going to mean it. You scared her to death."

"I know."

"She loves you with all her heart. You know that too, don't you?"

"She has a strange way of showing it sometimes, Dad."

"But you know, don't you?"

"Yes, I know."

"You're going to pay to have the car and the garage fixed, and you're not going to borrow either of the other cars. While yours is in the shop, you're out of luck. Besides that, you're grounded for the next two weeks."

"Might as well get the speech out of the way now too," Chloe said, "so I can put this behind me and start over."

Does that ever sound like me, Rayford thought. "Fair enough. Let me tell you what disappoints me the most, Chloe. This is so beneath you. You're smart, and not just academically. You have street smarts *and* you're intelligent. You start getting into this kind of nonsense and you're going to see your grades slip, your scholarship chances dry up, your acceptances to good schools disappear. You want to be a professional person, a successful, self-made woman. Well, this is self-made too, and it's a mess. Is this what you want?"

She shook her head.

"Don't do something now that will stay with you the rest of your life. Can you imagine if you'd hit another car while under the influence? Or a pedestrian? Killed someone?"

"Don't get dramatic now, Dad."

"Don't kid yourself, Chloe. This happens every day.

You'd never forgive yourself, and your life would never be the same."

Chloe wept openly now, her lip fat. "I don't want you to be disappointed in me, Dad. I want you to respect me."

"That's not easy tonight, is it?"

She shook her head.

He embraced her, rocking her as she sobbed. "Do me a favor?" he said.

She pulled back. "What?"

"Do the hard thing and do it first."

"What?"

"Your mother is still awake, and she needs to hear from you."

"Oh, Dad, no! Not tonight! Tomorrow?"

He just looked at her, and she trudged toward the master bedroom.

———

Irene wondered what was taking so long. She had to admit she was jealous that Chloe would talk to Rayford but never to her—at least not in a civil tone.

When the door opened and the dim light from the hall invaded, she could tell from the silhouette that it was Chloe and not Rayford. Irene quickly sat up and gathered her crying daughter in her arms.

"I'm so sorry," Chloe managed. "It won't happen again."

"I'm just relieved you weren't hurt worse," Irene said.

"I lied to you, Mom. I was only at the library long

enough to check out a couple of books, and then we were at Sherry's and we were all drinking. I didn't have a flat tire, and I ignored your phone calls till I thought I'd better try to buy some time. I shouldn't have been driving, and I'm sorry about the garage and the car."

"How's your mouth?"

"It'll be all right in the morning. Does this mean you forgive me?"

"Of course, sweetheart. I love you."

"Thanks, Mom. I love you too."

"I could use one more apology though."

"For what?"

"For how you talked to me today about Raymie."

Chloe sighed. "I'm tired. We'd better not talk about this."

"You're not sorry then?"

"I'm sorry if I was disrespectful, but I've got to tell you, Mom, we disagree on this. Raymie's way too young for you to be trying to push your religion on him."

"Good night, Chloe."

Abdullah Ababneh found himself preoccupied all day— not a good thing when flying fighter jets. He taught, he trained pilots, he flew test flights. And all he could think of was Yasmine. He felt responsible for her, and with good reason.

Such a sweet girl. She always had been. A good mother. A good wife. He wanted that she at least be happy, as happy as a woman could be in his culture. Life was harder for women than for men; he was sure of that.

Abdullah had always been able to tell when something was troubling Yasmine. Though she was naturally quiet, there was also something about her carriage, her very presence, that changed when anything was on her mind. She had acted this way when first she realized that he was not as rigid in his religious practices as he had been when they met.

What she didn't know, of course, was that he had never been as pious as he put on. He wanted to impress his own parents, who were true Muslim believers. And he wanted to impress Yasmine so she would marry him.

But when she had broached the subject about what was up with him, why he had seemed to change, he was surprised at what she had to say. He had feared, of course, that she was going to express alarm, disappointment, concern. Actually the opposite was true. She had danced around the subject for a long time, then eventually admitted that she had also been shirking her prayer life when he was not around. "I had no idea what you would think, Abdullah. What would you have thought if I refused to pray with you at the appointed times?"

He had to think about that one. It was one thing to decide such things for himself. And it might have been similar if he had decided for her that she could become more lax in her religious life. But for her, on her own, to choose to privately rebel like that, well, he didn't know what he thought or might have said or done had he known.

"Does it make you feel guilty?" he had said.

"Sometimes. Less now than at first. At first I wondered if Allah would hate me, cast me out, kill me. Did you fear the same, Abdullah?"

He smiled and nodded. "Yes, at first. But now I wonder if he even exists."

"Careful."

"I know. But if he is such an exacting, stringent god, how does he allow his people to turn on him like this?"

"Do you miss him, Abdullah?"

"Miss him? No. I never really knew him. You?"

She smiled shyly and shook her head.

Since that conversation a couple of years before, they had not discussed it. Neither prayed except in public, when it was expected and would have horrified others if they hadn't. But religion was not practiced in their home, not even with their children. They attended the mosque just enough to deflect suspicion.

But what could be on Yasmine's mind now? Could anything be as dire as, in essence, losing one's religion? All Abdullah wanted was to get home to see if she was ready to talk about whatever was on her mind. And yet another part of him dreaded knowing.

THIRTY-EIGHT

BUCK WILLIAMS—even he had embraced the nickname now—had never been to the White House. But now as he sat in the Oval Office with his boss and his boss's boss and a photographer, not to mention both President Gerald Fitzhugh and his wife, Wilma, Buck fought to keep his composure. Inside he felt like a kid, eager to get out of here and tell one and all where he had been, whom he had been with, and gush every detail.

But, of course, this was not about him. This was about a president elected for a second term and having been chosen a second time as *Global Weekly*'s Newsmaker of the Year. Buck could save his enthusiasm for later. Now he had to look and sound and act professional. He wanted this to not be the highlight of his career. He foresaw international assignments and—he hoped—more cover stories.

Buck wasn't even half the president's age, but his charm kicked in the moment he met the man and the First Lady. He maintained eye contact, listened, didn't talk about himself, and yet was able to empathize and show true interest when they talked about their home and their children. Mrs. Fitzhugh clearly seemed to connect with Buck, and the president had to notice.

Gerald Fitzhugh quickly lost his formal air, crossed his legs, gestured more broadly, was funnier than normal. At one point he stood and shed his suit coat, his wife whispering that he might want to reconsider that, due to the magazine photographer capturing every moment.

"Ah, it's all right, Wilma," he said. "It's not like I can run again anyway."

Cameron had expected the president to be vulgar and profane, which was his reputation. Fitzhugh had often been compared to a young Lyndon Johnson. Perhaps it was because of the presence of his wife, but Fitzhugh did not utter so much as a mild epithet the whole time. His outbursts were legendary among staff members, but Buck found him merely robust and youthful. Exuberant.

Buck's style was not to come in with a prescribed list of questions he would have to keep referring to. Rather, he listed on a small index card five areas he wanted the president to discuss. He hoped to not refer to it unless he thoroughly blanked, and he planned to base his follow-up questions on Fitzhugh's responses. That made it less formal, more like a conversation than an interview, and allowed Cameron to remain engaged rather than constantly scanning a notebook. His colleagues had proved more helpful than he had expected, suggesting tough questions and even tougher follow-ups, predicting the stock answers.

Every time Fitzhugh gave a canned response, Buck pressed him, respectfully but forcefully, making him explain himself to the public. Buck believed that was the highest calling of the journalist.

They discussed international trade, defense, the budget, health care, and Social Security. Finally Buck even delved into personal style. "Is it true?" he said. "Are you a shouter? a man with a short fuse?"

Fitzhugh didn't hesitate. "Guilty," he said, glancing at his wife. "Of course, I don't get away with that with this one in the private quarters. Can't fire her, know what I mean? But, yeah, I've been working on toning it down with my people. We've got a lot to do, and I don't have a lot of patience. I can improve in that area. Will I? I doubt it."

After a little less than an hour, Fitzhugh's chief of staff entered and signaled that the time was short. The president stood and put his jacket back on, thrust out his hand, and vigorously shook Buck's. "Don't think I don't know what a baby you are, son."

"Sir?"

"I've got a staff that researches all this stuff, no surprise to you. I know your age, your background, your credentials. And I got to tell you, this was as enjoyable an hour as I've spent with a journalist since I've been in office."

345

"Well, thank you, sir."

"He's not just saying that," Mrs. Fitzhugh said. "I seldom see him this relaxed. I trust you won't take advantage."

"Take advantage?"

"He was more forthcoming than his people would suggest."

"Well, ma'am, it was all on the record."

"I know," she said. "I just hope this wasn't an ambush. We have had people come in here and pretend to be allies, then go back and write awful things."

"Well, I can't say I'm an ally, but you may rest assured I am not going to ambush you either. This will be a straight-forward Newsmaker of the Year piece, giving the president a chance to speak his mind, which I feel he did here."

———

Maddeningly, Yasmine chose to wait until after the evening meal and the kids were in bed before being willing to talk seriously. That only added to Abdullah's frustration and worry. He found himself eating too quickly and too much, which was wholly unlike him. Then he sat studying her as she tidied up and put the kids down, searching her sad, tense face for any clue of what was to come.

Finally they sat together before an open window, Abdullah hoping for even a small breeze, anything to move the air inside the house where the temperature remained stiflingly hot.

For the longest time they just sat, Abdullah waiting, Yasmine sighing as if she was about to begin, then falling silent again. Abdullah thought he would go mad.

Finally he could take it no longer. "What is it, Yasmine? Tell me."

"I met someone," she said quietly.

Abdullah froze. Then he stood. "You *met* someone? There is another man?"

"Sit down, Abdullah. It wasn't a man."

"You think that makes it better? You met someone and it's a woman?"

"Sit. No, it's not like that. You need not worry about my loyalty to you. I am worrying about yours to me after you hear this."

"Hear what?" he said, sitting. "Please!"

"About three weeks ago I was in a market near the airport when tourists came through. They had a longer layover than expected, and someone at the airport suggested they get a taste of the local culture and sent them to the bazaar."

"So you met one of them."

Yasmine nodded. "Elle Lindquist. In her sixties, I would guess. Married, though her husband was not with her. They are missionaries to the United Arab Emirates. He is waiting there for her. She had been back to the United States to visit family."

"What kind of missionaries? CIA, oil, Catholic, what?"

"She called herself an evangelical Christian."

"You talked to her long enough to learn that?"

"It was one of the first things she said, Abdullah. She

was wonderful and sweet, but I did not know what to think. So often when you are accosted by a stranger in public, they want something from you. Money. Your time. Something."

"What did she want?"

"Elle just wanted to know me. She said she felt drawn to me in some way and was curious about our life and ways. The differences and similarities between here and the UAE seemed to fascinate her."

"Go on."

"Almost immediately, after courteously determining that I had time to talk—and I have to say, Abdullah, I felt a bond with her right away too; I have no idea why—she asked me directly about my religion. She said, 'I assume you are Muslim.'

"I said, 'You assume correctly.'

"Elle said she had studied our religion and wondered if I could confirm some things for her. She asked all about the mosque and rituals and the prayers, and I told her she had apparently studied good sources. Then she asked how I felt I benefited from Islam."

Yasmine looked Abdullah full in the face with a knowing expression. It had been the very issue he and she had talked about years ago.

"What in the world did you say?"

"I didn't know what to say, Abdullah. What could I say? I planned a lie. I wanted to tell her that I felt content and fulfilled and obedient and that I looked forward to eternal rewards someday."

"But?"

"But I could not speak. Every time I opened my mouth I had to choke back my tears."

"Your tears?"

"Elle was looking at me with such curiosity and love and sympathy that I was overcome with the need to tell her the truth. I did not understand it, Abdullah. I had known her only a few minutes and there I stood in public, trying to speak and able only to weep."

"What did she do?"

"She touched me. You know how rare that is here. She guided me to a tiny café, where we sat outside. She apologized for upsetting me and told me I did not have to answer, that I could collect myself and that she would carry the conversation for a while if I didn't mind. Not only did I not mind, but I was impressed anew at her sensitivity. It was just what I wanted and needed. I just nodded, and as we sat sipping coffee, she told me about herself."

"Americans are funny that way, aren't they?" Abdullah said. "Rayford Steele tells me things he does not tell his wife, and he has since the day I met him."

"She told me her life story, about growing up as the daughter of missionaries to South America, then moving back to the States when she was a teenager, meeting her husband at Bible college, and the two of them feeling called by God to be missionaries to this part of the world."

"'Called by God'?"

"That's what she said. I had finally calmed myself and found my voice. I said, 'And what has God called you to do here?' She said, 'To tell people the truth about Him. That He loves them and cares about them and wants to know them and have them know Him.'"

"That's a different God than I know," Abdullah said.

"That is exactly what I thought," she said. "Elle looked at her watch and said she had to start heading back to the airport, so did I mind if she just rushed through a few things with me. I told her I'd be honored to hear more, and she talked as we walked. She said she served a God of love who did not demand rituals and obligations and did not look for reasons to punish His children. She called herself His child, Abdullah. Have you ever felt like a child of God?"

Abdullah shook his head. Where was this going? It was one thing to be a lazy Muslim. It was quite another to consider defecting to another religion.

"I never have either," Yasmine said. "Elle asked if she could pray for me, and when I said yes, she bowed her head right there and talked to God. I was so embarrassed, and yet she talked to Him as if she knew Him, as if He was her friend, as if she simply accepted that He loved her and accepted her and cared for her. I was deeply moved."

"You still are. I can tell."

"She had to go then, Abdullah, but I was not willing to let her. I walked with her all the way to the airport, and she kept talking the whole way. I was hungry, thirsty for something like she had. She promised to e-mail me and to keep in touch. And she has. I go back and forth with her every day, often several times a day. She is teaching me, showing me things from the Bible, pointing me to the one true God who loves everyone, even if they have sinned."

"Have you sinned, Yasmine? Is that what you are telling me?"

"I am learning that we are all sinners. We are all separated from God. But He has provided a way back to Himself. He will forgive us and wash our sins away. It is the most beautiful love story I have ever heard."

"What has you so troubled?"

"Worrying about your reaction."

"My reaction to what? Are you converting?"

"I want to with all my heart, Abdullah. But I don't know what it will mean for you, for us. To have your wife, a mother, turning her back on the religion of her childhood, bringing disgrace on both sides of the family, making many think I am worthy of death . . . this would be no small decision."

"But what kind of a decision is it? What would be required of you? How will people know?"

Yasmine stood and moved to the window, then turned to face her husband. "There is no such thing as a secret Christian," she said. "I could not pretend to be something I was not, the way you and I have been practicing Islam for years. Part of becoming a Christian is throwing off the old life and taking on a whole new one. I could not become a believer in Christ without telling people."

"Muslims believe in Christ! You can be both!"

THIRTY-NINE

EVERYBODY AT *GLOBAL WEEKLY* had been calling Cameron Buck for weeks, so it caught him off guard when Steve Plank buzzed him and said, "Cameron, do you have a moment?"

Buck was also surprised to find Juan Ortiz in Plank's office, looking as if he'd rather be anywhere else on earth. He was chief of the international politics bureau for *GW.*

Ortiz began speaking first. "It isn't that I have anything against you personally, Williams."

"Now just hold on a minute," Plank said. "Juan came in here with a concern, Buck, and you know my style. He was questioning my decision to promote you from staff writer to senior writer, and I thought if a person of his stature has a problem with you, he ought to face you with it."

"But it's not a problem with him, Steve," Juan said. "It is, as you say, a problem with your decision."

"But my decision is all about Buck. And now that he's a senior writer, I want you to use him for stuff. If you've got a problem with him, let's get it on the table."

"It's not even your age, Cameron," Ortiz said. "I've worked with young people before."

"I heard you were a young person once yourself," Buck said.

Plank laughed.

Ortiz didn't. "I was young and I was inexperienced, just like you. You're a fine writer. It doesn't take a genius to see that. But international stories are complex, and a writer ought to have a lot of experience and background before he even attempts to—"

"I have a lot of experience with people, Mr. Ortiz. Hundreds of stories, interviews, profiles, features."

"On international subjects?"

"People are people, sir. Aren't their stories universal?"

"Sure, but there are differences in culture, background, protocol—you name it."

"Granted. And so where am I to get this experience?"

"Well, not here. Before coming to *Global Weekly* you should have had extensive experience in global issues, and then here you should serve some sort of apprenticeship, traveling with a seasoned writer and doing reportage for him or her."

"Like you did."

"Exactly."

"I'm willing to do that."

"You are?"

"Of course. And I'd be honored to serve under you, Mr. Ortiz. What are you working on that I can help with?"

Juan was clearly flustered. "It doesn't bother you that I am not as impressed with you as the boss seems to be? that I think you were promoted too soon?"

"I'd probably think the same if I had been around here as long as you have. I'm only a couple of years younger than you were when you were a senior writer though, right?"

"I guess that's true."

"In fact, weren't you the youngest before me?"

"I guess that's true too."

"Is that the problem, Juan?" Plank said.

"Absolutely not. I started right out of college as a copy boy, and I paid my dues, worked my way up."

Steve turned his attention to Buck. "Juan here has selective memory. He doesn't recall, as I do, that he took the same heat you're taking when Stanton Bailey, who had my position back then, made him a fairly young senior writer."

"Fairly young," Juan said. "But quite experienced."

"So, you willing to take me under your wing, Mr. Ortiz? If it's all right with Steve?"

Juan crossed his legs and leaned back. "Would you say you're teachable and want to learn?"

"This was my idea, wasn't it?"

"Mine too," Steve said, smiling. "I was about to suggest the same thing."

"You don't report to me," Juan said, "but you'd be expected to take direction—and directives—from me."

"Granted. I'd be honored."

"It won't be easy."

"I wouldn't expect it to be."

"And stop agreeing with me on everything."

"Sorry. I mean, I wasn't! How's that?"

Abdullah "Smith" Ababneh had trouble sleeping. His mind was a jumble. One thing was certain: he had caused this. He was to blame. Yasmine was about to turn her back on her religion and convert to Christianity, of all things. She could not be persuaded to simply embrace a respect for Jesus within the confines of her own faith. To her the Islamic understanding of Jesus was inadequate. They did not put Him on the same plane even as Muhammad, and they certainly did not think Him equal with Allah.

To Yasmine, Jesus was the Son of God, was God, divine, transcendent, and the Savior of mankind. Abdullah could have lived with that—especially given the laxness of his own religious practice—except that there was no easy way for her to do this. In her mind, he understood, true conversion meant something public. She could not be both Muslim and Christian, and being a Christian meant that the fabric of her faith included telling others.

Abdullah found himself pacing night after night.

Strangely, part of him envied Yasmine. For one thing, she had a friend, a confidante, someone who truly cared for her and for her soul. Elle Lindquist corresponded with her every day, often several times a day, and it was not beyond her to call Yasmine occasionally too.

"Do you not feel pressured?" Abdullah had said.

"Not in the least," Yasmine said. "I feel loved. I am learning so much, and it resonates with me, Abdullah. It feels right and true, as if I found what I had been looking for all my life without even realizing it."

After several days of agonizing over it, Abdullah prayed to Allah about it. He had never prayed about something specific before, other than when he was in danger. Otherwise his prayers had always consisted only of praising Allah and Muhammad. He had gone through the rote five-times-a-day prayers for years before he had begun to slack off. Suddenly he found himself becoming devout. If anything could get him into deep trouble with a god he still wasn't sure existed, it was losing his own wife to the other side.

And Allah, he now firmly believed, answered him. Deep within his heart and soul Abdullah became convinced that he had the answer for Yasmine. The trouble was, he waited too long to tell her. He ruminated about it for a few days, trying to shape his words in the most persuasive manner. The late evening when he had mustered the fortitude to raise the subject, she beat him to the point.

"I have news," Yasmine said as she lay beside him in their bed. "I finally made my decision. I prayed a prayer that Mrs. Lindquist walked me through, told God that I knew I was separated from Him by sin and that I needed forgiveness. I needed a Savior. I received His Son, Jesus Christ. Mrs. Lindquist says I am now born again."

Abdullah closed his eyes and rubbed his face with his hands. "You did this without telling me?"

"I told you, Abdullah. We have been talking about it a long time, and now it has happened, and I told you."

"But you didn't consult with me, didn't seek my permission."

"Your *permission*?" she said. "Do you consider me a child? a possession?"

"In a way you are my possession, yes. And I must tell you: I will not allow this."

Yasmine spoke just above a whisper. "I do not wish to defy you, Abdullah, but this was no small decision. This is my life. And this is the way I want to raise our children."

Abdullah had long heard the expression about one's blood running cold. Now he knew what that meant. A shudder ran through him, and a resolve began deep in his core. Guilt washed over him for being so bad, so inconsistent a Muslim that he was about to lose his wife. But his children also? He could not allow that. He simply could not. He would not be able to live with himself.

"My children are Muslims, Yasmine," he said. "They will be raised in Islam."

Yasmine rose and pulled on her robe, leaving the bedroom. He followed her, and they sat across from each other in the living room.

"My deepest prayer is that we not fight over this, Abdullah. You are no more Muslim than Elle Lindquist and her husband. It has become a religion of convenience for you. You do not believe in Allah. You do not believe in Muhammad. If you did, you would fulfill your duties and obligations to them, and not only when others are watching."

"I lapsed," he said, "and for that I am sorry. I have been a bad example to you, a poor husband. But this has awakened me. I am returning full strength to my religion. I believe there is no god other than Allah and that Muhammad is his prophet. Jesus is compatible with that. He is found in our holy writings."

"Jesus precedes your holy writings," Yasmine said. "And He said Himself that He was the way, the truth, and the life and that no one can come to God except through Him. If you don't believe that, don't say that He is compatible with Islam."

Smart and technically astute as he was, Abdullah had never believed he matched his wife's intelligence. He could not argue with her, could not persuade her. "I was going to talk with you about this this very evening," he said. "I was going to ask that you forgive me for the example I have been and give me time to get back on track. Hold off on your decision and return to the disciplines of our religion. There you will find the truth and happiness and contentment."

Yasmine looked down and shook her head.

"What?" he said.

"We have both been through our periods of devotion,"

she said. "There have been times in both of our lives when no one could have questioned our faith. Did it ever bring you contentment? happiness?" She did not wait for an answer. "Me either. Abdullah, I have found what I needed. I have truly come to God. I do not have to earn His favor. I cannot, and it is a good thing."

"You are to do nothing if you are a Christian? You are not expected to pray and worship and perform acts of goodwill?"

"Of course. But not to earn God's favor. Rather as a response to the gifts that have been bestowed."

"The gifts?"

"Forgiveness. Eternal life."

"You do not fear the anger of Allah?"

Yasmine sighed. "If I feared Allah, I would have remained a slave to the demands of Islam. So would you. Why do you now fear him?"

That was the question of the ages. Abdullah *did* fear Allah. He feared his god existed and cared and would now see Abdullah as a reprobate, an infidel, a failure.

Worse—if there could be anything worse—Abdullah took as a threat to his very manhood the fact that his wife was no longer reasonable. She had never before been impudent, obstinate, stubborn, resolute against him. And now she countered everything he said.

Abdullah wanted to be reasonable, to listen, to really hear, to discuss these deep things. But could he tolerate such rebellion from his own wife? Did he have no say, no sway over her? Could he compete with this divine suitor? And how was it that she had plunged ahead with what she admitted was no small decision without so much as consulting him or warning him?

They had discussed it, of course, but somehow Abdullah had missed that Yasmine was becoming so fully convinced. The draw, the lure of an older woman—so secure in her life and faith—had apparently proved irresistible to her.

They could sit and discuss this until dawn, but the bottom line was that Abdullah could not abide it. He could not accept it. He could not allow it.

"You need to tell Mrs. Lindquist that you acted too quickly. That you have changed your mind. That as you have prayed about it and talked it over with your husband, you have seen the error of your way. You will remain a Muslim, practicing Islam. You cannot do this to your husband and your children. You will not be a Christian."

FORTY

NICOLAE CARPATHIA HAD MORPHED into the consummate politician, diplomat, statesman, and international gadfly. He found reasons to travel, establishing alliances with heads of state who would not have thought to grant an audience to someone from the Romanian lower house, except that he was so persuasive. And he had become known as the most popular man in his home country, admired, respected, lauded by even his opponents.

He was a man of peace. A dove. Into disarmament. That tickled the ears of his colleagues in Europe and most of the world. He had not yet visited the United States, but he was certainly becoming known everywhere else. Carpathia's mental brilliance, business acumen, and accomplishments seemed somehow known by all, without his having to trumpet himself. And the way he deflected praise made people pour it on all the more.

The more he got, the more he needed, and often he nearly passed out from the thrill of it, only to come crashing down on his way from a public appearance.

Nicolae had learned the art of humility. Or at least of appearing humble.

His goal was to bypass the upper house and run for president of Romania when his second term expired. Pundits already called him the favorite.

———

Irene worried that Raymie, new in and excited about his faith, would not get all he needed unless she could somehow switch to New Hope Church. Rayford remained adamant against that, and Chloe was again making noises about dropping out of church altogether.

Irene took to rewriting everything she was learning from Jackie and putting it in language Raymie could understand. That had the double benefit of not only pouring solid Bible teaching into Raymie but also of solidifying it in her. Anything Irene was unsure about, that she might have glossed over in the past, she now pressed Jackie on. She wanted to understand everything completely so she could teach it.

Heartbreaking was Raymie's own growing sensitivity to the plight of his father and sister. He prayed for them every day, often asking Irene what it was they didn't see or get. "It's so simple," he said. "All I want is for them to have what we have."

———————

Cameron "Buck" Williams believed he had nearly won over Juan Ortiz. Oh, he still detected resentment, some irritation, and no question a generational divide. Juan had a family, and while his work ethic seemed good during the normal workday, naturally he found reasons to get home at reasonable hours. Buck didn't think Juan had ever loved the job as much as he did, which accounted for his constant clucking and head shaking at Buck's willingness to put in sixteen-hour days.

Traveling internationally was a new experience for Buck, and he also enjoyed getting to the various big-city *Global Weekly* offices stateside and meeting the bureau chiefs. Among his favorites was Lucinda Washington, a matronly African-American woman who ran the Chicago office. Assigned a story there, Buck spent three days in and out of that office, and he sensed Lucinda took a true interest in him.

"I'll not be calling you by that awful nickname," she said. "You need to know that."

"Really? Why? I've come to like it."

"*Buck? Buck?* Number one, it's not a nice word in my community, you understand."

"Never thought of that. Sorry."

"And I know where it came from for you. New York types tell me you're always bucking tradition. Well, let me tell you something: that's all right with me. If I didn't buck tradition, I'd still be in the mail room. Stay respectful and do your job and people will listen even when you go against the grain sometimes. The people who get my

goat are the ones who always gripe and complain and
say they have a better idea, but they don't work anyway.
Do it your own way, but do it; that's what I say."

"Me too," Buck said. "And you can call me whatever
you want."

"I will, Cameron."

Someday Buck would have to ask Lucinda about all
the artifacts in her office. She had a picture of Jesus right
between the picture of her and her husband and the pictures of her kids. On her wall a gaudy gold-metal heart
read "God Is Love."

He'd met people of faith, as he had learned to call
them, on the job before. But most were pretty laid-back
about it, almost secretive. It was as if they knew they
were in the minority and didn't want to look like
weirdos. Well, Lucinda Washington was no weirdo,
regardless of her religious persuasion or devotion. She
had a reputation as a savvy reporter and writer, and now
people loved working for her. She fought with New York
for her staff and for their space in the magazine, and the
brass respected her nonetheless.

Buck liked the way she looked at him, as if she could
see into his soul. She saw him as a mother would see a
child, he guessed, and her bemusement and look of
expectation seemed to bring out the best in him.

When Chloe Steele was a junior in high school she did
so well on her college testing that letters began arriving

daily for her from universities all over the U.S. She was on her way to a top-five finish in her class with an outside shot at salutatorian.

Irene was thrilled and proud, but her excitement was tempered by the change she saw in her daughter. Chloe had all of Rayford's best characteristics; that was fine. But she also had his worst, and that would not do.

On the pro side of the ledger she was inquisitive, studious, a hard worker, and—of course—brilliant. She could have slopped her way through her homework on the way to school and earned solid B's. But Chloe worked at it. She set aside a certain time early every evening to do her homework, and Irene could set her watch by Chloe being at her desk and working.

Chloe rewarded or punished herself by regulating her own fun time. If she finished what she was supposed to do by the time she had prescribed, she went out with friends. If she didn't, she stayed home and missed out, finishing her work. Irene was grateful she and Rayford had never had another incident with Chloe drinking or even missing curfew. In that way she had become the model child.

But on the negative side Chloe seemed to think the world revolved around her, that she answered to no one, and that she knew better than anyone else anyway—in particular, her mother. She believed only in what she could see and touch. To her God was okay as a concept, but He certainly didn't really exist, not as a person.

"If you want to treat Him like a real personality, worship Him, live your life for Him, study Him, all that, I say go for it," Chloe told Irene one night. "But I'm over it. I must insist you treat me like a fully functioning moral agent in this world and stop making me go somewhere and sit there having to be civil when I'm not buying a word of it."

"You don't believe in God?"

"I don't want to say it that way, Mom. At best I'm agnostic. I am honest enough to say I simply don't know. I lean toward atheism, but I'm not going to fall on my sword over that. But to pretend to worship and study and listen when this has less to do with my life than any other discipline I pursue, well, that's not intellectually honest."

"Well, I'd still appreciate it if you would accede to my wishes, and until you go off to college—"

"Mom, don't start with that again. I am not going to church with you. I mean, I'll go if Raymie's in some program or something, but that's it."

"Chloe, you're not at an age where you're going to tell me what you are or are not going to—"

"Mom, sit and listen to me. Now I mean it."

Against her better judgment, Irene sat. At least Chloe was being civil.

"The truth is, I *am* at an age where I am going to tell you what I won't do. What are you going to do to enforce this if I refuse?"

"I can ask your dad to physically make you go."

"Don't be silly. He's going to carry me bodily to and from the car and into the church?"

"I could ground you, take away your car."

"Mom, I appreciate the use of the car, but if you take it away I'll figure out something else."

"We won't pay your way to college."

"Mom! Where have you been? Have you read none of these letters? I'm getting full-ride scholarship offers. And from the places I want to go."

"You'll stay in the Midwest, won't you?"

"Not a chance. I'm leaning toward Stanford."

"You're not going off to college two thousand miles away, Chloe."

"Yes, actually, I think I am."

"We'll talk about this when your father gets home."

"He's on my side, Mom. Give it up."

———————

Nicolae noticed one morning that the challenges and tasks of his business magnate life had become routine and, worse, niggling. What used to motivate him, charge him up, spur him on, now made him say, "This again?"

He could have easily withdrawn from the business, let someone else run it at his behest. If Leon wasn't a chief operating officer, he could certainly find one. But within days of his realization that he was not as enthused as before, Nicolae found the emotion multiplying exponentially. Business bored him. Got in his way. Made him impatient.

He wanted to get on with life. It was time to move, to expand, to take what he believed was rightfully his. He had bowed the knee, worshiped his lord and master in exchange for the kingdoms of the world. Was something more required of him? He was the smartest, most well-read, articulate, multilingual man he was aware of.

It was time for Nicolae Carpathia to emerge.

He spent more than half his day in his office, poring over magazines and watching international news. He knew everything about everything and everybody. If he found himself in the same room with the most obscure emir of a sultanate, Nicolae would be able to converse with the man as if he were his best friend. He would know the man's wife's or wives' name or names, those of the man's sons and daughters. His cabinet. His advisers. His enemies. His strengths and weaknesses, his dreads and dreams. Nicolae believed he was more of a student of the world than any other man alive.

He and Leon had been discussing strategy to bypass election to the senate and go straight for the top prize— yes, directly from two terms in the House of Deputies. That would be no small feat, and regardless the plans they concocted, nothing really clicked in Nicolae's mind as a sure bet. He could leave nothing to chance. His move to pacifism had been perfectly timed, and his reputation and approval ratings were at all-time highs. Now if he could just find the pièce de résistance.

Within the space of a year or so, Rayford Steele realized that his life and career had reached both their zenith and their nadir at once. There was nowhere else for him to go within Pan-Con Airlines, unless it was management. And that held no appeal.

He was flying the flagships of the fleet, had his choice

Tim LaHaye & Jerry B. Jenkins

of routes, and virtually set his own schedule. Rayford
had mediated the latest skirmish between Irene and
Chloe, which resulted in Chloe's dropping out of church
and Sunday school altogether. If anything, Irene had
grown chillier than ever since then.

Rayford didn't know what her problem was with
Chloe. They could not have asked for a more ideal
daughter. She was a gem, a keeper, his friends would say.
She had recently inked her intent to accept a full-ride
academic scholarship from Stanford, and while he
couldn't imagine her being that far away when it seemed
she had been a toddler just a month ago, he was so
proud of her that he could hardly stand it.

He had the same high hopes for Raymie, but he worried about the kid. Was he becoming a mama's boy?
There was nothing soft or sissified about him, except
that he was so much into Irene's religion. That couldn't
be good. What other boy that age—and especially
older—was still so enamored with church? Something
was going to have to change there. Chloe may have been
able to talk herself out of having to go to church all the
time, but Rayford now had to deal with both Irene's nagging and Raymie's begging. Rayford was finding it
harder and harder to come up with excuses not to go,
let alone promises he could keep to make up for it.

The only interesting thing on Rayford's horizon
remained Hattie Durham. She had finally graduated
to international flights and occasionally rode on his trips
to England and other points east. Her goal was senior
flight attendant and enough seniority that she could

choose her routes. She had made it clear she would choose his flights, if that was all right with him.

Rayford had made it clear that this was his wish too.

That was ironic, because for as much of a thrill as it had given him to even say such a thing, it represented way more than had ever gone on between them. In point of fact, Rayford had never touched the woman.

He had been solicitous. He hoped his looks and gestures and tone of voice had made their points. But Hattie was the toucher in this relationship. She would lay a hand gently on his shoulder as she slid past him in the bulkhead. Would rest a hand on his back as she delivered coffee to the cockpit. She touched his hand while talking with him at the occasional dinner or while thanking him for the frequent rides home.

Rayford had never been inside her place, and they rarely saw each other alone. But with his life going the way it was and his midlife crisis kicking up alarmingly, Rayford began allowing himself to think of the possibilities. He told himself that if something broke, if he was tapped to fly *Air Force One* or *Two*, or if he was publicly lauded by the CIA or the Defense Department for his clandestine but admittedly limited consulting, that might get him back on track.

He could quit fantasizing about the beautiful young flight attendant and somehow talk himself into robotically walking through his boring married life.

FORTY-ONE

ABDULLAH "SMITTY" ABABNEH had made the biggest mistake of his life, and he was about to compound it. He
had tried to bluff Yasmine by threatening to take the
children if she persisted in her conversion to Christianity.
She had taken the kids, left him, and publicly declared
her new faith.

To save face Abdullah filed for divorce, but when she
countered by filing for full custody of the children, his
life began to fall apart. He stopped making payments
on his house and lost it. He took up residence at the air
base, thoroughly overthrew any semblance of loyalty to
Islam, and even took to drinking.

His morals failed as well, and when Yasmine was able
to prove that he had committed adultery before the
divorce was final, she had little trouble winning legal
custody of the children. Abdullah pulled himself together

only enough to keep his job within the Royal Jordanian Air Force, but he was nearly suicidal.

It was all he could do to get through a normal day, so remorseful and lonely had he become. In his anger and depression he wrote vitriolic, rambling letters to Yasmine, threatening to steal back the children—all the while knowing she was the best and only parent for them if they had to settle for just one.

Yasmine, in her steely and yet loving way, wrote Abdullah long, earnest missives explaining her faith and outlining the plan of salvation. The first two times she did this, Abdullah tore them into little pieces and mailed them back to her. The next time he stored the letter in a box of keepsakes. She wrote him a half dozen more times, pleading with him to read the Bible, seek counsel, pray, and turn to Christ. He quit answering her but saved her letters. It was good that he did, because apparently she wearied of no response and stopped writing.

Nicolae Carpathia seemed to notice things other people missed. At least people other than Leon Fortunato.

Strange thing: Nicolae didn't much care for Leon outside of what the man could do for him. He was not what Nicolae would call a friend. A confidant perhaps, but not a friend. They didn't socialize off the job. Leon wanted to; that seemed clear. But Nicolae found him clingy, and while he enjoyed being fawned over to a certain extent, he was addicted to the approval of the masses, not the sycophancy of one man.

Occasionally Leon surprised and delighted Nicolae, however. Like when they both got the same message from the netherworld. Nicolae had read an obscure item about an Israeli botanist, an elderly man named Chaim Rosenzweig, who was working on a concoction that he believed could make the desert sands bloom like a hothouse.

Nicolae passed over the item the first time but read it with more interest the second time. Then he forgot about it. Then it resurrected in his mind and began to play at the edges of his consciousness. People came up with bizarre ideas all the time, few ever coming to fruition. But this . . . if this had any legitimacy, was valid in any way, it could be bigger than the botanist ever dreamed.

What if it was true? What if the man could pull it off? The Middle Eastern nation that managed such a miracle would dominate the region, grow wealthy and fat, and throw the balance of power into disarray. Imagine what something like that could do for Romania.

Nicolae became obsessed with the idea. Why would the man, an old professor, announce what he was working on? Did he not fear competition? What of younger, sharper, brighter minds—perhaps some who had been working on the same thing, like a perpetual motion device, for years—beating him to the punch?

Nicolae set his own mind to the problem. What would it take? What would he need? He bounced it off his spirit guide one evening at dusk as he walked and prayed.

Sometimes these connections with the spirit world seemed like normal conversations. But this evening he sensed he had tapped into an angry spirit. Nicolae's mind was riddled with cacophony. Hissing. Spitting. Rage. In the depths of his being Nicolae sensed the spirit telling him, "Look to the North from whence come the power and strength emanating from me!"

"But this botanist," Nicolae pressed silently. "Is he on to something? Is it something I should pursue?"

"To the death."

"I do not understand."

"He is one of the enemy's chosen people. Worthy of hatred."

"I am willing to hate him, but should I not steal his idea?"

"Too late." More hissing and noise, as if Nicolae had reminded his spirit guide of something so distasteful he didn't even want to think about it.

"Too late? Really?"

"Win him with winsomeness."

"I do not understand."

"Get it. Take it. Lure it away, or I will take it by force with my minions from the North."

"So I am right? This is a worthy pursuit?"

"Inestimable."

Nicolae was always frustrated when he could not coax the spirit to continue a conversation. His connection to the netherworld went dead, and it nearly drove him mad. He rushed back to his office and jotted notes. The botanist's name. His university. His hometown.

Ideas on how to contact him. He would put Leon on it the next day.

But he didn't have to wait even that long.

Viv Ivins buzzed him. "Leon is on the line for you."

"What does he want? I am busy."

"He wants to come and see you."

"Tonight?"

"Right now."

"Tell him to come."

Leon arrived within twenty minutes, a rolled-up magazine in his hand. He spread it before Nicolae. "This struck me," he said. "And I believe it is something you should be aware of."

It was a story about Chaim Rosenzweig and his potential formula. "I am aware of it," Nicolae said.

"My spirit tells me we are too late to pirate it," Leon said. "Diplomacy is our only hope."

For whatever Leon was or was not, Nicolae trusted his instincts. Or at least his access to the spirits. Especially when they corroborated his own.

Buck Williams had been with *Global Weekly* nearly four years. He had already written more than thirty cover stories, including three Newsmaker of the Year pieces. He wanted to bag a fourth, so he went to the next staff meeting with his nomination in mind: Dr. Chaim Rosenzweig of Israel, the humble chemical engineer who preferred calling himself a botanist.

Buck was certain his colleagues wanted to go with an American, a pop or political star of some sort. But Rosenzweig was the only logical choice, at least in Buck's mind. It was a relief when Steve Plank opened the meeting with, "Anybody want to nominate someone stupid, such as anyone other than the Nobel Prize winner in chemistry?"

No one argued, but Buck wasn't going to leave this to chance. "Steve," he said, "I'm not angling for it, but you know I know the guy, and he trusts me."

The usual carping ensued with everyone else lobbying to be the writer, criticizing Steve for always leaning toward Buck, and Steve reminding them that the decision was his. In the end, the nod went to Buck. He had, after all, done the story when Rosenzweig had won the Nobel Prize.

In Israel Buck stayed in a military compound and met with Rosenzweig in the same kibbutz on the outskirts of Haifa where he had interviewed him a year earlier. Buck had found the wiry little man, with the Einstein thing happening with his hair, protected by security systems as complex as those for heads of state. Here was a warm, smiling, earnest-speaking man honored throughout the world and revered as royalty in his own country.

Rosenzweig himself was fascinating, of course, but it was his formula that had revolutionized Israel and changed the face of the Middle East. Irrigation was nothing new. But, as the retired professor said, all that did was "make the sand wet." His formula, added to the water, fertilized the sand. Buck was no scientist, but he knew Rosenzweig's formula had made Israel the richest nation on earth almost overnight. Every inch of available ground blossomed with flowers and grains, including produce never before conceivable in Israel. Flush with cash and resources, the nation made peace with her neighbors. Free trade and liberal passage allowed all who loved the nation to have access to it. What they did not have access to, however, was the formula.

Global leaders sought out Rosenzweig. Just ten days before Buck's visit, a Russian delegation had come calling, clearly imagining what a license to the formula might do if put to work on their own vast tundra.

Russia had become a great brooding giant with a devastated economy and regressed technology. All the nation had was military might, every spare resource invested in weaponry.

"Let me tell you something, my friend," Rosenzweig told Buck. "The Russians left here none too happy with my response. And I did not flatly refuse them. I merely told them that the rights to the formula technically belonged to the State of Israel and that I would not try to sway the government in what it chose to do with them. They will decide when they decide, and they may decide to share the formula with no one.

"The Russians told me they had already tried diplomatic channels to tender an offer for a license and that they had come to me only when that failed. I apologized that they had gone to all the time and expense to come to the wrong person."

"Who else has visited you?" Buck said.

"Oh, many. Many. Most all. It has been a joy, I confess, hearing their compliments and accolades. This has been a most interesting aspect. I was most amused by a visit from the vice president of the United States himself. He wanted to honor me, to bring me to the president, to have a parade, to confer a degree, all that. He diplomatically said nothing about my owing him anything in return, but I would owe him everything; would I not? Much was said about what a friend of Israel the United States has been over the decades. And this has been true, no? How could I argue?

"But I pretended to see the awards and kindnesses as all for my own benefit, and I humbly turned them down. Because you see, young man, I *am* most humble; am I not?" The old man laughed and relayed several other stories of dignitaries who had visited and tried to charm him.

"Was *anyone* sincere?" Buck said. "Did anyone impress you?"

"Yes! From the most perplexing and surprising corner of the world—Romania. I do not know if he was sent or came on his own, but I suspect the latter because I believe he is the lowest-ranking official I entertained following the award. That is one of the reasons I wanted to see him. He asked for the audience himself. He did not go through typical political and protocol channels."

"And he was . . . ?"

"Nicolae Carpathia."

"Carpathia like the—?"

"Yes, like the Carpathian Mountains. A melodic name,

you must admit. I found him most charming and humble. Not unlike myself!"

"I've not heard of him."

"You will! You will."

"Because he's . . ."

"Impressive, that is all I can say."

Later in the interview Rosenzweig said of Carpathia, "I believe his goal is global disarmament, which we Israelis have come to distrust. But of course he must first bring about disarmament in his own country. This man is about your age, by the way. Blond and blue-eyed, like the original Romanians who came from Rome, before the Mongols affected their race."

"What did you like so much about him?"

"Let me count," Rosenzweig said. "He knew my language as well as his own. And he speaks fluent English. Several others also, they tell me. Well educated but also widely self-taught. And I just like him as a person. Very bright. Very honest. Very open."

"What did he want from you?"

"That is what I liked the best. Because I found him so open and honest, I asked him outright that question. He insisted I call him Nicolae, and so I said, 'Nicolae, what do you want from me?' Do you know what he said, young man? He said, 'Dr. Rosenzweig, I seek only your goodwill.' What could I say? I said, 'Nicolae, you have it.' I am a bit of a pacifist myself, you know. Not unrealistically. I did not tell him this. I merely told him he had my goodwill. Which is something you also have."

"I suspect that is not something you bestow easily."

"That is why I like you and why you have it. One day you must meet Carpathia. You would like each other. His goals and dreams may never be realized even in his own country, but he is a man of high ideals. If he should emerge, you will hear of him. And as you are emerging in your own orbit, he will likely hear of you, or from you; am I right?"

"I hope you are."

FORTY-TWO

CHLOE HAD FALLEN in love with a senior at Stanford and believed it was the real thing. Ricky was tall, a former high school basketball star who had tried to make the Stanford team as a walk-on and failed. He excelled in intramurals and was a business major, skilled at public speaking.

He graduated early, spent three months touring Europe, sent Chloe a cheap souvenir from Switzerland, and disappeared from her life. Her letters went unanswered, and her devastation was complete when one of their mutual acquaintances returned from Ricky's wedding with photos and squeals of delight over his bride and how much Chloe would love her if only they would meet.

The setback had an interesting effect on Chloe. She settled into her task of being the best student she could be, and she quit trusting people, especially males. Her father was the only man she respected, but even he had little to offer other than condolence over her love loss.

"I won't try to make this better, Chlo'," he said over dinner during one of his four visits during her first year. "I'll just tell you that I would knock Ricky flat if he were standing here."

Chloe made her father promise he would never give Ricky the satisfaction of thinking he had affected her that way. "He clearly didn't care for me the way I cared for him, and I'd just as soon he not know what this did to me."

And that was the end of it. Except for how it helped forge Chloe's character and future.

Wholly sick of his business, bored with politics, and feeling a failure over his effort to curry real favor with Chaim Rosenzweig, Nicolae Carpathia took out his frustrations on everyone around him. He was short and sarcastic, particularly with Viv and Leon. And he was rude to the staff, shouting at subordinates over every slight or error.

He marched about his compound, barking at security first to give him space and then to not let him get so far from them. He raged at his spirit guide, demanding to know when his next assignment would come, when his next entitlement would be realized, and when he would take his proper place in the leadership of the world.

When the netherworld was silent he fumed that he would have to do something himself, would strategize the most sophisticated kidnapping plot in history, and would demand the fertilizer formula as ransom for Rosenzweig himself.

Finally his antics had gotten the attention of the spirits. "Patience, chosen one," he was told. "Retribution has already been scheduled."

Buck Williams had enjoyed a leisurely late evening meal with Chaim Rosenzweig a mile from the kibbutz and from the nearby military compound where Buck would stay before his dawn flight back to the States.

The old man was spent, his thick accent harder and harder to understand as he enjoyed his wine, and his eyelids drooped.

"I need to let you get some rest," Buck said.

"I suppose it is true, but this has been so invigorating. You must come visit me one day when we have no business to conduct."

"And when might that be?" Buck said, laughing. "I am always busy, and though you are more than twice my age, you are busier than I."

"We will have to carve out the time and schedule it. Just a time of relaxation and refreshment."

Buck couldn't imagine downtime like that, but he could think of no better companion for it.

Rosenzweig's driver dropped Buck off at the military compound, where he headed through the command center toward his more-than-comfortable quarters. It was already after midnight, and he was fascinated by the alert attention the strategy room personnel gave the glowing computer screens. Earlier in the week he had met the brass and been given full access to the technicians who kept their eyes on the night skies.

Israel seemed to be in such favor of all their neighbors that no serious threat loomed. Still, these proud soldiers spoke eloquently of their charge to defend and protect. Many nodded or waved as Buck moved through, and a couple of the command personnel called him by name.

A man of planning and systems, Buck rarely slept well when he knew he had to rise early. But he was eager to get home, and he prepared everything so he would be able to merely rise, shower, shave, and go. Always a light packer, he carefully loaded his leather bag and laid out his clothes for the next day.

Before undressing for bed he stood by his window and gazed into a starry sky. He felt keyed up, not drowsy. He would have trouble sleeping; he knew it. It was at times like this when he wished he enjoyed wine the way a man like Rosenzweig did. That would have put him out.

Maybe some late reading would do the trick. Just as he was turning from the window to dig a book or magazine from his bag, the raucous blat of sirens shook the place. A fire? Some malfunction? Buck assumed loudspeakers would advise occupants what to do, where to go. He was glad he was still dressed. He pulled on his leather jacket and was then drawn back to the window by something new in the skies.

It appeared surface-to-air missiles had been launched. Was Israel under attack? Could it be? Sounds from the air overrode even the ear-rattling sirens. When the skies lit up like noon, Buck knew this was the real thing—a full-fledged air battle. But with whom? And why?

He bolted from his room and ran down the corridor toward the command center. "Stay in your quarters, civilian!" he heard more than once as he darted among ashen-faced men and women in various stages of dress. Many had emerged from their chambers pulling on uniforms and jamming on caps.

The situation room was chaotic already, and this crisis was less than a minute old. Command officers huddled around screens, chirping rapid-fire commands at techies. One man wearing impossibly large earphones shouted, "One of our fighters has identified Russian MiG fighter-bombers."

From another corner: "ICBMs!"

Buck reeled. Intercontinental ballistic missiles? Against little Israel? From the Russians?

Suddenly no one was sitting. Even the experts stood at their keyboards as if staring at something they didn't want to see. Every screen seemed lit and jammed with blips and points of light.

"It's like Pearl Harbor!"

"We'll be annihilated!"

"Hundreds of MiGs nearly overhead!"

"Hopelessly outnumbered!"

Then the explosions began. Sections of the building went dark. Some screens. Bombs sounded as if they had landed right outside the windows. So this was no grandstand play designed to bring Israel to her knees. There was no message for the victims. Receiving no explanation for the war machines crossing her borders and descending upon her, Israel was forced to defend herself, knowing full well that the first volley would bring about her virtual disappearance from the face of the earth.

The sky was lit with orange-and-yellow balls of fire that would do little to slow a Russian offensive for which there could be no defense. It appeared to Buck that every command officer expected to be put out of his misery in seconds when the fusillade reached the ground and covered the nation.

Buck knew the end was near. There was no escape. Some personnel actually left their posts screaming, and their commanders did not try to stop them. Even senior officers dived under equipment and covered their ears.

As the night shone like day and the horrific, deafening explosions continued, the building shook and rattled and rumbled.

The first Israeli missiles had taken out Russian fighters and caused ICBMs to explode too high to cause more than fire damage on the ground. The Russian warplanes slammed to the ground, digging craters and sending burning debris flying. But radar showed the Russians had clearly sent nearly every plane they had, leaving hardly anything in reserve. Thousands of planes swooped down on the tiny country's most populated cities.

Buck's survival instinct was on full throttle. He crouched beneath a console, surprised by the urge to sob. This was not at all what he had expected war to sound like, to look like. He had imagined himself peeking at the action from a safe perch, recording the drama in his mind.

Cameron Williams knew beyond a doubt that he would die, and he wondered why he had never married. Whether there would be remnants of his body for his father or brother to identify. Was there a God? Would death be the end?

EPILOGUE

For the Lord Himself will descend from heaven with a shout, with the voice of an archangel, and with the trumpet of God. And the dead in Christ will rise first. Then we who are alive and remain shall be caught up together with them in the clouds to meet the Lord in the air. And thus we shall always be with the Lord.

1 Thessalonians 4:16-17

ABOUT THE AUTHORS

Jerry B. Jenkins (www.jerryjenkins.com) is the writer of the Left Behind series. He owns the Jerry B. Jenkins Christian Writers Guild (www.ChristianWritersGuild.com), an organization dedicated to mentoring aspiring authors, as well as Jenkins Entertainment, a filmmaking company (www.Jenkins-Entertainment.com). Former vice president of publishing for the Moody Bible Institute of Chicago, he also served many years as editor of *Moody* magazine and is now Moody's writer-at-large.

His writing has appeared in publications as varied as *Time* magazine, *Reader's Digest, Parade, Guideposts,* in-flight magazines, and dozens of other periodicals. Jenkins's biographies include books with Billy Graham, Hank Aaron, Bill Gaither, Luis Palau, Walter Payton, Orel Hershiser, and Nolan Ryan, among many others. His books appear regularly on the *New York Times, USA Today, Wall Street Journal,* and *Publishers Weekly* best-seller lists.

He holds two honorary doctorates, one from Bethel College (Indiana) and one from Trinity International University. Jerry and his wife, Dianna, live in Colorado and have three grown sons and three grandchildren.

Dr. Tim LaHaye (www.timlahaye.com), who conceived the idea of fictionalizing an account of the Rapture and the Tribulation, is a noted author, minister, and nationally recognized speaker on Bible prophecy. He is the founder of both Tim LaHaye Ministries and the Pre-Trib Research Center.

He also recently cofounded the Tim LaHaye School of Prophecy at Liberty University. Dr. LaHaye speaks at many of the major Bible prophecy conferences in the U.S. and Canada, where his prophecy books are very popular.

Dr. LaHaye earned a doctor of ministry degree from Western Theological Seminary and an honorary doctor of literature degree from Liberty University. For twenty-five years he pastored one of the nation's outstanding churches in San Diego, which grew to three locations. During that time he founded two accredited Christian high schools, a Christian school system of ten schools, and Christian Heritage College.

There are almost 13 million copies of Dr. LaHaye's fifty nonfiction books that have been published in over thirty-seven foreign languages. He has written books on a wide variety of subjects, such as family life, temperaments, and Bible prophecy. His current fiction works, the Left Behind series, written with Jerry B. Jenkins, continue to appear on the best-seller lists of the Christian Booksellers Association, *Publishers Weekly, Wall Street Journal, USA Today,* and the *New York Times.* LaHaye's second fiction series of prophetic novels consists of *Babylon Rising* and *The Secret on Ararat,* both of which hit the *New York Times* best-seller list and will soon be followed by *Europa Challenge.* This series of four action thrillers, unlike *Left Behind,* does not start with the Rapture but could take place today and goes up to the Rapture.

He is the father of four grown children and grandfather of nine. Snow skiing, waterskiing, motorcycling, golfing, vacationing with family, and jogging are among his leisure activities.

IN ONE CATACLYSMIC MOMENT
MILLIONS AROUND THE WORLD DISAPPEAR

Experience the suspense of the end times for yourself. The best-selling Left Behind series is now available in hardcover, softcover, and abridged audio editions.

1
LEFT BEHIND®
A novel of
the earth's last
days . . .

2
**TRIBULATION
FORCE**
The continuing
drama of those
left behind . . .

3
NICOLAE
The rise of
Antichrist . . .

4
**SOUL
HARVEST**
The world
takes sides . . .

5
APOLLYON
The Destroyer is
unleashed . . .

6
ASSASSINS
Assignment:
Jerusalem,
Target: Antichrist

7
**THE
INDWELLING**
The Beast takes
possession . . .

8
THE MARK
The Beast rules
the world . . .

9
DESECRATION
Antichrist takes
the throne . . .

10
**THE
REMNANT**
On the brink of
Armageddon . . .

11
ARMAGEDDON
The cosmic battle
of the ages . . .

12
**GLORIOUS
APPEARING**
The end of
days . . .

FOR THE MOST ACCURATE INFORMATION VISIT
www.leftbehind.com

FOR THE LATEST INFORMATION
ON INDIVIDUAL PRODUCTS, RELEASE DATES,
AND FUTURE PROJECTS, VISIT

www.leftbehind.com

Sign up and receive free e-mail updates!